REUNION

M.J. Arlidge has worked in television for the last twenty years, specialising in high-end drama production, including prime-time crime serials *Silent Witness*, *Torn*, *The Little House* and, most recently, the hit ITV show *Innocent*.

Steph Broadribb was born in Birmingham and grew up in Buckinghamshire. Along with her other novels in the Retired Detectives Club series—*Death in the Sunshine*, *Death at Paradise Palms* and *Death on the Beach*—she has also written the Lori Anderson bounty hunter series and the Starke/Bell psychological police procedural books (writing as Stephanie Marland).

Also by M.J. Arlidge:

Also by Steph Broadribb:

THE
REUNION

M.J.ARLIDGE
STEPH BROADRIBB

ORION

An Orion paperback

First published in Great Britain in 2024
by Orion Fiction,
an imprint of The Orion Publishing Group Ltd,
Carmelite House, 50 Victoria Embankment
London EC4Y ODZ

An Hachette UK Company

1 3 5 7 9 10 8 6 4 2

A CIP catalogue record for this book
is available from the British Library.

ISBN (Mass Market Paperback) 978 1 3987 1657 5
ISBN (eBook) 978 1 3987 1656 8
ISBN (Audio) 978 1 3987 1655 1

Typeset at The Spartan Press Ltd,
Lymington, Hants

Printed and bound in Great Britain by Clays Ltd,
Elcograf S.p.A.

www.orionbooks.co.uk

Prologue

Thursday 9 June 1994

It's almost time.

Jennie Whitmore pulls her rucksack towards her across the faded pink duvet on her single bed. This is her last chance to spot anything important she might have missed. She counts the basics: underwear, T-shirts, leggings. Then goes through her absolute essentials: Nirvana sweatshirt, acid-wash jeans, velvet blazer dress, red Converse, make-up, skin care. There's only one more item to add.

She takes her most prized possession from the bedside cabinet. The second-hand Nikon SLR camera might be a few years old, and a little battered around the casing, but it's the last birthday gift her dad gave her before he died, and she can't leave it behind. Carefully, Jennie places the camera into its padded travel case, and packs it into the top of her rucksack. It's a tight squeeze, but she manages to make it work and pulls the drawstring cord tight before buckling down the rucksack's top flap.

Jennie checks her watch; it's almost ten o'clock and she needs to get going. She hurries to the bookcase and takes a dog-eared hardback of *War and Peace* from the bottom shelf. She pauses before opening it, looking at the five brightly coloured 18th birthday cards that line the top shelf. There's one from each of her friends but nothing from Mum. Jennie's birthday was almost two weeks ago now, but her own mother still hasn't remembered.

Opening *War and Peace* reveals a hole cut out from the pages; it's the only hiding space that's ever managed to thwart Mum when she's on the rampage searching for more booze money. The roll of notes totals nearly three hundred pounds; the wages she's saved from her after-school job washing up at the Cross Keys. Saved for this moment. Jennie removes her money from its hiding place and tucks it into her purse.

Heart in her mouth, Jennie laces up her Doc Martens, pulls on her denim jacket, and swings her rucksack over one shoulder. She moves towards the door, pausing as she reaches it to take a final look around her bedroom. Kurt Cobain, Madonna, and Soundgarden look down from the posters Blu-Tacked to the wall behind her bed. Their cool clothes and enigmatic stares seem to challenge her to be brave. To finally get out of this hellhole. This place has always seemed like a stopgap, never a real home.

I'm ready now.

It's time.

Jennie creeps down the stairs, careful not to make any noise. Maureen Whitmore is sprawled on the sagging brown sofa, snoring loudly. One arm is draped across her stomach, clutching a nearly finished bottle of cheap gin. The other has flopped off the sofa, her fingers almost touching the two three-litre bottles of White Lightning lying empty on the floor.

Jennie tries not to feel angry that her mum has become like this, that the happy, laughter-filled family she used to be part of is now a distant memory. The news reports had called Frank Whitmore a heroic photojournalist, the man who captured many iconic and harrowing pictures of human conflict. But to her, he was simply Dad: the dad who wore a clown costume and juggled at her seventh birthday party; the dad who made chocolate pancakes with extra sprinkles for breakfast on Sundays; and the dad who taught her how to load a camera and frame a shot. She knows her experience isn't unique. There have been many casualties on all sides of the Bosnian war and her dad was just one of them. But when the IED detonated beneath the jeep he and his colleague were travelling in, it had torn Jennie's life apart too.

The cuckoo clock in the kitchen chimes ten times. She needs to go. Pushing away sad thoughts of the past, Jennie moves quickly across the lounge to the front door. She won't miss this drab house with its ever-present smell of damp and the hideous Seventies décor. She won't miss the anxiety she's felt every day on the way home from school, dreading what state she'll find Mum in. Jennie won't miss feeling like she's the parent rather than the child.

Because her life is about to change. After all their planning and saving, she's running away to London with her best friend, her heart sister – Hannah. Two girls taking on the big city. They're taking charge of their lives and making their dreams into a reality. The rest of her life starts right now.

Jennie's heart is racing as adrenaline buzzes through her. She can't believe she's actually doing this. *It's really happening.*

She takes a deep breath, and whispers, 'Bye, Mum.'

Then she slips through the front door, closing it softly behind her.

Head down against the rain, Jennie hurries along the lane to the main road. It's dark and the streetlights are spaced far apart, making it hard to spot the puddles. She squints through the downpour, doing her best to keep away from the kerb and the spray from the cars that whoosh past. The dampness seeps through her jacket and water drips off her hair but she doesn't care. Any amount of discomfort will be worth it when they get to London.

She checks her watch again; it's five past ten. The walk would usually take just over half an hour but she needs to do it in twenty. The night bus leaves at twenty to eleven but she promised to get there early.

Picking up her pace, Jennie follows the main road into town. The rain is getting worse and thunder rumbles overhead. She flinches as lightning flashes above the hillside beyond the town, briefly illuminating the ancient 85-foot-high chalk cross carved into it, the white cross that gave the town its name.

Refusing to be deterred, Jennie hurries on. As she passes the

Cross Keys pub, laughter from inside leaches out through the open windows. Jennie knows from working in the kitchen that the main bar has sport on the telly every evening – football, boxing, whatever is going on that day. A loud cheer goes up and there's the sound of pints being clinked together.

Moments later there's a loud wolf whistle behind her and she hears a bloke shout out the pub window, 'Hey, wait up, sweetheart, what's the big hurry?'

Ignoring him, Jennie presses on to the bus stop. Stepping inside the wooden shelter, she shakes the worst of the rain from her jacket and pushes her rain-sodden fringe out of her eyes as she searches for Hannah.

The time they'd arranged to meet comes and goes. Jennie checks her watch but isn't super worried; Hannah generally has a relaxed approach to timekeeping, so a couple of minutes late is nothing unusual. But as more minutes pass, anxiety starts fluttering in her chest.

She is coming, isn't she?

The rain becomes torrential. Jennie checks her watch for the second time in less than a minute. She moves from one foot to the other, feeling increasingly agitated.

Where is Hannah? She said she'd be here. She promised me.

Five minutes pass. Then another five.

A roar goes up from inside the pub. Another goal scored, no doubt.

Jennie sees the lights of the night bus approaching. She glances down the street, looking for Hannah, but the pavements are empty.

Has something happened? Did Hannah's dad ground her? Has she got into an accident on the way here? Please don't let her be hurt.

The bus is fifty yards away, then twenty.

Jennie feels as if she might be sick.

I can't go back home. There's no way. But I can't leave without

4

Hannah. We made each other a promise – the two of us together, always and forever.

Making a decision, Jennie steps out of the shelter with her hand up. The bus indicates and slows to a stop beside her.

Maybe Hannah got on at an earlier stop because of the rain?

The doors swing open and Jennie steps up into the bus. She scans the seats, looking for her friend. The bus is almost empty; there's a loved-up couple snogging, a disapproving-looking middle-aged woman with a bedraggled-terrier on her lap, and a couple of blokes who look a bit worse for wear. Jennie's heart sinks as she takes in the last few vacant seats at the back of the single-decker. Hannah's not here.

This is wrong. It's all going wrong. Where is she?

'You staying or going, love?' says the bus driver, a kindly-looking man in his fifties.

Jennie tries to swallow down her fear. She tastes bile on her tongue. 'I … my friend was meant to be getting the bus too but she's not here yet.'

The driver taps his fingers against the steering wheel. 'Sorry, love. I'm on a schedule. Can't wait all night.'

Should I go? Should I stay?

I can't do this without Hannah. It's meant to be our *adventure.*

'I …' Tears prick at Jennie's eyes as she steps back down onto the pavement.

Why isn't Hannah here?

Why didn't she come like she promised?

The bus pulls away, leaving Jennie standing at the side of the road in the pouring rain.

Alone.

Day One

Chapter 1

This is a bad idea.

As she climbs the steep woodland trail towards the top of White Cross Hill, Jennie trips over a rogue tree root and curses her decision to come here. Dusk is morphing into night and the beam of her phone's torch is doing a poor job of lighting the dirt path beneath the ancient oak, pine and silver birch trees. Their gnarled and twisted trunks loom up out of the darkness like woody spectres.

A dry branch snaps beneath her trainers and Jennie leaps forward, her heart pounding.

Get a grip. It's just a twig.

Thirty years ago, she'd known this route like the back of her hand. These woods were once her favourite place to photograph, and the top of the hill, marked by the 85-foot-high white chalk cross, was party central for all the kids who went to White Cross Academy. Jennie shakes her head. It's been thirty years since she took a proper photograph and it feels almost as long since she went to a party.

The summit's not far and as she gets closer, Jennie hears Duran Duran's 'Ordinary World' playing somewhere up ahead. Slowing her pace, she pushes the fringe of her shoulder-length black hair out of her eyes and smooths her T-shirt down over the waistband of her jeans. She hopes she looks at least half decent.

Reaching the edge of the treeline Jennie flinches as a sudden blast of laughter cuts through the darkness, causing the birds roosting in the tree above her to take flight. She can hear the sound of people talking now as well as the music. Her stomach flips and she wonders if it's too late to back out.

She hates parties. Why the hell did she say yes to this one?

Nostalgia. Betrayal. Regret.

When she'd first seen Lottie Varney's post on the Class of '94 Facebook group she'd scrolled past, not wanting the memories of that time in her life to come flooding back. But something about learning that her old school was going to be demolished and a shiny new apartment block erected in its place stayed in her mind, even though she'd only attended the school for the last year of sixth form. After thirty-six hours, she'd searched for Lottie's post – an invitation to an impromptu reunion up here where they'd partied as schoolkids – and marked herself as attending.

She regrets it now, of course.

As she reaches the summit, the ground levels out and Jennie gets her first glimpse of the party. It's far grander than she'd envisaged. Huge flaming torches are staked into the ground every few metres forming a large square party space. Groundsheets, blankets and cushions are spread artfully across the grass. Two trestle tables have been joined to form a makeshift bar laden with bottles nestling in enormous buckets of ice.

The party is already in full swing, with people silhouetted in the torchlight chatting and drinking. Jennie smells the unmistakable scent of weed and hears the braying laughter of Lorraine Chester, the ringleader of the mean girls.

This is definitely a bad idea.

Joining the sixth form for the final year hadn't been easy. Jennie had been wrenched from Solihull High School in Birmingham and inserted into White Cross Academy. There might have only been seventy-nine miles separating the two places, but from the way Lorraine Chester and her bitchy friends treated Jennie, she might as well have been an alien. They laughed at her Brummie accent, mocked her fashion sense and, when she tried to ignore their taunts and jibes, upped their bullying game and got physical.

Jennie grimaces. Why the hell would she ever want to see people like Lorraine Chester again? She's lived here in White

Cross for the past thirty years and has managed to avoid them. There's no sense in changing that now.

As her nerve fails her, Jennie turns away.

'Jennie? Jennie Whitmore? Is that you?'

Jennie freezes. The woman's voice is both a blast from the past and unfamiliar. Turning back towards the party, Jennie sees Lottie Varney hurrying across the grass towards her. She looks older than when they last met, but that was years ago, and her blonde hair is poker-straight and parted in the middle, rather than permed as it was back in sixth form. She's still petite with a ballerina's poise, and she looks expensive in the black Dior cocktail dress and spike-heeled sandals. Jennie has no idea how she's able to walk on grass in them, or how she's managed to hike up the hill for that matter.

'Hi.'

'Oh my God, it *is* you!' says Lottie, reaching Jennie and pulling her into a hug. 'It's been *forever*. I'm so glad you made it.'

Jennie feels awkward. What do you say to someone you used to be friends with but haven't seen in nearly thirty years? There's no rulebook for this, not given their history. 'I just—'

'Come and get a drink,' says Lottie, taking Jennie's arm and leading her into the torchlit area. 'And then I want to know everything that's going on with you.'

Jennie realises resistance is futile. Resolving to have one drink and then leave, she follows Lottie across to the makeshift bar. Duran Duran's slow-tempo song transitions into Corona's 'The Rhythm of the Night' dance track and Jennie feels her mood lift a little. She recognises a few people as they pass them. Johnny Mackenzie, the top scorer in the school football team, who looks greyer but as athletic as ever. Polly Bisley, the maths genius, who barely looks a day older than she did in sixth form. And the Winkleman twins, Carl and Daisy, who Jennie's shocked to see are still wearing colour co-ordinated outfits.

'Here we go,' says Lottie as they reach the bar. 'What's your poison?'

Jennie looks at what's on offer in the buckets of ice. There's Smirnoff Ice, Hooper's Hooch, pre-mixed Archers and lemonade, and several buckets overflowing with Bud Light. She hesitates. There don't seem to be any soft drinks and she's never been a big drinker. 'I—'

'Fun, aren't they?' says Lottie, her overzealous expression only rivalled by the whiteness of her teeth. 'I thought it would be nice to have retro drinks, you know, like we had back in the day?'

Jennie nods. She feels dull, lethargic even, standing next to Lottie and her megawatt smile. If she's going to survive this party, she's going to need some help. Forcing a smile, Jennie reaches into the closest bucket and takes a bottle.

'Smirnoff, great choice,' says Lottie. She grabs a bottle for herself, removes the cap and then passes the bottle opener to Jennie. Lottie clinks her bottle against Jennie's. 'To friends reunited.'

Jennie forces another smile. 'To friends.'

'So tell me, what have you been up to all these years?' says Lottie. 'You know I married Nathan? When we met at Exeter in freshers' week I just knew he was the one straight away. And I was so right. He's a sweetheart and he's doing brilliantly in his career. I mean, I know people don't like bankers very much, but the perks are just phenomenal and the quality of life we have makes it all so worth it.'

Jennie nods along. It's clear she'd have no hope of getting a word in even if she wanted to. Instead, she drinks the Smirnoff as quickly as she can without seeming rude. Once the bottle's empty she'll make her excuses and leave.

'So, we're out in Upper Heydon now,' continues Lottie. 'It's only four miles from here, but *so* much easier for the school run to Stockley House. Octavia, our eldest, started there last autumn, and Anthony and Katelyn are down for places when they leave

Bassington Prep. They're supposed to take the entrance exam too, of course, but the bursar says it's really just a formality.'

'Sounds great,' says Jennie, taking another swig of Smirnoff and taking a quick glance over Lottie's shoulder to see if there's anyone else here she recognises. She's hoping, and yet also fearing, that Hannah might have come, that this reunion might have lured her closest friend back to White Cross. That this might be the day Jennie finds out why Hannah abandoned her all those years ago.

Lottie doesn't seem to notice as she continues her monologue. 'Oh, and we have ponies now. Ponies! Of course everyone does really, these days, so it's no big thing, but Octavia is a such a keen horsewoman and her trainer tells us she has the most wonderful natural talent for it. It's so important to encourage your kids to follow their passions, don't you think?'

Jennie doesn't have kids and she's never wanted them. She's not sure how to answer. After all, it's not as if her own mum ever encouraged her in anything. 'I—'

'Oh look, there's Elliott,' says Lottie, waving frantically. 'Elliott, over here!'

Jennie turns to see Elliott Naylor walking towards them from the other side of the torchlit area. She hasn't seen him in years but aside from a few fine lines around his eyes and a smattering of grey in his otherwise black hair, he looks just as she remembers. She's relieved he's dressed as casually as she is, rather than in full glam mode like Lottie. His dark blue jeans, checked Superdry shirt and Converse trainers don't look that different from what he used to wear, but his glasses are stylish black Gucci frames rather than the round John Lennons he wore at school.

'Hey,' says Elliott. He air kisses Lottie on both cheeks and then grins at Jennie, his voice sounding as if he can't quite believe she's there. 'Jennie Whitmore? Wow. It's great to see you.'

Jennie feels her face flush. Elliott's always had this effect on her, even though she knows he's gay. 'It's good to see you too.'

Elliott gestures towards her bottle of Smirnoff. 'Another?'

'Please,' says Jennie. Anything to stop feeling so awkward.

'Good idea,' says Lottie, putting her hand on Elliott's arm and giving it a squeeze. 'Thanks, darling.'

As Elliott heads to the bar, Jennie manages to get a question in. 'There are so many people from school here. You must be in touch with loads of our year group?'

Lottie gives a little smile, clearly pleased with the compliment. 'I'm only in contact with them through the Class of '94 Facebook group really, although I catch up with Elliott and Rob from time to time.'

Rob Marwood was another of their friendship group. Super intelligent, but under a lot of pressure from his parents to get the best grades at every subject, Rob could be funny, moody, and rather off-the-wall. He was obsessed with *Flatliners* and wore a big grey coat like the one Kiefer Sutherland had in the film, even in the height of summer. When he'd told them he was applying to study medicine at uni, Jennie had been pretty sure he'd made his career choice based on that film.

'Is Rob coming?' asks Jennie, although what she really wants to ask is whether Hannah's coming tonight and whether Lottie has had any contact with her.

Lottie shakes her head. 'No, he's on another one of his luxury holidays. Jammy git, he's always off somewhere exotic or other. I suppose that's one of the perks being a super successful anaesthesiologist.'

'Here you go,' says Elliott, returning from the bar and handing both Jennie and Lottie a cold Smirnoff. 'You talking about Rob?'

'Of course,' Lottie replies, rolling her eyes, but smiling with it. 'It must be tough having all that money to spend.'

Elliott shrugs. 'We're not doing so bad ourselves, and money isn't everything, is it, Jennie?'

She opens her mouth to agree, but Lottie cuts her off.

'So says the man who just finished renovating an old chapel

into a home. I drove past it the other day on the way to hot yoga. That place must have cost you a fortune.'

'Not a fortune, but it was a bit of a stretch.' Elliott looks bashful. 'We felt it was important that the restoration was done as sympathetically as possible. It's our home now, and we wanted the community to be happy with what we'd done.'

'Where is it?' asks Jennie, taking a sip of her drink.

'In Whitchurch,' says Elliott. 'The station is just a couple of minutes' walk away, so it's handy for travelling to work. And Luke, my husband, works from home, so he can live anywhere.'

'Nice,' says Jennie. Whitchurch, a small town about fifteen miles away, is one of the most sought-after and expensive places in the area.

'And how's baby?' says Lottie. 'How long is it now?'

Elliott grins. 'Just over a month. We're so excited, but nervous too. There seems so much to prepare. Every time I come home from the lab Luke has ordered a whole load more baby stuff.'

'Congratulations,' says Jennie. She imagines Elliott will be an amazing dad. 'I'm really happy for you.'

'Thanks, I appreciate that.' He holds her gaze and reaches out to give her hand a squeeze. 'It really is great to see you, Jennie.'

'It is,' says Lottie, the over-brightness of her voice seemingly at odds with the rictus smile on her face. 'It's been *so* long. What happened to you, Jennie? It seemed like you just vanished after we got our A level results.'

Jennie drops her eyes to hide her anger and discomfort. That's not how she remembers it *at all*. At first, after Hannah had disappeared, she'd joined forces with Lottie and they'd spent hours together designing and photocopying 'missing' posters. They'd gone around town putting them up in shops and on community noticeboards and lampposts. They'd even spent a couple of weeks posting them through as many letterboxes as they could. But nothing had worked. And when, almost a month later, an eyewitness came forward saying they'd seen Hannah at the train station the night she disappeared, the police decided that Hannah was just another teenage runaway fleeing a troubled home.

The news had broken Jennie. She'd been certain Hannah had been taken against her will, that she had been on the way to meet her at the bus stop as they'd planned. That she'd *never* leave her without saying goodbye. When the evidence disproved that, Jennie's world imploded. She started to believe that maybe Hannah *had* chosen to leave without her, and she couldn't cope. The rest of the summer passed in a daze of grief and self-imposed isolation. She barely got out of bed and she listened to Metallica's *Black Album*, especially 'Nothing Else Matters', on repeat. By the time Jennie had felt able to venture out again, Lottie and the others had become distant, distracted by university and new relationships, until their friendship with Jennie seemed entirely forgotten. It was as if Hannah had been the glue that held them together, and without her their friendship group failed to function.

Jennie realises that Lottie is staring at her, still waiting for an answer to her question. 'I've always been here. I never left.'

There's an awkward pause in the conversation. Lottie gives Jennie another forced smile. Elliott looks sympathetic but unsure how to respond. Jennie fiddles with the label on her bottle, peeling it in thin strips from the glass. Behind them the conversations and laughter continue. On the speakers, Stiltskin's 'Inside' fades and Spin Doctors' 'Two Princes' takes its place. Jennie swallows hard. Hannah loved this song.

It's Lottie who finally breaks the silence. 'Have you heard from her?'

'Not once. You?' says Jennie.

'No, although there have been plenty of sightings reported on the Class of '94 page, and even that grainy photo of her taken in Ibiza a few years ago.'

So Lottie's just as much out of the loop. Jennie tries not to let the disappointment crush her. She knows about the sightings, and she saw the photo Lottie's talking about, although it was so out of focus it was impossible to tell if it really was Hannah or just some other flame-haired woman.

'I miss her,' says Lottie. 'She was my best friend, and I know I'm so blessed with my life now, but it still feels weird that she's not part of it.'

'Yeah.' *I miss her too.* Lottie always maintained that she was Hannah's best friend, but from the way Hannah acted it never seemed that way to Jennie.

'I got us some refills,' says Elliott, holding up three more bottles of Smirnoff.

Jennie hadn't even noticed he'd gone back to the bar, but she gratefully takes a fresh bottle, knocking back half of it in one long chug. She knows she's drinking too much and too fast, but she doesn't care. All she cares about is numbing the pain of the Hannah-shaped wound the conversation has reopened. The music isn't helping as the Spin Doctors fade and Prince's 'The Most Beautiful Girl in the World' begins. This song has always reminded her of Hannah.

'So what are you up to?' asks Elliott. 'Tell us about your life now.'

Jennie is grateful for the subject change, even though she hates talking about herself. Putting on a bright tone, she says, 'I joined Thames Valley Police in '95 and made detective a few years later. I'm a DI now and run a team in the Major Crime Unit based here in White Cross.'

'A detective, that's very cool,' says Elliott. 'Well done you.'

'Totally,' says Lottie. 'And do you have a husband, a family?'

Jennie takes another mouthful of Smirnoff before answering. 'I don't have time for that sort of thing. My work is my life.'

Lottie's expression changes to a pained look that Jennie's used to seeing from parents who learn she doesn't have kids. It's as if they can't comprehend why a woman might not want to have children. Lottie turns to Elliott and changes the subject. 'Speaking of time, I can't believe they're demolishing the school tomorrow. I

17

really thought the Historical Society's petition would've stopped the redevelopment plans, but the council don't seem to care about our town's history.'

'The place is falling down,' says Elliott. 'It's beyond saving.'

'But surely they could have done something?' Lottie replies, her voice getting louder. 'It's been standing over a hundred years. The developers should be renovating it, not razing it to the ground.'

Elliott shrugs. 'That school is a derelict death trap and the land it's on is worth a premium.'

Jennie agrees, but stays silent. She takes another gulp of Smirnoff instead and looks past the makeshift bar at the view beyond. The school building is too close to the foot of the hill to been seen from here, but across the valley the lights of White Cross town twinkle like stars in the darkness.

'It's the end of an era,' says Lottie, sadly. 'I'm going to watch tomorrow. I think it's important to bear witness to these moments in history, even if you don't agree with them.'

Later, Jennie wobbles her way home through the lanes, so drunk it's a struggle to keep her bike going in a straight line. She has no idea how many Smirnoffs she had; all she knows is that each one helped her feel less weird about seeing the schoolfriends she lost touch with so many years ago. She even managed to stay put when Lorraine Chester briefly joined their group to say hello. The weirdest thing was how Lorraine was so nice to her, greeting her like a long-lost friend rather than the Brummie-accented girl with the embarrassing mum who Lorraine and her mean-girl clique had bullied so mercilessly.

Braking to a halt outside the house, she dismounts and pushes the bike as she snakes her way up the front path.

As she tries for the third time to get her key in the lock, Jennie wonders if she'll hear from Lottie and Elliott. They hugged at the end of the night and swapped numbers with emphatic promises of staying in touch. Maybe they will. Maybe that would be nice.

Staggering up the front step, she wheels her bike inside and props it in the hallway before closing the front door. Bending down to pick up the post, Jennie's stomach lurches and the hallway seems to spin. The Seventies flowered wallpaper and peeling paintwork kaleidoscope before her eyes. She puts her free hand on the wall to steady herself and wonders if she's going to be sick.

Once the moment has passed, Jennie walks to the kitchen and downs a pint of water before refilling the glass and carrying it through to the lounge, along with the post. She flops down onto the threadbare brown sofa and starts to open the envelopes. There are a couple of bills in her mum's name, a letter from the solicitor handling the probate of her mum's estate, and a final statement and confirmation that the refund of her security deposit has been actioned by the estate agent she rented her apartment from until last month.

She looks around the lounge. It hasn't changed since her mum bought the place, back in 1993. Or rather, it's aged badly. Nothing has been mended or updated. The only modern things in here are Jennie's laptop and printer, and they're hardly state of the art. When Mum died seven months ago, Jennie had been adamant she wouldn't move back into the house. But when the landlord increased the rent on her flat, keeping the house going and renting an apartment didn't really make sense. So she moved in, telling herself that she'd clear out the place in her spare time.

Jennie's been here five weeks, but all she's managed to do so far is box up her mum's knick-knacks and start to recycle the mountains of old magazines her mum seems to have hoarded for the last ten years. She needs to hire a skip really, or a house clearer. The whole thing feels exhausting.

The cuckoo clock in the kitchen chimes midnight and Jennie flinches. She swears under her breath and vows that the stupid clock is going to the charity shop at the weekend. She's always hated it.

Putting the post down, Jennie takes another long drink of

water and tries not to think about how awful she's going to feel in the morning. This is why she doesn't usually drink.

Finishing her water, Jennie sits alone in the crushing silence, surrounded by the debris of her mum's life. She thinks about Elliott and Lottie, both married and living in fancy houses, and sighs. How the hell have things come to this?

Day Two

Chapter 2

Jennie wakes with her heart racing.

Yanked from sleep by the foghorn going off beside her head, she gropes for the phone and presses the screen, trying to silence it. It takes another few seconds to register that it's a phone call and not her alarm. She reads the caller ID: Zuri Otueome.

Jennie squints at the time: it's barely seven o'clock. Still groggy, she answers the call. 'Morning.'

'But not a good one by the sounds of it,' says Zuri, cheerful as ever. 'Sorry to wake you, boss, but we've got a body.'

Jennie's head is banging and her throat's so dry it feels like sandpaper. 'Where?'

'White Cross Academy. The old site, not the new one,' says Zuri. 'Over on Chalkton Road.'

'The Academy?' Jennie's voice is a croak. Her brain feels scrambled. As she sits up, she winces at how much her body aches after falling asleep on the sofa.

'Any more details?' Jennie asks, biting back the other questions flooding her mind.

'Not much, just that the body was found by the contractors working on the demolition and, from the description, sounds like it's been there a long time. They've paused all work for now. Shall I meet you there?'

'Yeah,' says Jennie, unsure whether the sick feeling in her stomach is due to last night's overindulgence or the thought of returning to her old school. 'Give me half an hour.'

Twenty-four minutes later, Jennie arrives at the old White Cross Academy site. Getting off her bike, she wheels it along the pavement towards the entrance. The once pristine black paint has flaked from the iron railings, which are now riddled with rust. The high arched entry gates, with the school's initials set into the iron, have been removed from their hinges and dumped in the dirt just inside the entrance.

Builders in hard hats and high-vis tabards are milling around the no man's land between the railings and an eight-foot-high wooden fence that's been erected to stop locals rubbernecking at what's going on in the buildings behind.

Pushing her bike through the open gateway, Jennie heads along the weed-lined pathway towards what looks like a gate in the new fence. The high-vis guys look over. A couple of them start walking towards her.

'You more police?' asks a well-tanned contractor.

'I'm DI Whitmore,' says Jennie. 'Has my colleague DS Otueome arrived?'

'Yeah, she went over to the main building, to the basement, with the doctor bloke and the others in the paper suits.'

Jennie smiles. 'Thanks.'

The contractor nods but doesn't return the smile. 'Any idea when we'll be able to get back to work?'

'Sorry, not yet,' says Jennie. 'We'll be able to give you a timescale once we've had a look, but it's unlikely to be today, and probably not tomorrow.'

The contractor swears under his breath. 'The boss isn't going to like that.'

'Like I said, we'll give you a timescale once we've assessed the situation.'

Leaving the contractor shaking his head, Jennie continues to the wooden fence and lets herself through the gate. Leaving her bike propped up against the fence, Jennie ducks under the tape. She looks across the yellowing lawn, past the uniformed officer standing at the bottom of the steps to the portico door, and up at the main school building.

The Victorian frontage is still as imposing as ever, but it's clearly been neglected. The grey stone is crumbling and the windows have been boarded up. Nature has started to take back the space; moss covers most of the black slate roof, and ivy has twisted itself around the once-white columns either side of the grand portico. Jennie supposes the decay was inevitable. After the school moved to a new purpose-built campus almost fifteen years ago, the old buildings were sold off to developers. Since then, they've stood empty and uncared for as the new owners tried and failed to get planning permission. Over the years, there's been trouble with squatters and with kids setting fires in the building. Maybe the body is a homeless person or junkie who sought shelter and died while they were here.

It can't be Hannah, can it? The police said she'd run away.

Behind the school, the woodland stretching up into the Chiltern Hills looks dense and foreboding. The early morning ground mist hasn't yet been fully burned away by the sun, its ghostly veil partially shrouding both the trees and the school building. It's almost impossible to see the huge chalk cross that dominates the hillside above.

As she walks towards the building, Jennie's stomach lurches. She's not looking forward to going down into the basement again after all these years.

As her footsteps echo off the stone floor, she repeats the mantra over and over in time with them, as if wishing something can make it true.

It can't be Hannah. It can't be Hannah.

With the boarded-up windows blocking any external light, and what's still working of the fluorescent strip lighting flickering overhead, the corridor seems far longer and much spookier than Jennie remembers. The last time she was here – the day she sat her last A level paper – this corridor was a bustling hive of activity. The football team had won the County Championship final the

25

evening before, and Johnny Mackenzie, who'd scored all three of the winning goals, was carried on the shoulders of his teammates through the corridors, accompanied by frenzied cheering. Only the twins, Daisy and Carl Winkleman, didn't cheer. They were frantically speed-reading the English paper set text, as if it would make a difference to cram information into their brains up to the very last second before the exam.

Mind you, it wasn't as if Jennie could talk. Following Hannah's disappearance Jennie gave up any pretence of revision and the A and two Bs she'd been predicted ended up being a C and two Ds. Considering she'd felt discombobulated and shell-shocked, and had very little memory of sitting the exams, she was amazed the grades were that high. Hannah's boyfriend, Simon Ackhurst, was captain of the school football team but he missed the championship match and failed to show up for any of his A level exams. Of their friendship group, Simon was the only person other than Jennie who truly fell apart in the vacuum left by Hannah's disappearance.

It can't be Hannah.

Jennie steps around a large pile of mouldy debris where the ceiling has caved in and continues on past the rows of grey metal lockers that line this section of the corridor. She stops beside number thirty-seven – her old locker – and can't resist opening it. The handle squeaks as she turns it, but the metal door swings open easily enough. The locker is empty, but it still bears the remnants of those who occupied it, with their stickers adorning the sides. Jennie looks at the pictures; the least faded are newer artists – Muse, Beyoncé, Foo Fighters – but beneath them, partially covered and their colours long-faded, Jennie sees Madonna, Jim Morrison, and Soundgarden. She smiles, and feels a warm hug of nostalgia: these are her stickers. On the inside of the door, remarkably intact even after all these years, is the *Give Peace A Chance* sticker her dad had put in her Christmas stocking a few months before he died. She wishes she could peel it off and take it with her. She has so few mementoes from her dad.

Closing the door, Jennie glances along the lockers towards forty-one and forty-two. The nostalgic feeling fades. Those were once Lorraine Chester and Becky Mead's lockers. Jennie remembers her first day at the school and shudders. She'd spent hours that morning putting together her outfit, opting for a smart calf-length skirt, a blue blouse and school blazer. Jennie was taking her packed lunch out of her briefcase to put into her locker when she first heard the laughing. Looking around she saw Lorraine and Becky, standing there in their mini-kilt skirts, Mary Jane shoes and tight vest tops. They called her a whole bunch of names that time, but it didn't take long for their bullying to become violent.

Hurrying away from the lockers, Jennie reaches the stairs leading down to the basement. The stone steps seem to be in good condition, unlike the rotten banister. As she descends, she feels the temperature drop with every step. The stench of damp gets stronger as she reaches the basement, and the air becomes thicker – chewy even. A sense of dread builds inside her. This basement is the place where she had the best and worst times at school. It's the place that reminds her most of Hannah.

It can't be her.

Jennie coughs. Her eyes start to water.

'Hey.' DS Zuri Otueome smiles as she hurries over to meet Jennie at the bottom of the stairs. She's smartly dressed in a grey trouser suit with an orange blouse. Her braided hair is twisted up into a bun, and she's wearing booties and gloves rather than a full white bodysuit. She looks the epitome of style and efficiency. Zuri gestures through the open doorway to their right. 'We're just through here.'

Jennie's stomach starts to churn. She knows where that doorway leads. 'What have we got?'

'Human remains. A full skeleton from what I've seen so far, but the doc will be able to tell you more. They were found this morning by the demolition team. They'd started work early, around 6am, to double-check the explosive charges before the detonation planned for 9am. When the charges down here didn't respond, a couple of the team were sent to investigate. They found part of the basement had flooded, probably due to the heavy rain we had during that thunderstorm early on Sunday morning. Anyway, they got to work pumping out the water, but as they were finishing up, one of the crew noticed the top of a skull protruding from one of the trenches where the charges had been laid. That's when they called it in.'

Jennie nods, unsure whether she can trust herself to speak. She puts on the protective booties and gloves she always carries with her. Then, hoping her voice will come out sounding normal, she says, 'Thanks, Zuri. You'd better lead the way.'

Following Zuri, Jennie goes through the open doorway and into the passageway beyond. Rather than taking a left into the basement darkroom that was Jennie's sanctuary during her time at the school, Zuri leads her further along the corridor. They pass several store cupboards and stop outside the old boiler room at the end of the passageway.

Zuri indicates for Jennie to enter the room first. 'The remains were found in here.'

Jennie steps inside. The smell of damp and decay is worse, and the floor is squelchy underfoot from the recent flooding. There are several white body-suited CSIs at work.

Forensic pathologist Hassan Ayad, a short, studious-looking man in his forties, is crouched down over a large trench. He looks up as Jennie enters the room. 'Good morning, DI Whitmore.'

'Hi, Hassan. What can you tell me?'

'Well, it's early days so far, but I'd say we have a female, probably a teen, who's been down here for a long time. If I was a betting man, which as you know I'm not, I'd put my money on it being more than twenty years, possibly nearer to thirty.' Straightening up, Hassan steps away from the trench to make room for Jennie. 'Decomposition is highly advanced. Take a look for yourself.'

Jennie's heart rate accelerates. Given the likely age at the time they died, and how long Hassan estimates they've been buried in the basement, this could be someone a similar age to her, to Hannah. She moves closer to the trench, apprehension growing with every step.

How could it be Hannah? A witness saw her at the train station. The police said she'd run away. She can't be here. She can't be dead.

Jennie stops at the edge of the trench.

Nausea rises within her. Her heart slams against her chest.

A skull looks up at her from the trench, but it's not the chalk-white bone and grimacing teeth that send Jennie reeling. It's the scraps of red plaid that cling to the skeleton's ribcage; the rusted but still distinctive Celtic Knot buckle of a belt still fastened around the long-deflated waist; and the heart-shaped gold pendant, its delicate chain snapped in two, that lies half a foot from the remains.

Hannah's favourite clothes.

The necklace Hannah *never* took off.

It can't be Hannah.

But it is.

Chapter 3

Struggling to get her breathing under control before Hassan and Zuri notice she's in trouble, Jennie forces herself to stay looking down into the trench. She can't show them the effect these remains are having on her because compared to a lot of the dead bodies she's seen in her time this is extremely tame. But the other dead bodies she's seen haven't been people Jennie knew.

Hassan, never one to like a silence, fills the void. 'It looks like our victim had been buried and concreted over, but the demolition crew took up that part of the floor to lay the charges last week. When the basement flooded, some of the earth surrounding her remains got washed away, revealing her.'

Jennie takes another deep breath. Doesn't respond.

Hannah never left. She's been here all this time.

'I had an initial conversation with the head of the demolition team,' says Zuri. 'He said there were old pipes in this section of the floor and they pulled some out when they were preparing the ground for the charges.'

Jennie frowns. 'They buried her under the pipes?'

'It looks that way. We also found a purple rucksack partially obscuring the body,' Hassan adds. 'The contents, mainly clothes as far as we could tell, looked rather worse for wear as you'd expect, but the bag itself was remarkably well preserved. Forensics will work whatever magic they can.'

A rucksack?

Jennie feels a rush of emotions. Questions too.

Was the rucksack Hannah's luggage for their move to London? Was Hannah killed before she could meet her at the bus stop?

Hassan, undeterred by Jennie's silence, continues, 'I've got a theory about what happened to her if you're interested.'

Jennie nods, but doesn't look at him as he moves alongside her at the trench.

'Well, you'll see the hyoid bone is broken,' says Hassan, gesturing down towards the skeleton's neck. 'My initial view is she was strangled.'

'So it's murder?' says Zuri as she scribbles down what Hassan's telling them into her notebook.

'I need more time with her back in the lab to be sure,' says Hassan. 'But, as a preliminary hypothesis, yes, I'd say there was definitely foul play involved.'

As Hassan and Zuri continue to talk about the details, Jennie finds it increasingly hard to focus on what they're saying. She finds it difficult to envision someone enacting that kind of brutality against Hannah, especially here, in what was meant to be her safe space.

Jennie, on the other hand, was no stranger to violence at school. Lorraine and Becky made her familiar with it. Quickly, too. The worst of it came only three weeks into her time at White Cross. Jennie had always hated PE. It wasn't that she was particularly unfit, but cross-country running wasn't her thing. She was slow, always falling behind the group and finishing as one of the final stragglers. Lorraine and Becky knew that.

On that day they hung back with Jennie, constantly mocking her with comments about her being a hippo, a tank, a sumo wrestler. She tried to run faster and catch up with the others, but she was soon breathless and exhausted.

Lorraine and Becky bided their time, waiting until everyone else was out of sight before they tripped her. As Jennie lay on the ground, fighting back tears and clutching her injured ankle, they laughed and taunted her.

'Ugly bitch. You pissed up like your mum?'

Becky joyfully told the story of how she'd seen Jennie's

'deadbeat' mum vomiting in the alcohol aisle of the local Tesco at the weekend. 'OMG, you should have seen it, your mum yelled at a shop assistant who was trying to help her and hit the security guard who escorted her from the store. It was *so* embarrassing. Who wants a shit mum like that?'

'Or a wife like that,' sneered Lorraine. 'Your dad probably got himself blown up on purpose so he didn't have to see you or your crap mum again.'

Struggling to her feet, Jennie lunged towards Becky and Lorraine, but that only made things worse. Becky pulled Jennie's arms behind her back while Lorraine whacked Jennie in the face. With blood pouring from her nose and a split lip, Jennie tried to fight them off. Eventually she managed to wrestle free from Becky's grasp, but Becky quickly grabbed for Jennie's cheap sports top and clung on tight. As Jennie twisted away Lorraine snatched at her top too and pulled hard. Seconds later there was a loud tearing sound as the side seam ripped, exposing Jennie's ancient grey bra. Becky and Lorraine had screamed with laughter. Tears pricked Jennie's eyes as she clutched the tattered fabric to her chest.

'Leave her alone.'

The shout came from behind them. Jennie didn't recognise the voice, but she saw fear flicker across Becky and Lorraine's faces. As she turned around, Jennie smelt the heady scent of Opium perfume, and then there was Hannah. She was wearing PE kit, but she'd added her own flare to it: a red plaid shirt over the regulation sports top and shorts, and long over-the-knee socks rather than the usual ankle length.

As Hannah came closer, Lorraine and Becky seemed to shrink back, away from Jennie. Hannah tilted her head to one side, seemingly amused by this. She was so vital and alive with this wild energy that just seemed to emanate from her; it was mesmerising. To Jennie she seemed like a kick-ass guardian angel.

Hannah had put her arm around Jennie and said to Becky and Lorraine, 'Touch her again and you're dead.'

As the bullies legged it through the gate and off across the playing field towards the school building, Hannah gave Jennie a dazzling smile. 'They tried to bully me when I started here. It didn't go well for them.'

Following Hannah, Jennie limped back to school and down into the basement. Hannah opened the first door off the hallway and told her to come inside. Jennie had never been in that room before. She didn't know what she'd expected but it wasn't what she found. The soft red light. The not-unpleasant smell of chemicals. A rickety old external door. A cosy space: dark wood-panelled walls, an old burgundy sofa, a long, thin table up against one wall with a stack of shallow trays and plastic bottles of chemicals at one end, and a washing line with what looked like photographs pegged along it.

A darkroom.

'This is Jennie,' said Hannah. 'I've said it's cool for her to hang out.'

The four people in the room all stared at her. Jennie looked down, feeling awkward. She hated to be the centre of attention.

'Welcome to the darkroom crew,' said Hannah. She gestured towards a long-haired, hippie-looking guy, who was wearing a long grey coat even though they were indoors and it wasn't cold. 'That's Rob, and over on the sofa are Simon and Lottie.'

'Hi,' said Jennie, smiling at them, even though it hurt her split lip.

Rob raised an eyebrow and then lifted his hand in a small wave. Simon, a broad, blond jock who she recognised as captain of the football team, gave her a casual nod. Lottie, her blonde curly hair perfectly styled and wearing an expensive-looking pink shift dress and black platform sandals, just stared back, unsmiling.

'And that's Elliott over there,' said Hannah, turning towards the tall, nerdy-looking boy with a mop of black hair, wearing jeans, a blue T-shirt and John Lennon glasses.

Elliott smiled a broad, generous smile. 'Hey, Jennie. Are you into photography?'

His eyes met hers and Jennie blushed. It felt as if a flock of butterflies had taken flight inside her stomach. 'Yes,' she said, inwardly cringing at how lame her voice sounded. She cleared her throat. 'I love taking pictures.'

Until that moment her life in White Cross, and at the school, had been hell. But meeting Hannah and the darkroom crew had changed everything. Jennie knew she'd finally found her people in this mismatched group brought together in a sanctuary beneath the school. She had wanted to be part of their group, whatever it took. And although she'd become firm friends with Hannah and Elliott almost immediately, it had taken a little while longer for the others to warm up to her. But they did. For the rest of the year, until they went on study leave before their exams, the six of them were inseparable. Then, suddenly, Hannah had disappeared.

'Don't you think, DI Whitmore?'

The sound of Hassan's voice pulls Jennie back into the present. Not wanting to look any more at what she is sure will prove to be her friend's remains, Jennie turns to face Hassan and Zuri. 'Sorry, I missed that.'

Hassan peers at Jennie over the top of his wire-framed glasses. 'I said if you're done with looking at the body, I can have her exhumed and transported to the lab.'

'Sure,' says Jennie. 'I've seen enough.'

'How long until you'll be able to do the post-mortem?' asks Zuri as they turn away from the trench and walk back across the boiler room towards the door.

'We're pretty stacked up at the moment, so it won't be today, but I'll try and get her first on the list for tomorrow,' Hassan replies.

'Thanks,' says Jennie. 'I appreciate that.'

Leaving Hassan to organise the removal of the body, Jennie and Zuri head back along the passageway towards the stairs. Jennie's still reeling from the discovery. Her legs are as wobbly as an hour-old foal's. Her mind feels scattered and confused. For so long she's believed Hannah left for London without her. She's hoped beyond hope for almost thirty years that one day Hannah would make contact, that she'd explain why she left the way she did, and where she's been all this time. That she'd be alive. But now that hope is gone. Hannah is dead. She was lying in a dirty, concrete-covered hole in the school basement for all these years.

'You okay?' asks Zuri, concern on her face.

'I'm fine. It's just weird being back at this school. It looks so different,' Jennie covers, trying to keep her tone light. 'And it smells bad, which with my hangover isn't the most fun.'

'I bet.' Zuri grimaces in sympathy. 'So, what's the plan for when we get back?'

'I'll brief the boss first, then let's gather everyone in the incident room.' Jennie checks her watch. 'In, say, an hour?'

'Sure thing.'

As they pass the door to the darkroom, the place that was once her and Hannah's sanctuary, Jennie feels an overwhelming urge to open the door and look inside. She wants to curl up on the old sofa, smell the reassuring chemicals, and feel cocooned and safe in the glow of the soft red light. She resists, though, just like she resists telling Zuri that she thinks she knows who the victim is, and that she was her best friend. Because although it might help to tell someone, and Zuri is the closest thing she has to a friend these days, she's also a stickler for the rules – which would necessitate that Jennie step away from this case and hand the reins to another DI. Jennie can't do that. She absolutely can't. She has to find out who did this to Hannah.

They leave the school building and pass back through the area cordoned off with police tape. Jennie collects her bike from where she'd propped it against the fence. As they exit through the school gates, Jennie's surprised to see the size of the crowd gathered at the barriers erected by the construction workers to keep people back from the blast zone. She recognises a few locals, serial rubbernecks, along with several ex-students, including Lottie Varney.

I'll have to tell Lottie about Hannah.

Pushing away the thought, Jennie looks at Zuri and raises her eyebrows. 'Busy out here.'

Zuri nods. 'Do you think they're here to watch the detonation or because word's got out about the body?'

'I guess we'll find out in a minute,' says Jennie, striding towards the barrier.

As she wheels her bike through the gap in the barrier, she sees Lottie pushing her way through the crowd to the front.

Lottie raises her hand, waving. 'Can you tell us what's going on in there? Rumour has it there's been a murder? Is that right? Surely it can't be right?'

'I'm sorry, we can't give any details,' says Jennie.

'But, Jennie, can't you tell me?' Lottie moves along the barrier towards her. 'I mean, a murder here in White Cross? That's just so unimaginable.'

Jennie stiffens. She can't appear too pally with Lottie, not if she wants to have any chance of staying the lead on this investigation. And she can't share the details either; if she does, she'll break down. So she shakes her head. Keeps her tone professional. 'Like I said, we can't comment at this time.'

A flicker of confusion passes across Lottie's face, quickly followed by hurt. Jennie keeps walking, heading along the cordoned-off section of the street towards the main road.

'I'm over here,' says Zuri, gesturing to the blue Toyota parked on the double yellows. 'See you back at base?'

'See you there,' Jennie agrees. Undoing her cycle helmet from the crossbar, she straps it on and climbs onto her bike. Before she starts pedalling, Jennie glances over her shoulder, back towards the school and the crowd gathered outside.

There's a woman standing slightly away from the group, facing towards the road rather than the school building. She's frowning, yet her expression is oddly hard to read. As their eyes meet, Jennie feels her stomach clench.

Lottie is staring directly at her.

Chapter 4

'So it's murder.' DCI Dave Campbell states it as a fact rather than asking a question. Leaning back in his chair, his attention is now fully on Jennie rather than the spreadsheet he was grappling with a few moments earlier. He indicates for her to take a seat.

Jennie sits down on the only free chair in the rather cramped office. 'Hassan thinks so. She appears to have been strangled, and was found buried beneath pipework and a poured-concrete floor.'

The DCI looks thoughtful as he runs a hand over his close-trimmed grey beard. 'Any idea who she is?'

'Nothing confirmed as yet, but the age, timing and some of the clothing found with the victim's remains suggest it could be Hannah Jennings.' She glances down at the battered-looking buff folder on her lap. 'I've had a scan of the old case file. Jennings was a local schoolgirl. She was reported missing in June 1994 but never found.'

'Jesus,' says Campbell, exhaling hard. 'This is all we need, yet another cock-up for the local press to bang on about.'

'Sorry, sir.' Jennie knows the DCI has been in damage control mode ever since there was public outcry over how one of the other teams mishandled the response to an attempted abduction of three teenage girls a few months back.

'Not your fault,' he says, the weariness clear in his voice. 'But we need a quick result on this, and zero errors. The whole town will be watching.'

Jennie nods. Stout, greying and with less than a year until he takes retirement, the DCI's physical appearance and usually unfailingly can-do demeanour has always made her think of him as an ageing hobbit. But that's changed since the attempted abductions and the problems highlighted in the force by the mishandling of the incident. Campbell seems to have aged ten years in just a few short months and his behaviour is decidedly more ogre-like. 'Forensics have expedited the comparison of the misper's dental records, so we should get confirmation of the ID soon.'

'Good. Let me know as soon as you have it,' says Campbell. 'We'll need to get out in front of this with the media.'

'Understood,' says Jennie. She's certain the dental record identification is just a formality. They've found Hannah after all these years. She can feel it.

The DCI frowns. 'You all right?'

'I'm fine.' Jennie looks away, glancing out through the glass wall of Campbell's office into the open-plan area where Zuri is gathering the team for a briefing in the incident room.

Campbell's expression remains concerned. 'This misper who disappeared in 1994, I assume they were a pupil at the academy?'

'Yes, she was in the upper sixth.'

The DCI rubs his chin, thinking. '1994 is a while before I moved here, but isn't that when you were a pupil at the school?'

Jennie feels suddenly cold. She knows where the DCI's going with this: he's wondering if she can really investigate a case impartially if she knew the victim. 'I moved to White Cross in 1993 and joined the school that autumn for my last year of sixth form.'

'You were in the same year group?' Campbell asks, raising his eyebrows. 'Were you friends with this...?'

'Hannah Jennings.'

'So were you?' asks Campbell.

She was like a sister to me.

Jennie knows she's on dodgy ground; the DCI can smell bullshit at a hundred paces. She shakes her head. 'I barely knew her, sir. It was a big sixth form and the other kids had known each other for years. I was the newbie and I kept to myself mostly.

It was just after my dad was killed so I ... I wasn't feeling that sociable.'

The DCI keeps his gaze on her. 'Nonetheless, it must have been unsettling?'

It felt as if my life had ended.

Jennie knows the DCI was an excellent detective in the field. On his desk, alongside the framed picture of his wife Lillian and their two daughters, there's a framed Community Policing Lifetime Achievement award that he was presented with the previous year. He's watching her now as if she's a suspect; one wrong move or word and he'll see past her lies. She fights to keep her neutral expression and hopes her voice doesn't give her away. 'I can only vaguely remember that time. There were a few posters up around the town and some stories in the newspaper, but I think most people believed she'd run away to London.'

'Still, it must have been traumatic having a fellow student go missing?'

I've felt adrift all these years, never able to move on from the jilted teen I was that night in the rain at the bus stop. I've been waiting for a call, an email, or a knock on the door. For Hannah to come back and tell me why she left me.

Jennie shakes her head. This isn't working; she needs to show him some emotion to sell him the lie. 'Not as traumatic as my dad getting blown up in Bosnia. I was still grieving for him, nothing else really registered with me for several years afterwards. That's why I flunked my exams and took a while to decide what to do for a career.' She injects her tone with a bit of anger. 'But you should *know* that; it's all in my personnel records.'

Campbell looks contrite. 'I'm sorry, I didn't mean to drag up—'

'It's okay,' says Jennie, relieved the deflection worked. 'So, like I said, I wasn't really fully aware of the original case, but I did go to the school. I know the layout, how the academy operated back then, and I have an awareness of the people who worked there. All that will be an asset to this investigation.'

'Perhaps.' The DCI still looks unsure. 'But if the media get even the slightest whiff that you knew the victim they'll be crying foul. I think it's safer if I shift the case over to a different team.'

'Which team?' Jennie asks, stalling for time as she tries to think of a way to ensure she keeps the case.

Campbell stares at her. Frowns. 'I haven't—'

'Because you're not exactly spoilt for choice, are you?' she continues, suppressing her fear and irritation in an attempt to keep her voice measured and professional. 'If you give it to Strickland's team you're going to have the same issue. He might not have been in the same year, but he and at least half of his lot went to the academy at that time. Plus if the media catch wind of them getting another high-profile case so soon after screwing up the abduction response that's hardly going to end well, is it?'

Campbell grimaces. Strickland's mishandling of the attempted abduction of two thirteen-year-olds walking home from netball practice had been front-page news in the local papers. The detective's delayed response had left the men free to make a second abduction attempt with another teen less than an hour later, the girl saved by two passing dog walkers who gave multiple interviews criticising the force, provoking outrage in the town.

'On the other hand, if you give it to Pearson and her team, you'll be giving what's likely to become a high public interest case to the most inexperienced DI. I mean, she was just newly promoted last month and has *never* led a murder investigation. Plus she's up to her eyes in those aggravated burglary cases at the moment, and you've already got the local MP and that *White Cross Gazette* journalist kicking off over the delays in arresting those responsible.'

The DCI looks through the glass wall into the open-plan area as if searching for another option from the staff working at the desks.

He has to realise I'm right.

'I'm the right person to lead this investigation, sir, you know that. My team has the experience and the capacity to do a good job and I've got inside knowledge about the old school site that will really help us. You said it yourself that we need to clear this case quickly, and I'm your best bet for getting that done. This might be a cold case, but it'll be important to the community, to the family, and to people who knew the victim. And as a member of this community, it's important to *me*.'

Campbell runs his hand across his beard. 'And you really don't think that being at school with the victim will cloud your judgement?'

Hannah disappearing clouded every aspect of my life. I need to atone for believing she'd left me behind on purpose. I need to get past the guilt about all the things I've thought about her for so many years, the anger, the grief and the hatred at her betrayal.

Jennie takes a breath. The DCI is coming round to her way of thinking. He's nearly there. She just needs to push him across the line. She shakes her head. 'It won't. Like I said, I hardly knew her, but it sickens me that a child was killed and left buried under the school for thirty years. Her family deserve the truth. This community *needs* the truth.' Jennie's voice is strong, impassioned, determined. 'I will find it for them. Let *me* take the case.'

Jennie can see in Campbell's expression that he's relenting. This case is hers. She just hopes neither of them will come to regret his decision.

Chapter 5

'It's Satvinder Neale from Forensics. I've got an ID on your White Cross Academy victim.'

Jennie stops walking. Grips the phone tighter, her heart rate accelerating. 'Okay.'

'The remains exhumed from the school this morning are a match for the dental records of Miss Hannah Jennings. She'd had a filling on the seventeenth of May 1994 and the dentist took X-rays before the procedure. Those X-rays show no changes in her teeth occurred between the time of the filling and the time when she died.'

Satvinder reels off Hannah's date of birth and the address she had registered with the dentist, but Jennie knows those details by heart. Instead, she thinks about all the sightings of Hannah posted on the Class of '94 Facebook group over the years, people claiming to have seen Hannah chilling out in the Wood at Glastonbury, dancing wildly at an Adam Lambert gig at G-A-Y, or hiking with the most enormous rucksack at Grasmere in the Lake District. Every time Jennie had seen a post reporting a sighting of Hannah, hope had flared that one day, maybe, she'd get to see her friend again. Now she knows for certain that will never happen.

Jennie thanks Satvinder for the information and ends the call. She takes a breath, steadying herself, then hurries to the incident room. There's no time to waste.

'So we've got a confirmed ID,' Jennie tells the gathered team. 'Our victim is Hannah Jennings, an eighteen-year-old pupil at White Cross Academy who was reported missing on Friday the tenth of June 1994.'

All eyes are on her. Squeezing her hands into fists to stop her hands from shaking, Jennie looks around the narrow room.

DS Zuri Otueome is sitting at the front, making notes on her scratchpad. In contrast, DS Martin Wright has removed his Ted Baker suit jacket and is lounging back in his chair looking relaxed. Behind the sergeants, DC Naomi Bradfield and DC Steve Williams look focused and attentive, even though, as is the norm these days, poor Steve has dark circles under his eyes and the look of a man who hasn't truly slept in months.

'Naomi, can you hold the pen on this one?' asks Jennie. Petite, with a mass of hard-to-tame black ringlets, fifty-something Naomi is the epitome of a reliable pair of hands. A career DC, she's diligent and thorough, and someone who Jennie has come to rely on a great deal.

'Sure,' says Naomi, getting to her feet and moving across to the huge whiteboard that covers the length of the end wall.

'Thanks.' Jennie takes a seat at the front. She doesn't trust her voice not to crack when talking through the details of this morning's discovery, so she looks at Zuri. 'Do you want to take us through what happened at the school?'

'No problem,' says Zuri, opening her notebook. 'We received a call from the construction manager at 6.43am. His workers discovered human remains during their final preparations for the planned detonation to demolish the school building. Initial pathologist observations are that the body had been in the ground for between twenty and thirty years, and the cause of death was likely to have been strangulation. Given she was also buried beneath the pipe work, foul play is strongly suggested.'

'No shit,' says DS Martin Wright dismissively, without making eye contact with Zuri.

'The post-mortem is scheduled for tomorrow,' continues Zuri, ignoring Martin's tone.

'How come the remains weren't visible before now?' asks Martin, looking at Jennie rather than Zuri.

Jennie nods for Zuri to take the question. She wishes the two sergeants would sort out whatever's going on. There's been a rift between them for several months and neither has been willing to speak about it. Jennie's even tried to get Zuri to open up on one of their regular cinema trips, but Zuri just brushed off the question, saying it was nothing. It doesn't seem like nothing, though. If they don't resolve whatever it is soon, Jennie knows she's going to have to intervene.

Zuri looks directly at Martin. 'Until last week, the basement floor had been concrete. The crew dug it up in order to bury the explosive charges. This weekend was the first heavy rain since the concrete was removed and the basement flooded, washing away soil to reveal the remains.'

Martin's nostrils flare but he says nothing.

'Thanks, Zuri,' says Jennie, pausing a moment while Naomi finishes noting down the information on the whiteboard. She clocks the look of irritation on Martin's face and wonders if it's due to him not managing to trip up Zuri or because Jennie thanked her. Either way, he needs to get over it.

Jennie continues. 'As I said, Hannah Jennings was reported as a misper back in June 1994. I've pulled the old case file and had a look through it. It's pretty light on detail, but what we know about our victim is that she lived on the Chairmaker's Estate with her father. Her mum had left them a few years earlier and was living in London at the time Hannah went missing, although there wasn't believed to have been contact between them. The file indicates that Hannah and her father, Paul Jennings, had a difficult relationship.'

'Was it the usual teenage rebellion type stuff or more serious?' asks Martin. 'Any suspicions of abuse?'

Jennie pauses. She thinks of the things Hannah told her about her dad, how he'd get angry and lose his temper, yelling and sometimes throwing stuff, like the time he hurled a full plate of spaghetti bolognese at the wall because Hannah had forgotten to put onion in with the mince. She shakes her head. 'The file doesn't indicate any physical abuse took place, but there's a witness statement that mentions a heated argument on the day Hannah disappeared.'

At the back of the room, DC Steve Williams clears his throat. With his thinning hair and the dark circles beneath his eyes, he's a shadow of the man he was a year ago, before his wife died of cancer, leaving him a single dad to their two young boys. 'Did they ever close the original case?'

'They did.' Jennie tries not to let the bitterness she feels about it come out too strongly in her tone. 'Hannah Jennings was deemed a runaway and they closed the case at the end of July 1994.'

'On what evidence?' asks Naomi from over at the whiteboard.

'Not enough. At first the investigation focused on the dad, Paul Jennings, and a teacher, Duncan Edwards, who Hannah was rumoured to have been in a relationship with, but the case file concludes no evidence of wrongdoing against either.' Jennie taps her finger against the buff file she'd put on the table beside her. 'It was after a witness, Siobhan Gibbons, came forward saying she'd seen Hannah at the train station on the night she disappeared that the investigation concluded Hannah was just another wayward eighteen-year-old who'd run off to London.'

'*Had* she been having a relationship with the teacher?' asks Zuri.

'Perhaps,' says Jennie. She knows that there'd been something going on between Hannah and Mr Edwards but whether it was more than a flirtation she wasn't sure. Whatever it was, it certainly wasn't serious as far as Hannah was concerned. But she can't say that, obviously, as it's not in the file. 'There's nothing conclusive. I was at White Cross Academy at the time, and I do vaguely remember the rumour mill blaming Mr Edwards even after he was dropped as a suspect.'

Zuri raises her eyebrows. 'Did you know the victim?'

Jennie shakes her head. 'I only moved to White Cross for the last year of sixth form. I didn't really know anyone at the school well.'

'But you think this teacher bloke could be dodgy?' asks Martin.

'I know the extra art supplies were kept in a cupboard in the basement corridor close to the boiler room where Hannah's body was found.' An image of her friend's remains half buried in the muddy trench flashes into her mind. Swallowing hard, Jennie pushes it away. 'We need to find Duncan Edwards as a priority.'

Naomi writes the action on the whiteboard. Martin and Steve nod in agreement. Zuri makes a note on her pad.

'Hannah went missing during the study leave period before sitting her A levels,' says Jennie, trying to strike the right balance between giving useful information and soft pedalling her connection to Hannah. 'But she was part of a photography group known as the "darkroom crew" who used to hang out in the basement space. They were one of a number of clubs that used the basement, each with their own spaces, both during and out of school hours. So although Hannah was on study leave, she might still have been going into school for that reason.'

Zuri looks thoughtful. 'Given it sounds as if her relationship with her dad was a bit fraught, it could be this darkroom crew were like a sanctuary for her to escape to when things at home were difficult. We should find them and see what they have to say.'

'There are statements from them in the old case file,' says Jennie, trying to sound impartial even though her heart is racing at the thought of having to bring her old friends into this. 'But, as I said, a lot of students used to hang out in the basement and the darkroom crew were just a few kids among many others. I don't think that's a useful line of inquiry at this stage. We need to focus on the two original suspects and see what else the first investigation missed.'

Zuri frowns, clearly disagreeing but not challenging Jennie's decision.

'Good plan, boss,' says Martin, giving Zuri a smug look.

Zuri ignores him.

'Can you give us an update on forensics, Zuri?' asks Jennie, wanting to step out of the spotlight for a moment. The effort of not appearing too upset and of not revealing too much is taking its toll. She feels mentally and emotionally exhausted.

'Several items of clothing and personal effects were found with the body,' says Zuri. 'There was a partially rotted plaid shirt, a belt buckle, a pendant found near the body, and a rucksack. The rucksack contained clothes, make-up and what looks like a modelling portfolio. They've all been sent to the lab for analysis. I've tried to impress upon them that speed is of the essence, but as it's essentially a cold case we might be waiting a few days for any results.'

While Zuri finishes speaking, Martin bends down and starts re-tying the blue and claret West Ham laces on his black Doc Marten shoes.

'Good work, Zuri,' says Jennie. She looks around the gathered team. 'Okay, so familiarise yourselves with the details of the original misper investigation. Just because this case is thirty years old, that doesn't make it any less important. Hannah Jennings lost her life and was written off as a runaway. This police force failed her back then. Finding the truth now falls to us, and we're going to get her justice.'

There are nods from the team. Naomi moves across to the section of the whiteboard with the action list. She looks at Jennie expectantly.

'Next steps, we need to find out how a body could have been buried in concrete in the school basement without anyone noticing,' says Jennie. 'And find the whereabouts now of any suspects and witnesses named in the original investigation. The teacher, Duncan Edwards, is top of that list. We'll inform next of kin, then start the interviews. No one is to let the press get hold of the victim's identity until I give the nod.'

There are murmurs of agreement from the team.

'I did a search for next of kin,' says Zuri. 'The victim's dad still lives in White Cross, although in a different part of town from before. Unfortunately, her mum passed away from Covid in 2020.'

'Thanks, Zuri,' says Jennie as a wave of sadness washes over her that Hannah's mother died before knowing what happened to her daughter. Hannah had been estranged from her mum since she left, but in the last few weeks before she'd disappeared they'd secretly been in contact. There was talk of meeting up away from White Cross and Hannah hoped it wouldn't be too long before that happened. Given how Hannah described her dad – an angry man who had zero respect for women – Jennie makes a decision. 'Zuri, can you get the actions assigned? Martin, come with me; we're going to notify Paul Jennings that we've found his daughter.'

She feels bad when she sees the disappointed look on Zuri's face. By rights, she should be riding shotgun on this, but having a man in the room feels like the wisest play, even though she hates that it's necessary. Martin, on the other hand, isn't disguising his delight, grinning like the cat that got the cream as he gets up.

Jennie glances from Martin to Zuri.

What the hell's going on between them?

Chapter 6

'Sorry the car's such a state,' says Martin as he manoeuvres his Rav4 out of the station car park and onto the main road.

'It looks fine to me,' replies Jennie. And it does – there's no untidiness that she can see.

Martin shakes his head. 'The kids are at that really messy age, you know? Me and Kath wouldn't be without them, of course, but they're a hell of a lot of work.'

'I can only imagine.' Jennie has never wanted kids. She's never wanted a partner either. Trusting someone enough to let them into your life, to give them the opportunity to hurt you? No, that's not her thing at all.

Martin indicates left at the roundabout, taking the road out of town towards the Lakemead development. 'So I found out a bit more about the victim's dad. He remarried a few years ago and works for Waterside Garden Centre, the big one over near the new shopping village, with his wife, Shelly.'

'And moved to a different part of town?' says Jennie.

'Yeah, he's moved around a bit over the years. He left the house he'd shared with Hannah about six months after she went missing, then it looks like he lived in a few different flats in the town centre over the next twenty plus years, before moving into the house in Lakemead last year.'

Lakemead is a smart new housing development designed around a couple of large man-made lakes. There's a yoga studio and an artisan bakery along with a gastro pub, a beauty salon and a variety of different water sports options. House prices on the development are a good ten per cent higher than in White Cross town. 'Did he have anything on record? Arrests, charges?'

'He's stayed clean for a long time,' says Martin, indicating right and turning into Lakemead. 'There's just a couple of drunk and disorderlies on there from back in the day, but nothing after Christmas 1994.'

'Okay, good work,' says Jennie, looking out of the window as they go over the bridge that crosses the smaller of the two lakes and get their first glimpse of the development beyond. The houses are painted in pastel colours: baby pink, powder blue, mint green. To Jennie they look more like American stucco properties than the sort of homes you usually see in the Chilterns, but maybe that's the appeal.

Beside her, Martin lets out a long whistle. 'From the Chairmaker's Estate to here? Paul Jennings definitely looks like he's living his best life.'

Not for much longer, thinks Jennie. She turns to Martin, her tone serious. 'Show a bit more compassion; we're about to tell him his daughter's dead.'

Martin looks contrite. 'Yeah, course. Sorry, boss.'

They leave the car parked on the street and walk up the driveway. The house is painted baby pink and looks like a three or maybe four bed, with a garage on the side and a porch with matching olive trees standing either side of the door. Jennie reaches the door first. She can't see a bell, so she raps three times using the chrome knocker.

Paul Jennings opens the door. Wearing a beige cardigan over a tattersall checked shirt and chinos, he's leaner and greyer than his picture in the old case file. He looks from Jennie to Martin and the colour seems to drain from his face. 'You've found her, haven't you?'

'Mr Jennings, I'm Detective Inspector Jennie Whitmore, and this is Detective Sergeant Martin Wright. Can we talk inside?'

Opening the door wider, Paul Jennings steps back to let them enter. His face is ashen, his eyes are watery, and his energy is subdued. He's nothing like the aggressive, angry man Jennie remembers Hannah talking about.

As he leads them along a tastefully furnished hallway, she wonders if Paul Jennings recognises her. There'd been no flicker of recognition in his gaze, and he looks too upset to be capable of masking his reactions entirely. But then, she'd only ever seen him once before and that was from a distance; Hannah was never keen to hang out at her house if her dad was around.

Paul leads them into a bright living room. He gestures to a homely looking lady in jeans and a navy jumper who is sitting on one of the armchairs. 'This is my wife, Shelly. Please, take a seat.'

He sits down on the armchair beside Shelly's, leaving Jennie and Martin no choice but to sit on the small sofa opposite the armchairs. It's only a two-seater so they're forced to sit far closer together than they would usually. It's awkward but she perches on the edge of the seat, her focus on Mr Jennings. 'Would you like to get yourself some water or a cup of tea—'

'I don't need tea,' he says, curtly. His expression is a mixture of hope and fear; after many years of delivering this kind of news, it's a look Jennie knows all too well. Paul clasps his knees with his hands, his knuckles quickly turning white. 'Look, we watch the news. The body found at the old school – it's Hannah, isn't it?'

'Yes, I'm afraid so,' says Jennie. 'I'm very sorry for your loss.'

'Oh Jesus.' Jennings slumps forward, his head in his hands. 'I can't … I knew …'

Shelly puts her hand on Paul's back, rubs him between the shoulders. 'It's okay, it'll be okay.'

'It won't be though, will it?' counters Paul. He looks up at Jennie. 'Where was she found?'

Jennie hesitates, her breath catching in her throat as she remembers Hannah's eyeless skull looking up at her from the bottom of the muddy trench.

'In the basement of the school building,' says Martin, bluntly. 'She'd been buried.'

Paul lets out a loud sob. 'So someone killed her?'

'That's what the evidence suggests,' says Jennie, recovering her composure. 'We believe she was strangled, but we'll know more after the post-mortem. In the meantime, I've opened an investigation into her death.'

'That's more than your lot did when she disappeared. They didn't give a shit about her,' says Paul, bitterness in his voice. 'A couple of weeks poking around in my life and then they had the cheek to say she'd just run away. Bastards. If they'd have investigated properly maybe she'd be here now, maybe she'd be alive.'

'I'm sorry, sir,' says Jennie.

'I just...' Paul shakes his head. He flattens his palms and presses them hard into the top of his thighs. 'Look, I want to help in any way that I can.'

Shelly puts her hand on his arm. 'Paul, you know what the doctor said about not getting stressed.' She looks at Jennie. 'He has a bad heart.'

'I'm fine, love,' says Paul, putting his hand over Shelly's and giving it a squeeze. 'I *need* to help them find out who did this to my sweet angel.'

'Thank you,' says Jennie to them both. She's trying to focus on the job but it's so weird talking to this man who Hannah described as aggressive and violent. She realises she still feels cowed by him, but she can't let old feelings distract her. *She's* the one with the power now. 'It would really help if we could go over a few details from the night Hannah disappeared.'

'Of course, not a problem,' replies Paul, keeping a tight hold on Shelly's hand. 'I was in construction back then, working nights building a new motorway slip road over on the M40. I'd left for work around five o'clock, as usual. Hannah was out when I'd woken up just after four, and still wasn't back by the time I left, but that was pretty normal. She liked to study with her friends.'

'Do you have the names of these friends?' asks Martin, looking up from jotting notes onto his scratchpad.

Jennie stiffens, wondering if her name is about to come up.

Paul thinks for a moment. 'Lottie and Elliott were the main ones, I think, but she mentioned a couple of others. Rob, I think, and Stephen – no, sorry, it was Simon. She'd had the same group of mates for years.'

Not me?

Relief and irritation mingle inside her. She's glad Paul didn't name her but it brings back the feelings she had when Hannah disappeared. No one spoke to her or asked her any questions – not Hannah's dad, the teachers at school, or the police. It was as if she didn't exist, had not been a part of Hannah's life. It was heartbreaking at the time, but she can use it to her advantage now. There's no record of her in the case file, nothing to show how close she was with Hannah. Nothing to prevent her leading this case. 'Thank you. What else can you tell us about the night she disappeared?'

'Well, you see, that night my machine broke down partway through the shift.' Paul fidgets in his chair. 'The engineer on-site couldn't fix it right away as one of the belts or gizmos had snapped and needed replacing but there weren't any spares to hand, so the supervisor sent me home.'

'Do you remember the name of the supervisor?' asks Jennie.

Paul runs his hand through his close-cropped greying hair. 'No, sorry, it was a long time ago and it wasn't the regular guy that night.'

'Okay, go on,' says Jennie, trying to get past how odd it feels to be talking with Hannah's dad as if Hannah were someone she'd never met.

'Anyway, so when I arrived back Hannah was home. I went into her room to say hello and that's when I found her packing clothes into a rucksack. I was gobsmacked. I mean, why was she packing her stuff? She was meant to be studying hard for her exams and looking after me while I worked all hours, not buggering off to God-knows-where.' Paul glances from Jennie to Martin, clearly looking for sympathy. He shakes his head. His tone switching from annoyed to full of regret. 'I'm sorry to say I didn't handle it well. I mean, I was tired and pissed off that I'd probably get my wages docked for the hours I couldn't work even though it wasn't my fault. So it didn't take much to wind me up. I asked Hannah what the hell was going on and banned her from going out. But she didn't listen. She just grabbed her bag and stormed out of the house.'

Jennie looks at the downcast man in front of her. She keeps her voice gentle as she probes further. 'Were you worried about her storming out?'

'Yes and no,' says Paul. 'You have to understand, Hannah was a very highly strung girl and she'd often explode at me and storm out, but she always came back a few hours later, or perhaps the next day after spending the night at a friend's house, once she'd calmed down. But she always, *always* came home.'

'But she didn't come back that time?' probes Martin.

Paul shakes his head, his voice cracking as he says, 'That's when I called your lot.'

Shelly squeezes his hand. Martin glances at Jennie.

'Did you have any idea why she'd been packing the rucksack?' asks Jennie.

'No, not right then, but later I assumed it was to do with the modelling.' Paul lets out a soft sigh. 'I'd known she'd wanted to be a model but it just seemed so pie-in-the-sky for people like us. I told her to be realistic, even banned her from talking about models and modelling, but it didn't do any good. I only found out she'd gone behind my back after I'd received a call from a modelling job in London asking why she hadn't shown up. It totally floored me. She was already missing by then though, so ...'

As Paul breaks down, Shelly gives Jennie and Martin a stern

look. 'That's enough. His heart can't take all this. Please, think of his health, he's been through so much.'

Haven't we all? thinks Jennie.

As she stands up to leave, Jennie hands one of her business cards to po-faced Shelly, but looks at Paul as she says, 'Thank you for sharing that with us. We'll be in touch as and when we get updates, and we might need to speak to you again. In the meantime, if you think of anything else, no matter how small or seemingly unrelated, please get in touch.'

Martin tucks his notepad back into his pocket and gets up to follow. As Jennie moves back across the room, she realises there are no pictures of Hannah here. There's a set of black-framed wedding pictures with Paul and Shelly smiling down from the wall behind the sofa, and a collection of silver-framed photos on the wall unit, but none include Hannah. If Hannah really was Paul's 'sweet angel', wouldn't he want at least one picture of her in his lounge?

Paul hurries up behind them as they reach the door. Turning, Jennie sees the anguish on his face. 'Mr Jennings?'

'Find them, please,' says Paul. His eyes are damp, his voice pleading. 'Find who did this to my little girl.'

Chapter 7

Rob

Rob Marwood climbs out of the black cab and shivers. London is a hell of a lot colder than St Lucia, that's for damn sure. He makes the short trip across the pavement to the white stone steps of his apartment building, then picks up his wheelie case and carries it up to the front door. It feels weird to be back in crowded, dirty London again. His building's five-storey, white-painted Georgian stone frontage, with its heavy black front door and matching iron balcony railings, is a far cry from the beach bungalow that he's called his home for the last two weeks.

Letting himself in, he takes the lift to the top floor and enters his penthouse apartment. It's spotless, as always, and bathed in the soft, amber glow of the setting sun. Rob smiles. He's lived in a few places over the years, but this is definitely his favourite. And, he supposes, it should be. He'd hired the much sought-after designer, Jared Dominic, to gut the place and redesign it in a masculine yet light-filled way.

Leaving his wheelie case just inside the door, Rob walks across the dark hardwood floor of the entryway to the open living space. After all the travelling, he's gasping for some caffeine. Thank God, his housekeeper Sandra has stocked the fridge and made sure there's freshly ground coffee waiting for him to brew. Switching on the machine, he picks up the neat stack of post that Sandra's left for him on the quartz countertop and flicks through the envelopes.

Credit card bill, wedding invitation to a distant cousin's nuptials, bill, bill ... His heart rate accelerates when he sees the official

NHS Trust logo on the front of one of the envelopes. Ripping it open, Rob speed-reads the letter.

Shit. Shit. Shit.

This is a nightmare.

His hand trembles as he dials his lawyer's number – his mobile, not his landline. Rob doesn't want to have to faff around being put through by an assistant. He needs advice. Now.

'Jefferson Barclay.' The lawyer's plummy tone sounds as self-satisfied as always.

'Jeff, it's Rob Marwood. There's a problem.'

'Rob, I thought you were off gallivanting in the Caribbean?' chuckles Jeff.

'I just flew back,' says Rob, talking fast. He needs to get Jeff's view. Needs help. 'Look, I've just received formal notice. The patient's wife has filed an appeal. They're saying I was negligent. That I killed him.' He glances back at the letter in his hand; the words seem to vibrate on the paper. 'They're saying further evidence has come to light; apparently there are several new witness statements alleging I was under the influence while on duty.'

'I see,' says Jeff. His tone is even: there's no judgement but no support either.

'What?' asks Rob, becoming more exasperated. 'You see what?'

'It's a figure of speech, old man,' says Jeff, amicably. 'Obviously I need to take a look at these new statements, but we faced down the previous investigation successfully, so I don't think you need to be losing any sleep over this.'

'Not lose any sleep? Jesus! This isn't a slap-on-the-wrist situation. They're saying I was high at work, Jeff. I'm invited to a disciplinary hearing in ten days' time.' Rob's hand is shaking. He sets the phone down on the countertop and puts it on speaker. 'They're going to strike me off and throw me to the goddamn wolves.'

'Now, let's not get ahead of ourselves,' says Jeff, his voice steady, calming. 'They have to prove the negligence.'

Rob feels anything but calm. He shakes his head. 'But I told the board already that it was a miscalculation. I've already put my hands up to that. And they said they weren't referring it on any further. They said it was done, gone away.'

'And it will be,' says Jeff. 'There were extenuating circumstances, I believe?'

'Well … I … The patient notes weren't very clear. We had a lot of emergencies coming in, stuff was coming through to me half completed or barely decipherable. It was like a bloody war zone …'

'Exactly. And you'd been working a double shift, and it was the fourth time that week you'd done a double,' says Jeff, smoothly. 'You were dog-tired, but they needed you and you're a loyal employee. I remember you told me there was a lot of sickness in the medical team so you were thin on the ground, and the patient was in a critical situation, yes?'

Rob nods. 'Life or death. He was bleeding out. I had to put him under quickly so they could operate.'

'Indeed, you were doing your best in extremely challenging circumstances,' says Jeff, his tone soothing. 'But in high-stress situations it's easy to make mistakes, especially when you've not had the legal number of rest hours. You had an old sporting injury that was playing up, so you'd taken something for the pain. If, as they allege, you made a mistake, it was tragic, yes, but a mistake none the less. And your employer is the negligent party here, they were responsible for your welfare and the patient's – they put you, their employee, in an impossible situation. They forced you to work far more hours than the law allows when you were already below par, without proper rest periods. Mistakes in that environment are sadly inevitable, and that is what we'll argue.'

Rob's silent for a moment, remembering the blond man in the Under Armour gear being rushed into theatre. He was an RTA victim, a rush-hour cyclist in his forties who'd been caught between an SUV and a bus, barely alive with his stats dropping by the second. There was blood everywhere. People were shouting.

The lights in the theatre seemed overly bright, the machines overly loud, but that was probably due more to the bump of coke Rob taken to try to stay alert on the double shift he was working. He should've known coke on top of Fentanyl was a bad combination. He's a bloody doctor. He should have bloody known.

'Rob, you still there?' asks Jeff.

He exhales hard. 'I'm here.'

'Look, I know it's troublesome, but really don't worry. We're well prepared to fight this and I had the team work on a number of strategies. Why don't you pop in to see me tomorrow morning, at, say, eleven? We'll have a chat to set your mind at rest and start getting you prepped for the hearing.'

'Okay,' says Rob, feeling sick to his stomach. 'What about my new job? I'm due to fly out in a few weeks. Should I tell the Dubai hospital board?'

'I don't think that's necessary,' replies Jeff, hastily. 'Let's see if we can squash this appeal first, shall we? There's no need to scare the horses just yet.'

Rob's left leg twitches, as if it wants to run. 'Okay, yes, sounds good. I'll see you tomorrow.'

'Good, good,' says Jeff, the jovial bounce back in his tone. 'See you at eleven.'

Hanging up, Rob puts his phone down on the counter beside the stack of post. He glances at the letter still in his hand and sees that it's shaking.

What the hell am I going to do?

In the aftermath of the fatality, Rob had found out all he could about the patient. It's amazing how much information you can find out about someone from Google, Facebook and the rest. He'd learned that the man had been forty-two when he died that evening on the operating table. He'd worked for a domestic abuse charity and volunteered every Friday night at a local food bank. He'd had a wife, Veronica, and two little girls: Bethany, aged 5, and Felicity, aged 7. They did a load of things together as a family – camping, wild swimming, horse riding, cooking. Rob had stared at the photos of them on Facebook for hours. They looked happy. So happy, Rob had been jealous of him even though the man was dead. His name was Angus Pearson and he had died within seconds of Rob injecting him with over six times the correct dosage of anaesthetic. All attempts to bring him back had failed.

Rob looks down at the letter in his hand and feels his stomach lurch. Whatever Jeff says, however confident he is about winning the appeal, Rob can't see a way to clear his name. Deep down he knows he doesn't deserve to, anyway.

He killed Angus Pearson.

As he puts the letter back into the envelope, Rob's phone buzzes on the countertop beside him. He glances at the screen, now lit up with a text notification, and reads the message: They've found Hannah buried in the school basement. It's awful. Call me. Lx.

For a moment it feels as if Rob's heart has stopped beating. *Hannah? Found? In the school? Jesus.*

This can't all be happening.

It's too much. Rob's chest tightens and it feels as if the panic is going to overwhelm him. He hurries across to the drinks cabinet at the other end of the kitchen and curses Sandra for tidying the decanters from the counter. Removing the best stuff from the cabinet, he pours a generous measure into a tumbler and downs it in one, barely registering the sharp, fiery taste.

His hand trembles as he pours another. He gulps it down. Feels the fire this time.

And pours another.

Chapter 8

The weather has turned. The torrential downpour makes the road conditions tricky in the half-light but tonight Jennie doesn't care. It's been one hell of a day and she's wrung out. Her brain feels like mush. Guarding her reactions and words, holding in the grief for her lost friend in front of her colleagues, has been unbearable. But here, cycling along the main road with the rain pelting her face, she can finally let the tears fall without fear.

She pedals along Prebendal Road and stops at the traffic lights before the main road, waiting for them to go green. An old Volvo with a mum and three kids inside pulls up beside her. The little boy in the seat closest to Jennie presses his face against the window and sticks out his tongue, waggling it up and down until his older sister pulls him away. The mum turns in the driver's seat, mouth opening to speak to the child. The lights turn green and Jennie sets off again. She wonders what the mum had been going to say to her son.

The standing water on the tarmac is worse along Main Street, and with the constant traffic swishing past her, it makes spotting the frequent potholes difficult. Jennie's got most of them memorised, but every so often she hits one and the jolt has her clenching her jaw. The bloody council needs to get them fixed. If she had the time, she'd write them a stingingly worded letter.

As she's pedalling out of town the traffic starts to thin out. Suddenly, Jennie shivers. The hairs stand up on the back of her neck as she gets the weirdest feeling that she's being followed. Glancing over her shoulder, she sees a car crawling along the road a little way behind her. While she's watching, it indicates left and pulls up on the kerb. Jennie shakes her head. They're not following her; they were just looking for an unfamiliar address.

As she continues on, a rumble of thunder sounds overhead and the rain worsens. She feels the damp starting to seep through the seams of her waterproof jacket and bows her head against the deluge as she pedals faster.

Not far now.

Turning off the main road, Jennie sets off along the narrower, darker lane that winds away from the town centre, past the park and children's playground, and towards her mum's house. There's barely any traffic here, and only a couple of cars pass her in as many minutes. Pretty soon it's just Jennie, the road, and the rain.

Rainwater cascades down her face. The bike's wheels slosh through the deepening puddles. Jennie can't believe Hannah was buried under the basement floor for all these years, so close to where she's been living and working. Her tears fall faster.

It's a few minutes later when she gets the weird feeling again and shudders. Looking over her shoulder, all she sees behind her is an empty road. She blows out hard. It's been a long and challenging day; maybe her mind is playing tricks on her. She *is* tired. But the uneasy feeling is growing. She can't shake the sense that someone's watching her.

The streetlights are sporadic in this part of White Cross yet there's still some light coming from behind her. At first, she thinks it must be from an approaching car's headlights, but no car overtakes. Glancing over her shoulder again, Jennie sees there *is* a car a little way back down the lane. It's travelling very slowly, maybe five miles an hour, ten at most. It's hard to tell, but the shape of the headlights makes her think it's the same one as before.

Weird.

She feels on edge, unsure what to do next. The road is getting narrower and the houses more spaced out. The pavement finishes on her side of the road, replaced with a high hedge. There are no pedestrians on the pavement opposite, the rain keeping people inside. No one to call out to for help. Jennie grips the handlebars tighter. She's cycled these roads for over thirty years, but she's never felt as vulnerable as she does right now.

She hears the rev of an engine behind her. The headlights illuminating the tarmac are coming closer. Jennie looks round again, the bike wobbling beneath her as she turns. The car is only a few metres behind her now, but it doesn't overtake, instead it matches her pace.

Her heart starts racing.

What are they doing?

She twists in her saddle, trying to see who's driving, but the face is in shadow, the darkness and rain blocking her view. Jennie curses. Her heart is pounding so hard it feels as if it's going to burst through her chest.

The car draws closer still. Its bumper is now barely a metre from her back wheel. It's so close she can feel the heat from the engine.

Why are they...? Shit.

Panicked, Jennie pedals faster, trying to put more distance between herself and the vehicle. But it's futile. The car matches her pace.

They're toying with me. Trying to intimidate me.

She doesn't need this, not today, not after everything that's happened.

Jennie feels a rush of fury. Yanking her handlebars to the left, she brakes hard, stopping at the side of the road against the hedge. Behind her, the car skids to a halt, then reverses back about ten metres.

'What the hell are you doing?' she yells at the car. 'You could have killed me.'

The car sits there, its lights shining directly at her. The engine purrs.

Fear rises within her. She's trapped. There's no pavement on this side of the lane, and the high hedge means the only way to escape is to cross the road in front of the vehicle.

With shaking hands, Jennie grapples with the straps of her rucksack, trying to get to her phone, but her fingers are numb from the pelting rain and adrenaline is making her clumsy. She yells towards the car, 'I'm calling the police.'

There's no response. No movement. Jennie peers through the rain, but it's too wet and too dark to get a proper look at the car. She still can't see the driver, and the number plate light is out, so she can't read that either.

Finally, her fingers undo the rucksack and she pulls out her phone. She holds it up towards the car, ready to record them.

Suddenly, the vehicle's full beams flick on. The engine roars and the car lurches forward, accelerating rapidly towards her.

Jennie freezes.

The headlights dazzle her.

There's nowhere to take cover. No way of escaping.

She braces herself for impact. Closes her eyes.

Jennie hears the car swerve at the last moment. Opens her eyes to see it miss her by inches. A shower of spray cascades over her as the car speeds away along the lane.

Jennie's heart pounds. Who the hell were they? Had they been following her? Or was her imagination playing tricks? She can't be sure it was the same car as earlier. Maybe it was just bored teenagers messing about for kicks and dares. That's the most likely explanation, isn't it?

Getting back onto her bike, Jennie's thankful that she's less than a minute from her mum's house now. But as she cycles along the lane two questions repeat in her mind.

Did they just try to drive me off the road?
Is my life in danger?

Chapter 9

Jennie's heart is still racing. Her legs feel shaky as she wheels the dripping bike into her mum's hallway and props it against the wall. Peeling off her drenched coat and helmet, she removes her shoes and stands beside the radiator, trying to get a bit of warmth into her bones. She's shivering, from the cold and the shock of what just happened. But the heating is cranky at best and the radiator's efforts don't offer her much comfort.

Walking through to the kitchen, Jennie unfastens her rucksack and removes her phone. She opens her helmet cam app and scrolls back to the incident with the car, hoping the tiny camera in the front of her cycling helmet has picked up something that identifies the vehicle, or the driver. The camera footage is grainy and largely out of focus; first the driver sits on her tail along the lane, then she pulls over and challenges them, and finally the car lurches forward and charges right at her.

Jennie flinches as the car swerves around her on the video. It looks as much of a near miss as it felt. She shudders. Her teeth begin to chatter.

They had me trapped. If they'd wanted to, they could have killed me.

She scrolls back to the best shot of the car and pauses the video. Zooming in on the image, she looks for identifying markings, the number plate, the driver's face, but the picture quality is too bad, and in close up the image is too blurred.

Jennie swears under her breath. She swipes back along the time-counter, looking for the moment earlier in her journey home when she'd first had the feeling she was being watched. Finding it, she replays the moment she looked round at the car. Again, the picture quality is too poor to make out any specific identifying details, but she's pretty sure it's the same car that almost hit her – the shape of headlights and the vehicle's size look the same, but she can't tell the make or model, or what colour it is, although she guesses it's black or dark blue.

Frustrated, Jennie closes the app and puts her phone down on the kitchen table. It didn't look random or accidental. It looked as if they targeted her on purpose. Kids muck about in cars, sure, but this felt – and on the video footage, looks – far more calculated.

Why does someone want to scare me?

She thinks about it as she takes a ready meal out of the fridge and puts it in the microwave. She's put a lot of people away during her time on the force; could one of them be holding a grudge? Or is it something to do with her new case, with Hannah's murder? Either way, she hopes whoever it was has got it out of their system tonight. She needs to stay focused on the case, not have to look over her shoulder all the time. Pressing *cook* on the microwave, Jennie peels off the rest of her clothes and chucks them into the washing machine, then heads upstairs for a quick shower.

Fifteen minutes later, she's sitting at the pine table in her pyjamas and big, fluffy dressing gown eating her mac and cheese for one out of the plastic tray. As she eats, Jennie checks her phone. There are many missed calls from Lottie Varney, all made one after another while Jennie was in the shower. Jennie sighs. She regrets giving Lottie her number now. She's bound to be calling to pump her for information. The announcement identifying the body found at White Cross Academy as Hannah Jennings was going out from the press team at eight o'clock and Lottie's first call to her was made one minute after.

Finishing the last of her meal, Jennie chucks the plastic tray into her recycling box and heads upstairs. All she wants to do is chill out on the sofa watching some rubbish reality show, but she can't rest; there's so much still to do in the house, decluttering and sorting out all the stuff. God knows what she's going to do with it all.

Up in her childhood bedroom, Jennie starts to sort through her own old things, figuring it might be easier than tackling more of mum's hoarding piles tonight. Jim Morrison, Kurt Cobain, Madonna, and Soundgarden look down from the faded posters still clinging to the wall behind the bed, put there to cover as much of the brown floral wallpaper as she could, and left there for the same reason.

Working her way through the first box, Jennie sorts the things into 'keep', 'donate', and 'bin'. A bunch of old tape cassettes go in the 'bin' pile, a Paddington Bear toy and her Barbie bedside lamp go onto the heap to donate. She looks into the box, ready to grab the next thing, and sees her old SLR camera – the one her dad gave her for her birthday just a few months before he died. Lifting it out, Jennie feels a wave of nostalgia. She spent hours following her dad's lessons about framing shots, using the light to create different effects, and perfecting her technique. 'You're a natural,' he'd told her, and she'd felt on top of the world. Even after he'd died, she continued taking pictures, just playing around really, but it gave her something of her old life to hang onto when her mum moved them to White Cross. Jennie quickly learnt to hide the camera, though. If mum ever caught sight of it, she'd lose her shit. But Hannah encouraged her, and that meant a lot.

In the box, beneath where the camera was, is a stack of photos she took while she was in the sixth form. Jennie flicks through them, stopping at a picture of Hannah. She remembers taking it as if it were yesterday. It was a couple of months before Hannah disappeared. She asked Jennie to take some pictures for her modelling portfolio. They went up to the woods and along the trail towards the top of White Cross, stopping in a small clearing where a couple of the huge oak trees had come down in the recent storms.

'Let's do it here,' said Hannah, putting her green velvet bag down against a small silver birch and kicking off her trainers. She ran her fingers through her hair, then gave Jennie a wicked grin as she climbed up onto the massive trunk of one of the fallen oaks.

Jennie took the lens cap off her SLR and lifted it to look through the viewfinder. Her breath caught in her throat as she saw Hannah. She was lying on her back along the oak's trunk with her face turned to the camera. She looked like a woodland spirit, ethereal in her white dress and no make-up, her long, strawberry blonde hair falling down over the side of the tree trunk.

'Perfect,' said Jennie, pressing the button to take a photo. She moved slowly, changing the angles, taking shot after shot. She captured the roughness of the bark, the dewiness of Hannah's skin, and the dappling effect of the light shining through the tree canopy. 'You look amazing.'

'Really?' Hannah said, for a moment sounding uncharacteristically vulnerable.

'Really,' said Jennie. 'The camera loves you.'

As Hannah looked directly into the lens, Jennie felt her stomach flip. She took another photo, trying to capture the look on her friend's face. She was like an enigma: happy and sad, brave and afraid, womanly and childlike. Jennie had no idea how she could emote such a range of contradictions in a single expression, but it made the pictures phenomenal.

Later, when Hannah saw the developed photos from the shoot, she pulled Jennie into a hug. 'Oh my God. These are amazing. I have to use them in my portfolio. There's this job coming up and with these pictures I'm totally going to get it. It's like you're looking right into my soul.'

Jennie blushed. 'You think?'

'I *know*. You're a real talent, Jen.' Hannah held up the photo of her lying on the tree trunk. '*This* is your superpower.'

Jennie smiled to hide how self-conscious she felt. 'I'd love to be a photographer.'

'Then do it,' said Hannah, grabbing Jennie's hands. 'You know my plans – get modelling work, move to London, and become the next Kate Moss.'

Jennie nodded. She didn't want to think about Hannah leaving town.

'You need to come with me,' said Hannah, pulling Jennie closer until she was entirely enveloped in the heady scent of Opium perfume. 'We can make a new start, together. You'll take amazing pictures and I'll be booked for all the fashion shoots.'

'That sounds a lot better than staying here,' said Jennie, feeling hope flare inside her for the first time since her dad died.

'It will be.' Hannah held Jennie's gaze, her eyes bright with excitement. 'We *have* to do this. Promise me you'll come with me? Promise we'll take the city together?'

'Yes.' Jennie nodded, a smile spreading across her face. 'Yes, I promise.'

Back in her old bedroom all these years later, Jennie stares at the photo. In that moment everything felt possible. But just a couple of months later Hannah was gone and nothing felt possible any more.

Putting down the picture, Jennie picks up a photo she took of the darkroom crew sitting on the old burgundy sofa in the basement. Hannah's in the middle, Simon is on her left with his arm around her, Lottie is on her right, her head resting on Hannah's shoulder. Rob is next to Lottie; he's sitting on the arm of the sofa, with his feet on the seat and his long, grey, Kiefer Sutherland-style coat hanging over the side. Elliott, safety glasses still on because he'd been developing photos when Jennie had insisted they let her take one 'formal' photo of them as a group, is beside Simon. They're all smiling at the camera, at Jennie.

The darkroom used to be her sanctuary, a warm, low-lit space that felt as cosy and welcoming as a hug. She loved the sexiness of the red lamps, the smell of the chemicals, and the ritual of the developing process as the true image was gradually revealed on paper. In that place, with her friends, Jennie had the feeling she could be anything, *do* anything. She loved it there. But after Hannah was gone the memory of the place was forever tarnished. Without Hannah nothing felt the same, including Jennie.

Putting the stack of photos onto the 'keep' pile, Jennie picks up her old SLR again. Holding it to her eye, she looks through the viewfinder and focuses the camera on the poster of Madonna behind the bed. Adjusting it until she's sure it's perfect, Jennie presses the button as if taking a shot. Click. The camera whirrs into life, making her jump as it automatically forwards the film to the next exposure.

What the . . . ? There's still film in it?

She looks at the picture counter. It's on number 14.

Jennie roots through some of the other boxes looking for her photo developing kit, but can't find it in any of them. Frustrated, she puts the camera on the pile of things she wants to keep. She'll order some developing supplies when she's finished sorting through the boxes.

After another half an hour, and having sorted through several boxes, she moves across to the wardrobe. Flicking through the rail of her old clothes, she sorts them onto the 'donate' and 'bin' piles. Pulling out a purple velvet blazer dress, she pauses. This is the dress she wore the day she took the group shot of the darkroom crew. Walking across to the full-length mirror, she holds it up to herself, covering her navy pyjamas. She washed up in the kitchen of the Cross Keys every evening for a month to be able to afford this dress.

For a moment, Jennie sees her teenage self staring back from the mirror: the unruly hair, the sun-kissed freckles over her nose, the slightly too big mouth and the eyes full of hope for the future. Then she shakes her head.

That girl was snuffed out a long time ago.

Day Three

Chapter 10

Post-mortems are never easy, but this one is the worst. She's been here for the whole thing, but still Jennie can hardly bear to look at Hannah's remains lying on the steel mortuary table. She's tried to keep her feelings hidden but she's not sure she's doing a good job of it. Hassan Ayad, the forensic pathologist, hasn't seemed to notice; his focus is on examining the remains, dictating his notes into the old-fashioned dictaphone he always uses. But Zuri keeps glancing over with a concerned expression on her face.

Jennie looks away, avoiding Zuri's gaze. Instead of watching Hassan as he completes the last of the examination, she stares at the stainless-steel cabinets behind him and the white tiled wall beyond. Hannah was always so vivid and full of life, her being here seems so wrong; the only thing this clinical, impersonal place is full of is death.

The memory of the last photoshoot she did with Hannah fills Jennie's mind. It was early June and they'd gone back to their favourite spot in the woods by the white chalk cross. The weather was hotter than usual for the time of year and Hannah was channelling festival chic in a white bikini, undone cotton shirt, straw cowboy hat and calf-length Doc Marten boots. She'd never looked more beautiful. Jennie kept shooting film as Hannah twirled in the small wooded clearing. She blushed as Hannah removed her bikini and posed topless against a tree, mimicking Kate Moss in her iconic Calvin Klein campaign. Then felt fear as Hannah climbed high into one of the oaks, walking along one of the branches and throwing back her head, laughing at Jennie's protests that she might fall.

The sound of Hassan loudly clearing his throat pulls Jennie back into the present. Both Hassan and Zuri are staring at her.

'You okay?' asks Zuri. 'Do you need some air? You look a bit out of sorts.'

'I'm fine, honestly,' says Jennie, waving away her DS's concern. She looks at Hassan. 'So what are you thinking?'

'As I was saying,' continues Hassan. 'While we don't have the usual material to work with here, her skeleton can tell us a lot. There are a number of signs of trauma here, inflicted both ante-mortem and peri-mortem.'

'What trauma did she experience when she was alive?' asks Jennie, her tone sharper than intended.

'Join me and I'll show you,' says Hassan, gesturing for Jennie and Zuri to come closer. He points a gloved finger towards a hairline fissure on Hannah's left wrist. 'Now, if you look here, you'll see a fracture callus that took place ante-mortem. You'll see the signs of healing, but the callus has not entirely remodelled.'

'Does that suggest the injury happened not long before she died?' asks Zuri, making a note on her scratchpad.

'It's hard to give an exact timeline, but I'd say within the last year of her life.'

Jennie nods. Hannah broke her wrist during the winter of 1993; she'd slipped over on the ice outside her house and ended up with a plaster cast for weeks. Jennie can't tell Hassan and Zuri, though.

'The potentially more interesting trauma is here.' Hassan points to three of Hannah's ribs. 'You can clearly see the line of the fractures, but the more distinct characteristic is how they've healed in a slightly angulated manner, with the lowest rib being misaligned.'

'What does that mean?' asks Zuri, leaning over the table to study the ribs more closely.

'Well, it occurs naturally during the healing process, but in this day and age it's more often than not a by-product of when medical attention isn't sought, or indeed followed, after an injury is incurred: the bones being allowed to heal without the correct alignment or support.'

Jennie frowns. 'But doctors don't do anything if you break your ribs anyway, do they?'

'True, the practice now is often to leave ribs to heal unaided.' Hassan indicates the lower of the three ribs. 'But this case is rather more complex. You'll see here that there's a fine web-like pattern of multiple fractures in this bone. This, combined with the concern that lower rib fractures can cause damage to the liver and spleen if not managed correctly, makes me think that if a medical practitioner had reviewed this on an X-ray, they would have made a surgical intervention.'

'Any idea on the timeline?' asks Zuri.

Hassan looks thoughtful. 'They're more recent than the wrist trauma, so I'd say within the last six months of her life.'

Jennie frowns again. Hannah had never mentioned anything about hurting her ribs. Why would she hide that? And why didn't she get medical treatment? The answer explodes in her mind like a grenade.

She didn't question her friend's wrist injury at the time, but looking back at it now, with this other information about the cracked ribs that Hannah hadn't told any of them about, Jennie is seeing it in a different light. She's not a naive child any more, she's an experienced copper, and all her instincts tell her these injuries were inflicted *on* Hannah. She did tell Jennie that her dad was losing his temper more; it was one of the reasons she wanted them to leave for London before rather than after their exams. Back then Hannah told her he would often hurl things – a plate of spaghetti, a mug, Hannah's CD player. Had he started chucking them at Hannah? Or maybe it was punches he'd thrown at her?

Jennie shudders. She feels tears prick at her eyes and blinks rapidly.

I mustn't break down here. I can't.

'Do you have a theory?' asks Zuri, glancing at Jennie.

Trying to keep a poker face, Jennie shakes her head. 'No, I was just thinking we need to check with the local A&E and compare the injuries with her medical notes.'

'Agreed,' says Zuri, jotting down a note. 'I'll get onto it when we're back at the station.'

'So then we come to the peri-mortem trauma,' says Hassan. He points towards a small horseshoe-shaped bone in the neck that has clearly been broken into two pieces. 'As I said yesterday during my preliminary examination at the school, the hyoid bone has been broken.'

Zuri keeps making notes as she asks, 'And you think this is what killed her?'

Hassan nods. 'I would say so; a fracture can be fatal due to both the initial trauma and further complications from secondary issues such as upper airway oedema and the risk of infection.'

'So a break like this *is* survivable?' asks Zuri, looking across at Hassan. 'But you're sure it happened peri-mortem?'

'As you can see, there's no sign of healing,' says Hassan. 'That suggests the trauma occurred peri-mortem. Although it is possible to survive this kind of fracture, the way in which it occurs usually means that the person doesn't survive. As I said yesterday, it's incredibly difficult for a person to inflict this injury on themselves, unless they hang themselves. The more usual explanation is strangulation. And given our victim was also found buried under a concrete floor, something she would not have been able to do herself, I would suggest someone did this to her intentionally.'

Jennie trudges back to the car in silence. No matter what she does, she can't push from her mind the image of rough hands around Hannah's neck, choking the life out of her.

Grief and anger rise within her. She tries to breathe through it.
Inhale. Exhale.
Inhale. Exhale.

78

'It's so rough, isn't it?' says Zuri, walking in step beside her. 'It never gets easier, seeing a young life reduced to bones.'

Jennie nods. She doesn't speak. Can't trust her voice not to crack.

'I know Loretta is only eleven, but every time I see a young girl hurt or worse it makes me so fearful.' Zuri slowly shakes her head. 'The thought of something like this happening to her makes me feel sick to my stomach.'

'No life should ever be cut so short,' says Jennie, clenching her fists. 'But you and Miles are brilliant parents. You're doing everything you can.'

'Sometimes the world just feels so hostile.' Zuri exhales hard.

It's not like Zuri to sound so defeated. Jennie reaches out and gives her arm a squeeze. 'I know. But we'll catch whoever did this. And Loretta is the happiest, most loved kid I know. I don't think the same could be said for Hannah Jennings.'

'Thanks. You're right. We'll find them,' replies Zuri, with quiet determination. She unlocks the car and opens the driver's door. 'I'll get onto the medical records request as soon as we're back.'

'Thanks,' says Jennie, climbing into the passenger seat.

As Zuri drives back to the station, Jennie takes out her phone and switches it back on. Alerts ping onto the screen, notifying her of two missed calls and a text from Lottie Varney. She reads the text message.

I'm still in shock about Hannah. It's just so awful. Are you leading the investigation into what happened to her? I hope so. I trust you'll do everything you can to get justice for my very best friend. If there's anything I can do, please tell me. I so want to help. Lx

Lottie's getting far too full on for her liking. Jennie realises that she wants to help, but Jennie needs to keep her at arm's length if she's to have any hope of keeping her own friendship with

Hannah under the radar. Lottie never was any good at keeping secrets.

Jennie deletes the message without replying, instead messaging DS Martin Wright:

How are you getting on tracking down Paul Jennings' old neighbours?

Martin replies a few seconds later.

Closest neighbours moved away, but found a new address for one of them.

Jennie taps out another question.

Next steps?

The reply from Martin comes almost immediately.

Just arrived at the address. Heading in to see them now.

Good, thinks Jennie. They need the neighbour's input. Paul Jennings might have put on a convincing performance as the grieving father last night, but as far as she's concerned, the jury is still out on him.

She shudders, remembering Hassan's words about Hannah's misaligned ribs being a result of an untreated break. Did Paul Jennings force her to hide the wrist and rib injuries? Could he have inflicted them?

Jennie blinks, trying to push away an image appearing in her mind. She clenches her fists as in her mind's eye she watches Jennings clamp his rough hands around Hannah's neck. Nausea rises inside her. Did Paul Jennings strangle his own daughter?

If he did, I'll make him pay.

Chapter 11

Elliott Naylor is waiting in reception. He stands up as he sees Jennie coming through the door into the station. 'Can we speak? There's something I need to tell you.'

Maybe it's the lack of greeting, or the intimate way he speaks, or just the fact he's clearly been waiting for her, but Zuri gives Jennie a questioning look and raises her eyebrows. Jennie almost laughs out loud; the idea of there being anything romantic between her and Elliott is absurd. She cringes inwardly, remembering when she initially got to know him. He was the first one of the darkroom crew, aside from Hannah, to really warm to her. He was kind and attentive, spending hours talking her through how to develop her own photographs using the various chemical baths, and then coaching her through her first few attempts.

It was the first time Jennie had had that kind of closeness with a boy, and she'd thought maybe she had a chance with him. When Hannah had realised, she'd laughed and teased Jennie mercilessly about how her gaydar was off. Jennie had been gutted, but she'd tried to put a brave face on it. Even so, Hannah had sensed her discomfort and backed off quickly. But Lottie persisted in mocking her, often making kissy faces at her behind Elliott's back and trying to get her to play 'straight or gay' as she pointed at different kids in assembly. Jennie made a point of never telling Lottie who she had a crush on after that.

Jennie smiles at Elliott. Careful to keep her tone professional rather than overly friendly, she says, 'Can I ask what it's about?'

'Hannah,' he says, a pained expression fliting across his face as he looks from Jennie to Zuri. 'I need to tell you something important about Hannah Jennings.'

Jennie glances at Zuri. 'Can you find us a free room?'

Her DS looks confused, but she recovers quickly. 'Sure.'

As Zuri heads over to the desk sergeant to find out which interview rooms are available, Jennie leans closer to Elliott. 'What's going on?'

He shakes his head, the pained expression back on his face. 'It's bad, Jen. I have to …'

'We can use room two,' says Zuri, rejoining them.

'Great,' says Jennie. 'Could you take a seat here for a couple of minutes while we get set up?'

Elliott frowns. 'Erm, sure … Okay.'

'Thanks,' replies Jennie, giving him a reassuring smile. 'We won't keep you waiting long.'

Leaving Elliott in the waiting area, Jennie and Zuri stride along the corridor to the lifts. Jennie's wondering how to play this; it must be obvious to Zuri that Elliott knows who Jennie is, and that she knows him well enough to be on first-name terms. But she *can't* let Zuri know just how close they once were or it could give away the strength of her connection to Hannah.

Reaching the lift, Zuri reaches out and presses the button for level two. As the lift doors open and they step inside, she turns and looks questioningly at Jennie. 'What did I miss?'

The question throws Jennie for a moment. 'Miss?'

'When I was getting the room organised,' says Zuri. 'He was telling you something?'

'Nothing of note,' Jennie replies, keeping her tone light. 'Just that he's really anxious to talk with us.'

'Interesting,' says Zuri. 'You think he's about to confess?'

'I doubt that,' Jennie answers, quicker than she should. 'I mean, he didn't give any indication of that.'

'Sometimes they don't,' says Zuri. She shakes her head. 'Whatever it is, he looked wired.'

'Yeah.'

Elliott has always been highly logical and structured in the way he does things. He's not an impulsive guy. For him just to turn up at the station and wait for Jennie is completely out of character.

What's going on with him?

The lift doors open on the second floor and they head towards the open-plan desks.

'Anyway, how did you know who he was back in reception?' asks Zuri. 'The way he spoke to you, he seemed to be very … familiar.'

Stay cool.

Jennie shrugs, trying to act normal. 'I recognised him from school. Weirdly, he looks pretty much the same as he did back then.'

'Right.' Zuri looks away.

At her desk, Jennie grabs Elliott's statement from the original misper case file and her notebook. She hunts around for the silver fountain pen she likes to use, but can't find it anywhere. Looking over the desk divider, she asks Zuri, 'Do you have a pen I can borrow?'

'Sure,' says Zuri, passing her a biro. 'Keep it.'

'Thanks.' As she takes the pen from Zuri, their eyes meet. Jennie wonders whether it's just her imagination or if her DS has a hint of doubt in her gaze.

Interview room two is Jennie's least favourite. It's smaller than the others and, being an internal room, has no natural light. Even the white walls, light wood-effect laminate table and pale wood-effect vinyl flooring can't brighten up the space enough to make it feel less like a dungeon.

They take their seats, Jennie and Zuri on one side of the table, Elliott on the other. In the unforgiving strip lighting, Elliott looks even worse than he had downstairs. There are dark circles under his eyes and his hair seems greyer and unkempt.

Jennie sets the audio recorder going and parrots the usual start-of-interview preamble before asking, 'What is it that you want to tell us?'

Elliott takes a deep breath. 'Okay. So on the day Hannah went missing I was in the darkroom, the school basement, developing some of my photographs. I'd been there most of the afternoon and stayed on into the evening. I was almost done when Hannah rushed in.'

'What time was this?' asks Zuri, looking up from the notes she's taking.

'Erm. Later on in the evening sometime, I'm not exactly sure when.' He looks at Jennie. 'I always lost track of time when I was in the darkroom.'

'And you were alone?' asks Zuri.

'Yes,' replies Elliott. 'There was a supply delivery in the afternoon, around four o'clock I think, but after that I didn't see anyone.'

Jennie nods. 'What happened after Hannah arrived?'

'Yeah, so she was in a real state. She'd been crying, her mascara was all down her cheeks, and really shaky. I was trying to find out what had happened when the darkroom door flew open and her dad stormed in yelling...' Elliott presses his hands together, clasping and unclasping his fingers.

'Go on,' says Jennie.

'I hate any kind of arguing and I didn't really know Mr Jennings at all. It was awkward. I felt really uncomfortable.' Elliott stops speaking and looks down at the table, seemingly conflicted.

'What happened next?' asks Zuri, gently. 'Anything you can tell us, no matter how small or inconsequential you think it is, could help us find your friend's killer.'

Elliott keeps looking at the table. His voice is softer, more vulnerable-sounding now. 'I left them both there. I... there was so much shouting. Mr Jennings was telling Hannah she had to go home and she was screaming that she hated him. I just... it was too much.' He looks up at Jennie. 'I didn't want to be caught in the middle of their family argument, I had enough of that with my own parents, so I made an excuse and I left. I doubt they even noticed I'd gone.'

Jennie stares at him, shocked. There's nothing about this in the original case file, and he'd never told her or the others that he'd seen Hannah that night. 'Did you mention this to the police at the time?'

'No.' Elliott blows out hard and runs a hand through his hair. 'I didn't think it was relevant and, if I'm honest, I was pretty scared of Mr Jennings. Especially that night. He was so riled up ...'

'In your statement,' says Jennie, scanning the one-page state-ment Elliott had given after Hannah had gone missing. 'You said you'd been in the darkroom from mid-afternoon until after dark. Is that correct?'

Elliott nods. 'Yes, I was. It was dark when I left.'

'And you told the detectives that the last time you'd seen Hannah was two days before she disappeared?'

'I had seen her two days earlier.' Elliott's voice is meek, like a penitent child. 'But I also saw her that night.'

Jennie can't fully suppress the anger in her voice as she asks, 'Why didn't you think it was relevant for the detectives to know about the argument between Hannah and her dad?'

'I was an idiot, okay. I know that.' Elliott presses his hands together, interlacing his fingers and clenching them tight. 'But the papers said Hannah had been seen by a witness at the train station later in the evening, so it wasn't relevant that she'd argued with her dad earlier, was it? He couldn't have done anything to hurt her because she'd been seen several hours later looking perfectly okay. I was convinced she was fine.'

She thinks back to all the sightings of Hannah posted on the Class of '94 Facebook page over the years. Eyewitness statements, even when made with the best of intentions, are often inaccurate on some level.

Elliott, seemingly unsettled by Jennie's silence, continues talking. 'The witness came forward, didn't they? The police ruled that Hannah had run away and I believed them. We all believed them. How was I to know they were wrong? I mean, back then, it seemed that me having seen her earlier was irrelevant and her dad was already going through hell, so ...' He hangs his head, looking as if stress is eating away at him as he scratches the raised pink eczema on his hands. 'How was I to know she never left the basement?'

Jennie wants to shake him. No matter how scared he'd felt of Hannah's dad, he should have told the police this at the time. Or her, he could have told *her*.

Glancing at Zuri, Jennie sees the thinly disguised disgust on her colleague's face. Jennie feels it too, but she's also fighting back fury. Elliott had been both her friend and Hannah's. He was the person she trusted most after Hannah. She thought they had no secrets, yet he kept something to himself that could have been critical to finding Hannah. She can't get her head round it.

Forcing her feelings down, she swallows hard and does her best to sound composed. 'Is there anything else you missed out in your original statement?'

Elliott shakes his head. He looks up at her, utterly guilt-stricken. 'Is Hannah's death my fault? Did I leave her when she needed me most?'

Jennie wants to say no, but she can't help thinking, *Yes. Yes, you did.*

Chapter 12

'What else have we got?'

The team is gathered in the interview room. Jennie has summarised the information from her conversations with Elliott Naylor and Paul Jennings, and Zuri has walked them through the post-mortem findings. Jennie feels increasingly disturbed by the growing evidence of Hannah's turbulent family life. She knew it was volatile, but Hannah never let on exactly how bad.

'I've checked the local A&E records looking for cross-reference to the post-mortem findings,' says Zuri, from her usual seat at the front of the room. 'There was no reference to the rib injury, but the notes from when she attended with a broken wrist indicate the doctors didn't believe it was caused by the fall Hannah described to them. There's a note in the record asking for social services to follow up, but when I checked with social services, there's no record of that happening.'

'Was Hannah's dad with her at the hospital?' asks Jennie, ignoring the vibrating of her phone in her pocket; the caller will have to wait.

Zuri nods. 'Yes, but he wasn't at the visit she made four weeks before she disappeared. On that occasion she was treated for a heroin overdose and had light bruising to her chest and neck, following her friend's attempt to resuscitate her.'

What the . . . ?

Jennie knew nothing about this. Surely Hannah would have told her? She struggles to keep an even, calm tone to her voice as she says, 'You're sure?'

'Totally,' says Zuri. 'There's a comprehensive write-up on Hannah's patient record.'

'So who was the friend?' asks Martin, putting his mug of coffee down on the desk beside him.

Good question, thinks Jennie. Who *was* the friend?

Zuri flicks over the page of her pad and reads from her notes. 'Robert Marwood.'

Rob?

Jennie battles to keep the shock from her face. She knew the darkroom crew had smoked weed in the basement; they even offered her some. That was the reason Rob first warmed to her – her willingness to try smoking a joint even though she nearly coughed her lungs up the first few times. But taking hard drugs – heroin – that was in a whole different league. Hannah never told her about taking harder drugs, or about the overdose. She also never said she met up with other members of the darkroom crew without her. She remembers Hannah telling her multiple times that it was only Jennie she got together with outside the group.

Jennie's blindsided. She never suspected Hannah lied to her, ever. She was like her sister, like her real family. Getting together in the darkroom with Hannah and the crew had been Jennie's refuge from her shitty life, the one good thing about that time. Now, with the revelations about Hannah's drug taking and Elliott hiding the truth about seeing Hannah the night she'd disappeared, it's starting to feel like their tight-knit friendship was a lie.

'Rob Marwood? He was one of the witnesses the original investigation spoke to, right?' asks Steve, rubbing his eyes and looking as knackered as ever.

'Yes,' says Jennie, her voice coming out as more of a croak. She clears her throat. Tries to push away the emotion that feels as if it's tightening around her throat.

Focus. I have *to focus.*

She looks around the room at the team. 'What else do we have?'

Martin makes a show of sitting up in his chair and smoothing out some creases in the front of his Ted Baker shirt. 'I spoke to Morris Walker, the elderly man who lived next door to the Jenningses back when Hannah went missing. Old Morris was a bit of a talker, and seemed to have a pretty good memory for what went on back then. He told me he heard shouting and glass breaking, like stuff was getting thrown about, through the party wall between his place and the Jennings' place. He also said it wasn't the first time; the walls in the terrace were very thin, and he'd often heard screaming matches between Jennings and his wife before she left. He clearly didn't like Paul Jennings. Morris said Paul was always being aggressive and menacing to his neighbours. Apparently, there had been a big hoo-ha earlier that year when Paul had punched the man across the street for parking outside the Jennings' house.'

Zuri glances at Jennie and she can tell from her expression that her DS is thinking the same as her: the more they find out about Paul Jennings' behaviour back in the early Nineties, the more it seems he might have harmed his own daughter. She looks at Martin. 'Good work.'

'Thanks, boss,' says Martin, looking very pleased with himself. 'Morris also said that on the evening Hannah went missing he'd heard the front door slam twice, and then a few moments later there was shouting in the street. He wasn't sure of the exact time but thought probably around seven or seven-thirty.'

'And he's absolutely sure it was Paul and Hannah Jennings?' asks Zuri.

Martin rolls his eyes. 'Yes, I just said that, didn't I? Morris looked out of his front window and saw Paul and Hannah arguing in the street. Then, suddenly, Hannah ran off into the night.'

'That doesn't chime with the account Mr Jennings gave us,' says Jennie, looking across at Naomi. 'Can you add this as something to follow up on with Paul Jennings?'

As she waits for Naomi to finish updating the board, Jennie's phone starts vibrating again; another call. Whoever is trying to get hold of her is certainly persistent. Pulling out her phone, she looks at the name on the screen: Lottie.

Shit.

Jennie rejects the call. The last thing she needs right now is to be pumped for information by Lottie.

'There's something else he wasn't honest about,' says Martin. 'I got in touch with the motorway construction firm that Paul Jennings worked for back then. They're still going but the personnel files from the Nineties have all been destroyed because so much time has passed. Luckily, there was still a record of him on the old HR system, and although it held limited information, it did say that Jennings had been fired from the job. The date his employment was terminated was Thursday the ninth of June 1994. The day Hannah disappeared.'

'So he lied to us about several things,' says Jennie, thoughtfully. 'The argument in the street with Hannah, and the real reason he was at home earlier that night.'

'Getting fired would be enough to put anyone in a foul mood,' says Zuri. 'Add that to his anger issues and finding Hannah packing a bag when she should be studying, and it doesn't take much imagination to see how things could have taken a bad turn.'

'Indeed, very easy,' says Jennie. There's a sick feeling churning in the pit of her stomach. Swallowing hard, she looks at the others. 'Anything else to add?'

'Steve and myself tracked down the construction workers who were laying the new pipes in the basement around the time Hannah went missing,' says Naomi, putting the whiteboard pen down and picking up her scratchpad to consult her notes. 'We spoke to them all and have discounted them as suspects. None had a key to the basement, so they had to wait for the school secretary to arrive and unlock the place each morning.'

'Yeah, the foreman said working there was a bloody nightmare because of having to wait around to be let in,' adds Steve. 'But they didn't see anything suspicious on the dig site, and never once found the basement unlocked.'

'Even though we know Hannah was hidden in the trench beneath their pipes?' says Zuri, her tone disbelieving. 'You'd have thought they might have noticed the trench had been disturbed.'

Steve shrugs and looks apologetic. 'That's what they said.'

'I spoke to the school secretary,' adds Naomi. 'She confirmed their story. Unfortunately, the headmistress moved to Australia back in 2016 and it's taking a bit longer to locate her.'

'Okay, keep on it,' says Jennie. She feels her phone buzzing in her hand. Looking at the screen she sees the same name: Lottie. She rejects the call again, switches off her phone, and looks back at the team. 'Steve, how did you get on with finding the photographer?'

'It's a dead end,' Steve replies. 'Unfortunately, he died six years ago and the company he'd booked our victim for went bust ten years before that, so that's a dead end too.'

'Have you had any luck locating the witness who saw Hannah at the train station on the night she disappeared?' asks Jennie.

'So that's an interesting one,' says Naomi, reaching for her notes again. 'Siobhan Gibbons, the woman who claimed to have seen Hannah at the train station, is flagged in the system as an unreliable witness. Apparently, she's tried to insert herself into a number of misper cases over the past thirty years and give fake sightings of the missing person.'

Jennie feels her blood go cold.

'Sounds a real crank,' says Martin, a smirk on his face.

A real *something*, thinks Jennie, rage building inside her. Siobhan Gibbons was the key witness in the original case into Hannah's disappearance. Her sighting of Hannah at the train station was the reason they closed the case. 'Are you sure, Naomi? Have you checked this thoroughly?'

Naomi bridles, clearly taken aback at being questioned so sharply. Her tone is more formal than usual when she replies.

'Of course. DC Williams and I visited the witness. She lives in a flat near the train station, the same one she lived in when Hannah Jennings went missing. She gave us a tour of her flat—'

'And her creepy rabbit dolls in dresses collection,' interjects Steve, shuddering.

Martin laughs. 'Sounds a right weirdo.'

'Not helpful,' says Naomi. 'As I was saying, we checked the layout of the flat and got Siobhan Gibbons to run through her witness statement again. What very quickly became clear was that there is no way Gibbons could have witnessed what she claims, because the view of the train station from her first-floor window is entirely obstructed. It seems the detectives in the original case never checked out the flat layout; they just took Gibbons' statement as gospel.'

Jesus.

'So she lied,' says Jennie. 'She bloody lied.'

Jennie tries to control a rush of anger. Siobhan Gibbons' witness statement was the main reason the police stopped looking for Hannah, the reason she was ruled a runaway. That was the moment Jennie began to doubt herself and the relationship she'd had with Hannah. Why she started to believe that Hannah *had* left town without her. Over the months, with still no word from Hannah, Jennie came to believe Hannah had betrayed her trust. That their friendship meant far less to her than to Jennie. And the realisation had destroyed her.

'The team leading the original investigation screwed up,' says Zuri, looking pissed off.

'Yeah. They did,' says Jennie. Sloppy coppers doing a half-arsed job make her sick to her stomach. So do members of the public like Siobhan Gibbons, craving attention so much that they give false information on a misper case. It would be easy to get lost in the anger, the injustice of it all, but she can't. Hannah deserves justice, and she needs the truth.

She looks around the room at her team. 'We can't change the

cock-ups of the past, but we can make sure we don't make the same mistakes. Paul Jennings has lied to us, and in the original investigation. We need to bring him in and talk to him formally.' Jennie looks towards Martin. 'Set it up. We'll interview him here this afternoon. You can ride shotgun. Book room two; let's make him as uncomfortable as possible.'

'No problem, boss,' says Martin, a triumphant grin on his face as he looks towards Zuri.

Zuri's expression is impassive, but Jennie knows she must be frustrated not to get in on the interview. It's a shitty situation but although the way Paul Jennings presented last night was very different to the violent, woman-hating man Hannah had complained about, he could revert to type under the stress of being more formally questioned. If that happens, Jennie needs options in the room and it's a sad truth that a man who doesn't respect women is far more likely to respond to Martin than to her or Zuri. Jennie knows it's messed up, especially in this day and age.

'Okay, thanks everyone,' says Jennie. 'Keep working through the action list. We'll regroup end of day.'

As the others file out of the incident room Zuri stays behind. 'I think we should broaden the search to include everyone who used the basement space, like Elliott Naylor, Rob Marwood and the rest of this darkroom crew.'

Jennie frowns. 'They were just kids though.'

'Kids can be killers,' counters Zuri. 'You know that.'

'No, I think the dad is our strongest lead at the moment, we need to focus on him.' Jennie shakes her head. She doesn't want this discussion. Doesn't want to think about Elliott and the rest of the crew in that way; her friends couldn't have had anything to do with Hannah's death.

Could they?

Chapter 13

'I'd *never* hurt her.' Paul Jennings glances from Jennie to DS Martin Wright. 'She was my world, my little girl. You should be finding her killer, not wasting time harassing me.'

Jennie holds his gaze. 'Tell us about the trips to A&E, Mr Jennings.'

'A&E? I…' Paul's clearly surprised by the question.

'On Hannah's medical records there are details of two visits to the local emergency department within the last year of her life.' Jennie picks up her notebook and reads from it. 'She received treatment for a broken wrist on one occasion, and a drugs overdose on the last visit, four weeks before her death.'

Paul looks horrified. 'A drugs overdose, I never—'

'The pathologist who examined her remains also found evidence of other injuries sustained within the six months before she died, including three broken ribs for which she appeared not to have received medical attention.' Jennie looks at Hannah's dad over the top of the notebook. 'What can you tell us about that?'

'I don't know anything about a drugs overdose or her breaking any ribs,' Paul Jennings replies quickly, not making eye contact as he speaks. 'A broken wrist, yes. She did it falling over on the ice. I took her to the hospital myself.'

'Are you sure about the broken ribs?' Jennie asks.

'Very,' snaps Paul, his face reddening.

He did it.

Rage builds inside Jennie as she imagines Paul beating her friend. Her tone is harder as she asks, 'And the overdose?'

Paul frowns and shakes his head. 'My Hannah didn't do drugs. No way.'

Jennie isn't sure if he's being evasive about the drugs or just in denial, but he's definitely lying about breaking Hannah's ribs. The softly-spoken man who came into the room barely ten minutes ago has morphed into someone far more sullen and guarded. 'How do you know? From what you've already told us you were out at work most evenings. Can you be sure what she was doing in your absence?'

'I had to earn a living, didn't I,' Paul Jennings retorts. 'I was a single dad, it was up to me to put food on the table, clothes on her back.'

'So losing your job on the motorway construction team must have come as a real blow then?' says Jennie.

Paul Jennings jerks his head up as if she's just slapped him.

'We spoke to the company you worked for, Paul,' says Martin, his tone casual. 'You left the site early on the night Hannah disappeared because they sacked you. You'd been drunk when you showed up for your shift and it wasn't the first time.'

Paul Jennings bows his head. 'Shit.'

'Yeah, mate,' says Martin, conversationally. 'Best if you tell us the truth now.'

Hannah's dad swears under his breath. Shakes his head again. 'Look, I loved that girl, I really did. She was the only good thing I had left in my life back then, but I was angry after my wife buggered off, and bitter. Really bitter. Sometimes I had too much to drink. Other times, I'd take it out on Hannah.' He looks from Martin to Jennie. His voice cracks as he continues. 'I'm not proud of the man I was back then, in fact, I'm really bloody ashamed of him. But I'm different now. I got help, stayed with the pro-gramme, and turned stuff around. I just wish Hannah was here to have seen it.'

Jennie's not sure what to believe. Paul Jennings has lied to them, but he also seems genuinely penitent. 'What happened that night?' she asks, gently.

'Site security escorted me from the job after I was sacked. It was humiliating. I was raging, and that made me thirsty, so I stopped at a 7/11 on the way back and picked up a bottle of cheap whiskey. I'd drunk most of it by the time I got home.' Paul pauses. Blows out hard. 'I was in a bad way, so when I found Hannah with a packed rucksack, clearly about to leave the house, I got mad. We argued and she told me she was leaving home. I told her no, she was grounded, but she just laughed. She told me she'd be better off in London with her mum and her new husband. I felt rejected and I...'

'It's all right, you can tell us,' says Martin, nodding encouragingly.

'The red mist descended – it did that a lot after I'd been drinking.' Paul Jennings pauses again. Blows out hard. He looks at Jennie. 'I hit Hannah. Did it before I even knew what I was doing. It wasn't the first time, but it was the worst. She fell. Hit her head on the floor...'

Jennie stares at him. The strip lighting flickers. The walls seem to be closing in.

He killed Hannah?

'Next moment she was up and screaming at me. She grabbed her rucksack and ran out of the house. I tried to follow. Managed to catch up with her along the pavement but she pulled away from me and I was too drunk, too unsteady on my feet, to keep up.' Paul shakes his head, his disgust at his own actions clear on his face. 'The last thing I said to my little girl was that she was dead to me. She died thinking I hated her. I never got to tell her I was sorry.'

Hannah's dad slumps forward, his head in his hands, and cries. Jennie stares. He's admitted to hurting his daughter while under the influence of alcohol, but is he a remorseful man, someone to be pitied as much as he is to be reviled? Or is he a drunken, vengeful killer who is still trying to get away with murder thirty years later? She's not sure. 'Is that the last time you saw Hannah?'

Paul Jennings straightens up. His cheeks are damp and his eyes bloodshot. 'Yes. After she'd run off I went back into the house. I thought she'd stay with a friend and come back the next morning, but when she still wasn't home by lunchtime I called the police and reported her missing.'

'You sure about that, mate?' asks Martin, shifting forward on his chair.

Paul Jennings nods. 'Completely. I passed out on the sofa pretty soon afterwards. Didn't wake up until gone ten the next morning. I had the hangover from hell and felt sick to my stomach at what I'd done to Hannah.'

'Did you go to the school?' asks Jennie.

Hannah's dad looks confused. 'The school, why would I ...?'

Jennie keeps her tone matter of fact. 'We have a witness who puts you at the school after dark on the evening Hannah disappeared.'

Paul Jennings shakes his head vehemently. 'I never went near the school.'

Jennie consults her notes. 'So you didn't go into the darkroom in the school basement that evening after you and Hannah argued?'

'The basement? I've never been in the basement of the school. Why would I have been?' Paul Jennings looks from Jennie to Martin, confused. His tone hardens. 'Who said I was there?'

'I can't disclose that, Mr Jennings. But we have a witness who says that they left you in the basement darkroom with Hannah that evening. They reported you as being extremely angry and aggressive.'

Paul Jennings stares at Jennie with thinly disguised fury. 'That's a lie, it's a bloody lie.'

She holds his gaze, refusing to let him intimidate her. 'The witness said Hannah turned up a few minutes before you looking very distressed. Then you arrived and the pair of you argued. The witness left because they felt uncomfortable and your behaviour scared them.'

Paul shakes his head vigorously. 'No, it's not true. I was never there. Never. I only found out that darkroom was her "special place" after she'd disappeared. It was all over the papers, you know? Nasty rumours about what my little girl had been doing at that school with that bloody teacher, the pervert. If Hannah went to the school basement that night it wasn't me she was with, it was him. Duncan Edwards, her so-called art teacher. The papers made a big thing about how close she was with him. I bet they used the darkroom for their "assignations".' Paul Jennings slams his fists down hard on the interview room table and it vibrates from the blow. 'That man violated my child and no one did a bloody thing about it, did they? You should be questioning *him*, not me.'

Jennie keeps her expression professional. She can't let Jennings' anger derail her.

Paul Jennings squares up. His calm facade is gone, showing them the violent man he was before. He glares back at Jennie, defiant. 'I never set foot in that bloody school.'

Chapter 14

Alone in the incident room, Jennie stands in front of the whiteboard, her mind whirring. The feelings of betrayal and hurt that she's harboured all these years about her friend ditching her have finally started to subside, but in their place are new emotions: rage, injustice, and most of all, the absolute necessity to find out who killed Hannah. Paul Jennings had inflicted horrific injuries on his daughter. Is it possible he murdered her?

Blinking rapidly, Jennie tries to hold back tears and focus on the facts. Scanning the whiteboard, she takes in the information the team have gathered so far. In under forty-eight hours, they've found fundamental flaws in the original misper case and uncovered new evidence, and had an admission of guilt, of Paul Jennings' violence towards his daughter. But even with his history of lashing out in anger, Jennie isn't fully convinced Hannah's father was her killer.

She gazes at the photo of Hannah taped up in the centre of the whiteboard. It's the photo many of the papers used to accompany their articles back when Hannah first went missing – a picture Jennie herself had taken as part of her art portfolio, a close-up portrait of Hannah in black and white. Even in the two-dimensional, make-up-free image, she's never seen a person who looks as truly alive as Hannah. But there's more than just her beauty on display here. The image shows a fragility, a vulnerability, that was usually hidden behind Hannah's bold personality; a deeper sadness rooted in her friend's troubled home life.

The irony is that things were looking up for Hannah in some ways. In the weeks before she'd gone missing, she'd been in contact with her mum, who'd returned to the UK after living in

Spain. Hannah had confided in Jennie that when they moved to London, she was going to arrange a reunion. Finally, after so many years without her mum, Hannah was going to see her again. Jennie had hoped it would free her friend from the sadness she tried so hard to disguise. Instead, Hannah was murdered, never seeing her mum or getting closure. The injustice of it stabs at Jennie's heart.

'How did it go with the dad?'

Jennie turns to see Zuri standing in the doorway of the incident room. 'He admitted getting violent with Hannah on the night she disappeared, and that he was fired earlier that evening for being drunk at work, but he strongly denied being in the school basement.'

'Did you believe him?' asks Zuri, stepping into the room and joining Jennie beside the whiteboard.

'Maybe,' says Jennie, thoughtfully. 'He pointed the finger towards Hannah's art teacher.'

'I assessed the microfiche archives and read through a lot of the media articles on the case,' says Zuri. 'There was a lot of speculation about her and the teacher, Duncan Edwards.'

'Yeah,' says Jennie. 'From the limited notes in the original misper file it looks as if the investigation team were still trying to get to the bottom of the rumours when Siobhan Gibbons came forward and the case was closed. Have we had any luck locating Edwards yet?'

'Not yet. We've got some old addresses but after the early 2000s he seemed to fall off the grid. Naomi is on it, though.'

'Okay, good. We need to talk to him as a priority.'

Zuri nods, then turns towards the whiteboard, frowning.

From her DS's expression Jennie can tell she's got something on her mind that she's not sharing. 'What is it?'

Zuri stays silent a moment, then turns to face Jennie. 'I think the investigation is too narrow. Focusing just on Hannah's dad and the art teacher is what the original investigation did, and we know they got things wrong.'

'But they closed the case before they knew all the facts,' says Jennie, surprised by the strength of feeling in Zuri's voice. 'Who knows what they would have found if they'd stayed on them.'

'We're being too blinkered,' says Zuri, emphatically. 'We *have* to widen the search.'

'I know what I'm doing,' Jennie replies. Zuri's a friend and they work well together usually. She doesn't want to pull rank here; she needs to get her DS onside. 'Look at all we've discovered in just a couple of days.'

'Yes.' It's clear Zuri isn't convinced. 'And we could uncover a lot more if we broadened out the investigation to look at more people – like those who used the basement darkroom. There's already discrepancies coming to light. If we dig even deeper we could find more.'

Jennie bristles. Until now Elliott might have withheld the information about seeing Hannah and Paul Jennings in the basement on the night she disappeared, but that doesn't make him a suspect. Sure, either Paul Jennings or Elliott has to be lying about that night, but her money is on Hannah's violent dad.

'They were just kids mucking about in a basement. Let's prioritise the strong leads first, the dad and the teacher. I think we're on the right track with them.'

Zuri frowns, confused. 'They weren't really kids, they were eighteen. We need to pursue as many leads as we can.'

Jennie knows Zuri's right, but she's still reluctant to back down. Her old friends can't be involved, surely? They all loved Hannah. 'I was at the school. I never got any vibes that—'

'You're not being objective about the case.' Zuri shakes her head, not attempting to hide her disappointment. 'Just because you went to the school back then, it doesn't make you right.'

Jennie says nothing. She knows Zuri has good instincts. Glancing back at the board, at Hannah, she feels a wave of emotion rise up and fights to push it back down. She *has* to do whatever it takes to get her friend justice. And although she doesn't want to think that their friends had anything to do with what happened, she knows that Zuri is right – they should be looking at everyone who had access to the basement and was close to Hannah. The list of Hannah's friends isn't particularly long, and the number of people who frequented the basement is small too, limited to those who were allowed to use the key.

No matter how unpalatable it is, although Paul Jennings and Duncan Edwards are currently the key persons of interest, there *could* be others in the frame for Hannah's murder: people Jennie knew and liked. If she's going to do the right thing for Hannah, they have to be thorough. 'Okay.'

'Okay?' says Zuri, raising an eyebrow.

'We'll widen the search,' says Jennie quickly, before she changes her mind. 'Paul Jennings is still in play, as is Duncan Edwards. We've spoken and discounted the drainage workers and the school secretary, but we still need to speak with the headmistress, and the janitor. We also need to interview Hannah's close friends – Lottie Varney, Rob Marwood, Simon Ackhurst – and we should speak to Elliott Naylor again. Let's double-check where they were on the ninth of June 1994. And get Naomi to compile a list of any other groups that used the basement space in case we want to take the search even wider.'

'Got it,' says Zuri, scribbling down the names in her notebook. 'Do you want background checks, financials and employment records?'

Jennie feels disloyal to her old friends, but she takes the decision anyway. 'Yeah, do the full work-up; we need to explore every avenue.'

Zuri smiles. 'Great, I'll get onto it. Talking to all Hannah's friends is the right call.'

Jennie forces herself to smile back. The list doesn't have *all* Hannah's friends on it.

She didn't include her own name.

Chapter 15

Simon

Simon Ackhurst is on a date. The fancy new wine bar on Summerley Street isn't his usual type of place – it's all statement wallpaper, gold furnishings and jaunty neon signs – but Clare seems to love it, so Simon tries to hide his awkwardness. It's only their second date and he doesn't want to screw it up.

He raises his eyebrows at the price of Clare's prosecco and his alcohol-free beer – it'd be half the price at the Cross Keys – but pays the girl behind the bar anyway. Then he carries the drinks across the crowded bar to the table in the corner where Clare is sitting.

'Here you go,' he says, handing the prosecco to her before sitting down on the bench seat.

'Thanks,' Clare replies, smiling and taking a sip.

He likes her smile. Her lips aren't all pumped up with filler like some girls', and she doesn't wear lipstick – which he's thankful for because he hates the taste and texture of the stuff. 'So how was your day?'

'Same old, same old,' Clare says, but she's still smiling. 'You know how little kids are.'

He doesn't, actually, but he keeps that to himself. Instead he smiles, pretending like he does. That's the thing about dates, isn't it? You're never yourself. You put on a show, or at least that's how Simon always feels when he's meeting someone new. It's why he hasn't dated in a long time, because the effort of pretending can be a real drain. It's hard work acting like you're a regular person. A good man. Presenting your best self to the person you're with and trying to get them to like you. But there's no harm in it, is there? Everyone's faking it because no one wants to reveal their secrets, especially him. 'Some of the older kids are pretty challenging too.'

'I bet,' says Clare, taking another sip. 'I don't know how you do what you do. Working with young offenders must be so hard.'

'It can be tough, but I love it.' Simon smiles. His work is a topic he can talk about happily, and honestly, for hours. 'Working with someone who's taken a wrong turn and helping them turn their life around can be very rewarding. Addiction is highly complex. I've been there myself, many years ago, and if I hadn't been given the support to fight it, I probably wouldn't be here today. So for me it's about paying it forward.'

'That's so admirable.'

Clare's voice is so sincere it makes Simon blush. Seconds later the guilt comes. She wouldn't think he was admirable if she really knew him. He takes a gulp of his alcohol-free beer and changes the subject. 'I don't know how you do your job. I can't imagine having to control a bunch of under-fives all day; it must be mayhem.'

She laughs. 'It's pretty manic, and noisy, but I love it. I've worked at the nursery for a while now, so I know the kids and the parents fairly well.' Clare takes another sip of her prosecco. 'Did you grow up around here?'

'Yeah,' says Simon, taking another mouthful of his beer. 'I was born at Moreton Hospital; lived in White Cross my whole life.'

'So did you go to that old school where they found the body earlier in the week?' asks Clare.

Simon's smile freezes on his face. 'Yeah.'

Clare keeps talking. He can see her lips moving but he's not focused on her words. All he can see in this moment is Hannah: long strawberry-blonde hair, those piercing blue eyes, and her lips naturally pillowy and pinker than any other girl he'd known.

'Simon, are you okay?'

Clare's voice brings him back into the moment. He pushes the image of Hannah away. 'Yes, sorry, I'm fine.'

Clare's still looking at him funny, but he's not sure what else to say. He certainly isn't going to tell her the truth; that the body found at the school belonged to his first girlfriend, Hannah Jennings. That her being the talk of the town again is bringing all the old memories back from when Hannah disappeared. The memories that he thought he'd escaped from. The memories that had pushed him to take solace in drugs in the first place.

Simon tries hard to keep his answer vague. His tone normal. 'I was at the school when she disappeared, I vaguely remember it, but I was pretty young. Feels weird, something like that happening here in White Cross.'

Clare nods. 'Totally. I couldn't believe it.'

Simon can't think of what to say next. Around them the chatter seems to grow louder. The girls on the table behind them – three peroxide blondes with heavy eye make-up and glossy lips – laugh raucously at something. The Weeknd's 'Blinding Lights' is playing over the speakers. The lyrics mirror how Simon's feeling. He needs to snap out of it and say something. Start a new topic of conversation. Lighten the mood. But he can't think of anything else to say.

Clare finishes the last of her prosecco.

He nods towards Clare's empty glass. 'Would you like another?'

'No, I'm fine thanks.'

Simon's heart sinks. He's blown it. She clearly can't wait to get away from him.

Then Clare gives him an impish smile. 'Do you fancy some dinner? I could make us something at my place. Nothing fancy, just pasta or—'

'Sounds great,' says Simon, eager to put off going back to his houseboat and a dinner of beans on toast in front of the telly again. Hurriedly, he drinks down the last of his alcohol-free beer. 'I'm ready when you are.'

Dinner turns into a nightcap on the sofa, and kissing on the sofa turns into getting naked in Clare's bedroom. Simon feels self-conscious as she unbuttons his shirt. He's in okay shape for his age but a far cry from the toned athlete he was back in his glory days. Clare doesn't seem to mind, though. Sliding her hands into his boxers, she takes him in her hand. He feels himself respond. Kisses her harder.

Hannah's face appears in his mind's eye. Pushing it away, he sits down on the bed and pulls Clare down on top of him. He runs his hands over her body. Kisses her skin. But when he opens his eyes and looks up at her it's Hannah's face that he sees. It's as if she's haunting him. His erection withers in Clare's hand.

He presses himself harder against Clare. Kisses her again, trying to spark life back into his stubbornly flaccid penis, but it's no use. All he can see now is Hannah. She's staring at him with those pale blue eyes of hers, as if to ask him why.

Why, why, why?

He rolls out from under Clare and sits up on the side of the bed with his back to her. This is a bloody nightmare.

'It's okay,' says Clare, moving across the bed towards him. She leans against his back, her hands around his waist. 'It happens to a lot of guys.'

Simon doesn't turn to look at her. Can't bear to see the look on her face. This isn't who he is, who he *should* be. Bloody Hannah. She's been gone thirty years but she *still* haunts him. Will he ever truly be able to move on?

Stepping off the bed, Clare kneels in front of him and takes hold of his limp penis. She kisses the inside of his thighs as she starts trying to coax his dick back to life. Simon knows it's a lost cause. As Clare gazes up at him, he's sure he can see pity in her eyes.

'Just leave it, will you?' shouts Simon, standing up and pushing her away.

Clare looks hurt, confused. 'What's the matter? I thought we were having fun.'

Grabbing his clothes, Simon quickly pulls them on. 'It's not working.'

'But I—'

'It's done, yeah?' says Simon, shoving his feet into his trainers. He heads towards the door. 'We're done.'

Clare starts to reply, but he doesn't hang about to hear what she has to say. Slamming the door behind him, Simon jogs down the road towards the canal. This is why he never goes on dates. One way or another they always end badly.

Chapter 16

Arriving home from work, Jennie wheels her bike into the hallway and goes through to the kitchen. The smell of mould seems to be getting worse. She assumes there's a leaking pipe somewhere, but until she's got the place cleared, it's hard to get a plumber in to investigate. Dumping her stuff on the table, she moves over to the fridge and extracts a microwave lasagne. She pierces the film lid and sets it to cook.

On top of the pile of things beside the microwave is her old SLR camera. Seeing it reminds her of the half-used film inside it, and how she'd been meaning to get a new developing kit and chemicals. While the microwave meal cooks, Jennie goes online and orders the supplies she needs to develop the film. She has no memory of what's on it – it was so long ago that she last used the camera – but she's intrigued to see the pictures. It's strange, but if she'd found the camera before Hannah's body was discovered she might not have had the same reaction; she's spent the last thirty years trying not to remember that time in her life. But now it's as if the floodgates have opened. Memories of her time with Hannah and the rest of the darkroom crew are pushing their way to the front of her mind whether she wants them to or not. She's already hurting – the loss of Hannah so much more acute, and final, than it's been before – so what more harm can a few pictures do?

After eating the distinctly average lasagne and washing it down with a glass of red wine, Jennie rinses out the plastic tray and puts it in the recycling, then girds her loins ready to tackle some more decluttering. The job seems endless, but until it's done, she can't do anything with her mum's old place – renovate it or sell it, whatever she decides once probate has come through. Pouring another glass of red, she heads into the dining room. This is the worst of the downstairs rooms, every inch of the space rammed with piles of her mum's crap. Newspapers dating back through the years, magazines, bric-a-brac, clothes that she'd bought in the local charity shops but never worn. And bottles. *Lots* of empty bottles.

She goes through the stuff, sorting it into the three usual piles – bin, recycle and keep. As she works, she thinks about the case, about Hannah. In the last few days, everything she's believed for the past thirty years has been turned on its head. More and more, it's looking as if Hannah *had* been coming to meet her at the bus stop – that her friend didn't abandon her as she'd believed all these years. Someone stopped her, and Jennie has to know who. But the effort of keeping her personal relationship with Hannah a secret from the rest of the team is taking its toll. Zuri, especially, has picked up that Jennie isn't her usual self. And she can't afford to let any of them know the extent of her friendship with Hannah. If the DCI gets wind of it, he'll have no choice but to pull her off the case, and she can't have that. She has to find the truth, and fast.

After a couple of hours sorting through her mum's hoarded belongings, the bin pile is huge and the keep pile non-existent. By ten o'clock Jennie's had enough, and is ready for a bath and then bed.

Going upstairs, Jennie heads into the bathroom. She turns the taps on to fill the hideous limescale-stained avocado bath, adds some bath salts and then lays the bathmat over the top of the watermarked old grey carpet. The bathroom needs gutting – another job to add to her already long to-do list – but she's too tired right now to think about it.

Instead, she leaves the bath to fill and walks across the hallway to the magnolia-painted guest room that she's been sleeping in since she moved into the house. It felt weird to stay in her childhood bedroom, and wrong to sleep in her mum's room, so this one was her only option. It's an okay size and she's already managed to clear most of the clutter out of it. Without turning on the light, she puts her bag on the bed, hangs her suit jacket on the wardrobe handle and moves across to the window, reaching for the curtain.

Jennie freezes, her hand on the fabric.

She stares out of the window. Heart pounding.

Down below, in the shadow of the high hedge and the large acer tree in the corner of the front garden, is a person. Jennie can't see them clearly, but they're definitely out there. They're looking up, watching her.

What the hell...?

With her heart thumping in her chest, Jennie grabs her pepper spray from her bag and hurtles down the stairs. Flinging open the front door, she flicks on the porch light and runs out and down the steps into the front garden.

'Who's there? Show yourself.' She braces for attack, her finger on the pepper spray trigger.

There's no answer.

Jennie hears footsteps running along the pavement. Sprinting to the gate, Jennie yanks it open and hurries out onto the street. A lone figure is running away along the road to her left. The streetlights are spaced far apart, their illumination sporadic. She can't tell if it's a man or a woman, only that they're dressed in dark trousers and a hoodie.

They can't get away.

Racing after them, Jennie keeps her eyes on the trespasser. She follows to the top of the road and around the turn into Wildflower Meadows, straining to keep up. The street is empty of cars and people and the figure takes advantage of this, avoiding the uneven pavement by running up the middle of the road.

Jennie's lungs are burning. Her fluffy UGG slippers are hampering her usual speed. The fugitive moves quickly, extending the distance between them. Frustrated, Jennie kicks off the slippers and continues barefoot. The tarmac is rough against her feet but she's faster now. Gaining on them.

Up ahead, the figure reaches the end of Wildflower Meadows and cuts left into Longdown Close.

It's a dead end. They can't know that, surely?

This is my chance.

Jennie pumps her arms, forcing herself faster. Her quarry does the same. They're starting to pull away again.

Shit. I can't lose them.

On the other side of the road the fugitive runs past a thirty-something man out walking an elderly Jack Russell. The man doesn't look up from scrolling on his phone as they pass. The dog continues sniffing around the base of a lamp post.

'Stop them,' Jennie yells at the dog walker.

The guy looks up, confused, but does nothing.

Swearing under her breath Jennie powers on. They're almost at the end of the cul-de-sac now. There's nowhere to go. Up ahead, she sees them slow their pace. They must realise they've made an error.

Got you.

Suddenly the figure veers right and leaps up and over a wooden garden fence.

Shit.

Jennie shoves the pepper spray canister into her trouser pocket and jumps for the top of the fence. It must be six foot high, and as she grabs the top and scrambles over, splinters pierce the soles of her feet. She ignores the pain.

Can't stop now.

Landing in the back of someone's garden, she races across the lawn, looping around a large trampoline and a children's rusty swing set. The fugitive is scaling a brick wall on the opposite side.

'Stop,' shouts Jennie. 'Police.'

Her quarry doesn't stop or turn to look at her.

Jennie reaches the wall as they disappear down the other side. Cursing, she clambers up and over, landing in a heap on the tarmac the other side. Scrambling to her feet, she looks around, searching.

There's no one there. The narrow alley is empty, silent. It looks like an accessway along the back of the gardens.

Where are they?

Jennie stands still, listening. The only thing she hears is her own breathing.

Dammit.

How the hell did they disappear?

She doesn't know this part of town. All the houses seem to be in darkness and there are no street lights in the alley. Taking the pepper spray out of her pocket, Jennie keeps her finger on the trigger as she searches the alleyway again in both directions. She checks for signs of someone hiding behind the wheelie bins parked outside the back gates, behind an overgrown elder bush, and behind a couple of wooden pallets propped up against a fence. But there's no movement, no sound. No one.

They can't have just disappeared. They must still be here somewhere.

She shivers. Takes a breath.

'What do you want?' Her voice seems unusually loud in the quiet alley.

There's no response.

Still on high alert, Jennie becomes aware of the pain in her feet. Looking down, she sees blood. Her feet are torn up from the chase. Her hands are cut from the climbing. She's a real mess.

What was I thinking?

I shouldn't have given chase. I should have called it in.

Something's stopping her calling it in, even now. Could it have been Lottie, or Paul Jennings outside her house? Or was it someone else? Jennie has no idea why anyone would want to watch her. Outside work, her life is as boring as it gets.

She scans the alleyway again. Shudders.

How long were they watching me? What were they doing out there? And will they come for me again?

Day Four

Chapter 17

'Are you okay?' Zuri looks at Jennie over the top of her computer screen with a concerned expression on her face.

'I'm fine, I just didn't have a great night's sleep,' Jennie replies quickly, brushing off her colleague's concern. Usually, she'd confide in Zuri about how she's feeling, but today something makes her hold back. She sees Zuri frown, and attempts to lighten the moment with a rueful grin. 'I do come in early sometimes.'

Zuri smiles. 'Sure you do. Actually, it's good you're here. I've lined up an interview with Charlotte Varney for nine o'clock over at her house in Upper Heydon, and then Robert Marwood is going to come in later this morning.'

'Brilliant,' says Jennie, putting her cycle helmet and bag down on her desk. 'That's fast.'

'Well, I'm still looking for the current addresses of Hannah's other two school friends,' says Zuri. 'But I've got the janitor's address.'

'Good work.' Jennie switches on her computer. 'Give the janitor's details to Martin, he can pay them a visit while we talk to Ms Varney.'

'Okay, I'll give the information to DS Wright,' says Zuri. Her tone is light, but there's a tension in her jaw that wasn't there a moment earlier.

Jennie softens her tone. 'How was your evening anyway? Better than my exciting night of a microwave meal for one and decluttering my mum's house?'

'A bit better,' replies Zuri, laughing. 'I took Loretta to the Mission Impossible double bill playing at the Empire. I needed something to help me decompress, you know? And she can't get enough of those films. She always says if she can't make it as a novelist, she'll become a stunt actor.'

Jennie knows Zuri's daughter is the school's champion gymnast; she doesn't doubt she would make a great stunt actor. 'Were the films good?'

Zuri nods. 'Yeah, or at least I think so. The first one was fine, but I fell asleep in the second. Loretta told me I snored.'

Jennie laughs. 'I wouldn't have made it to the end of the first.'

As Zuri continues looking into the current addresses for the witnesses, Jennie makes them both coffee and then settles down at her desk to read through what the old case file has on Lottie Varney. There isn't much, just a fairly short witness statement. In it, Lottie says she last saw Hannah two days before she disappeared, when they'd been in the basement darkroom listening to music, just the two of them. Jennie frowns, wondering how often they used to do that. She knew that Lottie and Hannah had been friends for years but over the time that Jennie had known them they'd seemed to grow further and further apart. Hannah had confided in Jennie that she found Lottie's constant need for validation tiring, and Jennie had noticed how clingy Lottie got whenever Hannah spoke about doing something that didn't include her.

When she reaches the section that covers Lottie's movements on the day Hannah went missing, Jennie is brought up short. In the statement, Lottie explains that she'd gone to the youth club disco in Farnby Square that night. Jennie knows Farnby Square, as does everyone in White Cross; it's a music venue that back in the day saw the Rolling Stones, Blondie and The Who play, but had fallen into a shabby, dilapidated version of its former glory by the early Nineties. It was used for various discos and raves. On the night Hannah disappeared, there was a youth club disco, but Lottie Varney definitely wasn't there. Jennie's sure because she'd been there herself.

Lottie claims to have arrived at 6.30 and stayed until 10.15.

Jennie wasn't at the disco the whole night, but she was there from seven until almost nine o'clock; at that point she hurried home to pack her bag and go to meet Hannah. The disco wasn't especially busy that night, and at no time did Jennie see Lottie. Whatever Lottie said to the police who took her witness statement, Jennie knows she must have been lying. The question is, why?

'Jennie, have you got a minute?'

Looking up from the file, Jennie sees Naomi hovering on the other side of her desk. 'Sure. What is it?'

'Zuri asked me to start working up the financials on all Hannah's friends.' Naomi hands Jennie some bank statements. 'These are Elliott Naylor's. He has a monthly standing order paying Simon Ackhurst a thousand pounds. It's been going out every month for nearly thirty years.'

'Nearly thirty years?' Jennie frowns as she scans the top page of the financials. 'You're sure about that?'

Naomi nods. 'I've double-checked it. It's weird, right?'

'It's certainly curious,' says Jennie. Especially when Elliott said he didn't see Simon much any more. 'Thanks, Naomi. I'll take a look.'

'We should get going,' Zuri announces, standing up from her desk and pulling her jacket off the back of the chair.

Jennie glances at her watch; it's just gone 8.30. She puts Elliott Naylor's bank statements into the file for later, then gets up and grabs her bag. 'Okay, let's go.'

As they walk towards the lift, DS Martin Wright emerges through the door from the stairwell. He's supposed to start work at eight o'clock.

'Nice of you to join us,' says Zuri, sarcastically. 'I've left a note on your desk; can you follow up on the janitor?'

Martin ignores Zuri and instead fixes Jennie with a charming smile. 'Sorry I'm late; the baby's teething and Matilda was having one of her pre-nursery tantrums. I couldn't run out and leave Kath to deal with it all.'

'Okay, see you later,' says Jennie, following Zuri into the lift. As they start to descend, she turns to Zuri. 'What's going on with you and Martin?'

'Nothing,' says Zuri, quickly.

Jennie raises an eyebrow. 'The two of you have been at loggerheads for weeks, months, now. Something must be going on?'

'It's ...' Zuri shakes her head. Sighs. 'It's nothing. He's just ... Martin, you know?'

Jennie nods, but she doesn't know, not really. She needs to focus on Hannah's murder investigation right now, but she adds the issue between Zuri and Martin to her list of things to get onto once this case is finished. She needs her detectives to be working well together, not barely tolerating each other's presence. Once Hannah's murderer is caught, she *will* get to the bottom of whatever's going on.

Chapter 18

Upper Heydon is four miles from White Cross, but the rush-hour traffic makes the journey take more than three times longer than it should. They pull into the driveway of Hermit's Rest just after nine o'clock and wait, the engine idling, for the automatic wooden gate to open.

'Nice place,' says Zuri as the gate slowly opens giving a first glimpse of the huge imposing mock-Georgian mansion beyond.

'Yeah,' says Jennie. She'd known at school that Lottie's family had money; after all, Lottie was always splashing the cash and paying for stuff. But she'd never realised quite *how* wealthy she was. Places in Upper Heydon don't come cheap, and Hermit's Rest must have at least five or six bedrooms, plus there's a tennis court off to the side and what looks like stables beyond. The place must be worth millions. 'Very nice.'

They park in front of the detached double garage and walk across the gravel to the front porch. Hermit's Rest is a huge red-brick mansion, with a square-fronted portico supported by four white pillars forming the entrance. Twin bay trees with fairy lights adorning them sit on either side of the stone steps leading to the black gloss front door. Ignoring the heavy iron door knocker, Jennie presses the Ring doorbell and steps back, waiting.

It takes Lottie more than two minutes to answer the door, even though they're late and the automatic gate opening must have let her know when they arrived. Still, she pulls open the door without apology and ushers them through into the kitchen, offering tea, coffee and a range of chilled soft drinks. It takes a few minutes of buzzing around for Lottie to fetch the drinks and settle down at the kitchen table with them. Jennie takes the opportunity to scan the room. It's a large kitchen diner, with a huge island in the middle, a massive gas range cooker and an American-style fridge with an ice-maker in the door. It looks like the sort of room you'd see in a magazine, all marble countertops, two-tone cabinets and Farrow and Ball paint. The kitchen table is solid oak with ten seats around it. Jennie tries, unsuccessfully, not to compare the space to her recently inherited, mould-smelling kitchen.

'So how can I help?' asks Lottie, sitting down opposite Jennie. Her expression is keen, her eyes overly bright. 'I want to do whatever I can to help you find who did this. Hannah was my best friend. It's just so awful to think that someone killed her and hid her body away all these years.'

'It would be really helpful if you could talk us through what happened in the weeks leading up to Hannah's disappearance back in 1994,' says Zuri, getting out her notebook and opening it up on the table in front of her.

'Oh, well, okay, if you need me to.' Lottie smiles and glances at Jennie.

Jennie nods. She agreed on the way here that Zuri should take the lead on this interview. She didn't tell her it was because Lottie might think it weird if the types of questions they need to ask came from her. 'Please, go ahead.'

'Okay.' Lottie takes a deep breath. 'I'd been friends with Hannah a long time; she was my best friend from primary all through school to sixth form. We were inseparable; anyone we were at school with will tell you that.' Lottie looks at Jennie then back to Zuri. 'Hannah was always the life and soul of the party, larger-than-life, you know the kind of person? But she hadn't been acting herself in the weeks before she disappeared. Something was off.'

Zuri makes a note, then leans closer across the table. 'What sort of thing?'

'I'm not a hundred per cent sure, really.' Lottie looks thoughtful. 'Hannah was always super easy-going. She was kind of carefree and adventurous, always looking for a new experience, but in the weeks before she went missing, she started seeming kind of secretive, withdrawn almost.'

'Why do you think that was?' asks Zuri.

'I don't know.' Lottie looks down at her hands. She clasps them together. 'I've been so angry with her for all these years. After the investigation back then decided she was a runaway I assumed she'd been planning to leave White Cross for a few weeks and that's why she distanced herself from me and the rest of her friends. I was hurt that she didn't tell me she was going, or ask me to go with her, but now ... now I find out she didn't leave, she was at the school all this time and I never even knew ...' Lottie sniffs loudly and reaches for a tissue from the box on the countertop.

'It must be hard,' says Zuri, sympathetically. 'Please take your time.'

Lottie dabs at her eyes with the tissue. She looks at Jennie. 'It's been a lot to process, you know?'

Jennie nods. 'You're doing great. This is all really helpful for our investigation.'

Lottie sniffs loudly again and then blows her nose. 'I do so want to be helpful. I was convinced that Hannah ran away, and now I know the truth I've been trying to make sense of it. I feel so terribly guilty ... You see, we'd been arguing a lot in those last few weeks.'

'What did you argue about?' asks Zuri, gently.

'About Hannah being a model. She'd always wanted to be a model in London. She'd talked about it for years. I'd assumed she'd grow out of it, you know, like a kid who says they want to be an astronaut or whatever, but she never did.' Lottie shakes her head. 'A few weeks before our exams, she said something about her results not mattering because models didn't need A levels, and I said surely she'd grown out of her model fantasy by now. Anyway, it went down like a lead balloon, as you can imagine, and after that I never felt like she really wanted to hang out with me.

I tried to apologise, and she said it was fine, but I knew it wasn't. Something had changed between us.'

'You said that you were arguing?' says Jennie. She remembers the tension between Hannah and Lottie in the months before Hannah disappeared. Lottie had tried to ease the tension by buying Hannah presents – bits of No 7 make-up, CDs of the bands Hannah loved most, like Soundgarden and The Doors, a fluffy jacket thing that had cost over fifty quid. Hannah had accepted the presents but the atmosphere between the two of them never seemed to improve.

'Yeah, it was over stupid little things mainly, like why she went to see a film with Simon and not me, or why she wouldn't come shopping with me to buy my end-of-school party dress.' Lottie tilts her head to one side. 'Or why she didn't buy me a sandwich when she got everyone else sandwiches.'

In her peripheral vision, Jennie sees Zuri glance at her inquisitively. Ignoring her DS's gaze, she stays focused on Lottie. 'Did you ask her why she was acting like that?'

Lottie hangs her head. She starts to shred the tissue in her hands. 'No. I couldn't. I didn't want to give her an excuse to tell me I wasn't her best friend any more.'

'Is that what you thought?' asks Zuri, making a note on her pad.

'I think that's what Hannah thought,' says Lottie, her eyes remaining on Jennie. 'I think *everyone* thought that.'

Jennie needs to move the conversation away from this topic. It feels unsafe, as if Lottie is about to say something that will reveal her as a friend of Hannah's and blow her leadership of the case out of the water. 'And now, how do you feel now?'

Lottie's eyes become watery. 'I think we were just kids. Teenagers. And teenagers feel things so acutely, you know? But it didn't matter, not in the big scheme of things. We'd have got through it, I know we would. We were best friends for life.' She shakes her head again. The tissue is shredded into a small heap on the marble countertop now. 'But we never got the chance because someone killed her. I just can't get my head around it. I'm never going to see my best friend again, am I?'

'We're sorry for your loss,' says Zuri. Her tone is sympathetic, but Jennie can tell she's keen to move the conversation on.

'Thank you,' says Lottie. 'I feel so helpless, you know? Like I should *do* something. I'm organising a candlelit vigil for Hannah at Cross Keys Park this evening. Something to honour her, to let us all come together as a community to mourn. I think we need to do that, to let out the pain and hurt and anger that we're all feeling right now. Don't you think?' Lottie looks at Jennie.

Jennie avoids eye contact with Lottie. 'That's a good idea.'

'It's the least I can do.' Lottie reaches out and takes Jennie's hand. 'You will come, won't you?'

Jennie's thrown. Not sure how to react. 'I ...' She glances at Zuri who's watching her closely now. 'Yes, I'll be there. Of course.'

'Thank you,' says Lottie, gripping Jennie's hand tighter. 'I really appreciate that.'

Jennie nods, and slowly removes her hand. This is a nightmare. She needs to get Lottie focused back on what happened when Hannah disappeared, and away from her. 'Is there anything else you can tell us about the time that Hannah went missing?'

Lottie thinks for a moment. 'We all had a lot going on. Our exams were coming up, and there was a lot of pressure to do well. So I don't think any of us were spending quite as much time together as we usually did, were we? Before we went off on study leave, we'd get together every day in the darkroom to hang out and decompress, but in the week or so before Hannah went missing, she'd become a bit distant. Not just with me, but with some of the others too. I know she'd argued with a few of us. I mean, her and Rob were always having little tiffs, but Elliott had been having a tricky time with her for a while, and that was super unusual.'

'Do you know why?' asks Zuri.

Lottie bites her lower lip. Lowers her voice. 'So there was this rumour going round the school about Elliott getting beaten up by this guy he'd fancied. Elliott told me he thought Hannah had started the rumour.'

Jennie frowns. She never heard that rumour and she hadn't seen any awkwardness between Hannah and Elliott either. Of the group, the two of them were her closest friends. How had she missed something like that? She wonders if Lottie's telling the truth.

Zuri finishes jotting something in her notebook. 'And had she?'

Lottie shakes her head, dolefully, and picks at the mound of shredded tissue. 'I don't know.'

'Tell us about when Hannah disappeared,' says Jennie. 'What did you do that night?'

'It's like I told the police back then, I'd been out at the youth club disco in Farnby Square that night. I was feeling sad that me and Hannah weren't in a good place, so when some of the girls from my ballet class said they were going and invited me, I decided to tag along. I think we arrived around six-thirty and left just after ten. I took a cab home.'

Lottie's lying, she has to be. I would have seen her at the disco if she'd been there.

She's incredibly convincing, though. Jennie leans in closer. 'You're sure you were there that night?'

Lottie holds her gaze. 'Absolutely.'

Jennie recognises the obstinate look in Lottie's eyes from when they were in sixth form, but she doesn't back down. 'Because from what I remember the youth club disco ran several times a week. You're sure it was the night Hannah disappeared and not another night?'

'I told you, yes, I'm completely sure.' Lottie looks confused. Her words become rushed, emotion clouding her voice. 'Hannah disappearing is the worst thing that's ever happened to me. Where I was – what I was doing instead of being with her – is forever etched in my mind. Of *course* I'm sure.'

Jennie knows she's lying. She can't drop it. 'Sometimes the stress of a situation can warp our memories and make us—'

'Jen, please.' Lottie puts her hand over Jennie's again. 'I know where I was. I didn't see what happened to Hannah. I wish I did. I wish I could have stopped whoever did this, whoever killed our dear friend, but I didn't. I couldn't. I …' Tears well up in Lottie's eyes. She grips Jennie's hand tighter. 'None of us could.'

Zuri looks from Lottie to Jennie, frowning.

Shit. This looks bad.

Slowly, Jennie tries to extract her hand from Lottie's. She has to stop pushing her about what she was doing the night Hannah disappeared. But it's infuriating. Clearly, Lottie is lying, but she's so good at it. Now Zuri is looking at her suspiciously and she needs to do some major damage control if she's to pull this back. 'Okay, so—'

'Can you tell us about this picture,' says Zuri, talking over Jennie as she pushes a printout of the 'Justice for Hannah' Facebook post that Lottie recently published on the Class of '94 school alumni page.

Lottie takes the printout. She shakes her head sadly. 'It's the last picture of us all together.'

Jennie holds her breath. The photo is the one Jennie took of the darkroom crew on the day they went on study leave, all sitting on the old sofa in the darkroom. She remembers how she and Lottie had used a cropped version of the photo on the makeshift 'missing' posters they'd made and pinned up all over town in the days after Hannah disappeared.

'Can you name the other people in the picture?' asks Zuri.

'Sure,' replies Lottie. She points to each person as she says their name. 'Simon Ackhurst. Rob Marwood. Elliott Naylor. Hannah. Me.'

'That's helpful, thank you,' says Zuri as she writes the names on her notepad. 'Do you know where they are now?'

Jennie tries to keep her expression neutral. Where's her DS going with this line of questioning?

'I guess,' says Lottie, glancing from Zuri to Jennie. 'I'm in semi-regular contact with Rob and Elliott. Rob's based in London now, but Elliott's still fairly local in Whitchurch. I know Simon still lives in White Cross – he's got a houseboat moored along the canal somewhere, I think – but I haven't seen him in years. I think maybe Elliott still catches up with him sometimes.'

'That's really helpful,' says Zuri, closing her notebook. 'I think we've got everything we need for now.'

Jennie feels relief flood through her. She can't wait to get out of here.

'Lovely,' says Lottie, with a forced-looking smile. 'Like I said, I'm really happy to help in any way that I can, but you could just ask Jennie about most of this stuff.'

Jennie freezes.

'How's that?' says Zuri, frowning.

'Well, she took the photo of us all of course,' says Lottie, laughing. 'She was almost like one of us.'

This can't be happening. Lottie has simultaneously managed to out her as a friend of Hannah's and belittle her connection to her and the darkroom crew.

Zuri doesn't say anything, but that doesn't mean there's nothing to worry about. Her DS is utterly professional and would never show her emotions in front of a potential suspect, but knowing her as well as Jennie does, she can see from the tightness in her jaw and her pursed lips that Zuri's confused, and maybe even upset.

Lottie tilts her head to one side, smiling. Seemingly blissfully unaware of the damage she's just inflicted, she adds brightly, 'Shall I show you both out then?'

Chapter 19

Jennie's reading the details of the candlelit vigil that's been organised for Hannah on the Class of '94 Facebook page when DCI Campbell steps out of his office and beckons for her to join him.

She feels her heart rate accelerate. The DCI looks *furious*.

Getting up, she moves through the open-plan area to his office. Her team is hard at work: Steve and Naomi are on their phones, Martin is tapping out an email, Zuri is going through some paperwork from the original file. None of them look up as she passes by.

As soon as she's inside, her boss gestures for her to close the door, but says nothing. It's a bad sign. The DCI prides himself on a largely open-door policy. Only when the shit is *really* hitting the fan does he choose to have it closed.

She sits down on the only free seat; the others are still piled high with old computer equipment. Butterflies swarm in her stomach, wings whirring, making her feel sick.

Campbell's expression is serious as he pushes the printout of the 'Justice for Hannah' post from the Class of '94 Facebook page across the desk towards her. He taps his index finger against the picture of the darkroom crew bundled together on the basement sofa. 'Explain how *you* came to take this photo.'

Shit.

What she says and does in the next few minutes will decide whether she keeps the lead in Hannah's murder investigation or gets thrown off the case. She can't let the DCI dump her off the team. She has to be smart.

Jennie runs her hand through her hair, feigning confusion.

'You know I was in the sixth form at the same time as Hannah Jennings. We discussed it.'

'In the same year as her, yes, but if a witness says you took this…' The DCI taps the picture again. 'It puts you in the basement with the murder victim.'

'Yes, it does,' replies Jennie slowly. 'But lots of kids hung out in the basement.'

'If lots of kids were there, why were you the one taking the picture?' says her boss, eyeing her suspiciously.

Jennie shrugs. 'I don't know. Because I was there at the right moment, when that group wanted someone to take their picture? Because I majored in photography for my A level art project? Because my dad had been a famous photojournalist?'

The DCI stares at her, clearly irritated.

Jennie holds his gaze. Keeps up the confused expression. She can't let him realise how close he is to exposing the truth of her friendship with Hannah. 'Sir, I don't understand why this is—'

'You took the last known photo of the victim alive, for God's sake. Don't you get how that looks?' Campbell blows out, frustrated. 'You can't stay on the case.'

'Of course I can,' says Jennie, not needing to fake the outrage she's feeling. 'This is my case and we're making progress. It should be no surprise that I was at the school – you already knew that. It stands to reason that, as I was there, I'd have bumped into the victim from time to time; and I did. This picture means nothing; I didn't even remember taking it until Lottie Varney mentioned it. It was just a moment in time on the last day of school before my year went on study leave. Everyone was signing each other's school T-shirts and hugging and taking photos. I must have snapped a dozen shots of different people. It means *nothing*.'

The DCI shakes his head.

'Come on, you know me. It's just a picture, no one's going to care that—'

'No,' says the DCI, his tone louder now, firmer. He drops the pen back onto his desk with a clatter. 'It's not *just* the picture. DS Otueome says the witness, Lottie Varney, knew you. That she was referring to things you already knew, and that she held your hand during the interview. What the hell is all that about?'

Shit. Shit. Shit.

'She was getting emotional, sir, that's all,' says Jennie, trying to keep her voice calm, even. 'I think she just wanted support and I was there. She grabbed for my hand a couple of times. It was nothing.'

'And she knew you from school?' says Campbell, looking hard at Jennie.

Jennie holds his gaze. 'We knew *of* each other, yes.'

The DCI swears under his breath. His face starts to turn red. 'Do you know any of the other key witnesses or suspects, Jennie?'

'I know all of them to some extent.'

Campbell balls his right hand into a fist and thumps it against the desk. 'For God's sake!'

Jennie tries not to flinch. She's never seen the DCI look so incensed. The butterflies start dive-bombing. A wave of nausea hits her and she swallows hard.

Hold it together.

'Like I said, I was at the school for a year. I probably had contact with most people in the sixth form over that time, but that doesn't mean that I—'

'No. Don't play smart with me, Jennie. You clearly knew Lottie Varney far better than you told me or your team, and that's just not on. You should have declared the connection up front, but you lied and now you're leaving me no choice but to—'

'Sir, I didn't—'

'I don't want excuses,' says the DCI, holding up his hands. 'You're off the case, and that's the end of it.'

The butterflies in her stomach dive in formation. Fear grips her. She can't be taken off the case. She *has* to find out what happened to Hannah.

Pushing away the fear, Jennie tries to keep her voice calm, her reasoning objective. 'We're making progress, sir. Surely that's what matters most? So what if I knew the victim a little – it just makes me want to catch her killer *more*.'

'I said no.' Campbell is red-faced, adamant. 'That's the end of the conversation. DI Strickland is going to take the lead from here.'

'Strickland?' Panic rises in her chest. This can't be the end. She *has* to pull this back. She knows if she's going to get her case back she's going to have to play dirty. 'How will it look to the press if I'm pulled off the investigation at this stage?'

Campbell frowns. 'What are you—'

'When the press ask what made you take me off the case, what will you tell them? Will you tell them it's because I took a photograph of some fellow students when I was a kid at the school?'

The DCI is clearly angered by her sarcastic tone but says nothing. At least now she's got his attention.

'They won't buy it, which will make them suspicious. And angry. This case means a lot to the people of White Cross. They want justice for Hannah – one of their own who was failed by the authorities before. The community, and the press, have placed their trust in *me*, the top-ranking female DI at this station.' She shakes her head, disbelieving. 'And you're thinking of replacing me with Strickland? A male DI with a chequered record who's already under investigation for his handling of the teen abduction case?'

'Where are you going with this?' growls the DCI.

'Think of the optics, how the media, and the local community, will react. There'll be lots of bad press, a slew of negative headlines, more ill will towards us from the community…'

There are several pings from the DCI's computer as new emails land in his inbox. He doesn't seem to notice, his attention fully on their conversation. 'What happened with the abductions wasn't DI Strickland's fault.'

'I think we both know that's not true.'

'What are you implying?' The DCI's voice is gruff but Jennie detects a whiff of fear too.

'Strickland got the call right after those girls were offered cash to get into that car, but he stayed at the Long Service Awards drinks *for another 50 minutes*, only leaving when the second call came in.'

'Jennie, let's not get into—'

'The details? Why not? If he'd left immediately it might have prevented those same men trying to abduct another teen less than an hour later.'

The DCI is silent. A muscle pulses rapidly in his jaw.

'A child could have been abducted or worse, yet you fobbed off the media with a bunch of lies – Strickland was on another case, staff shortages, blah blah. You got a lot of bad press, and the community believe we're all incompetent now, but it could have been much worse for you personally, couldn't it?' She narrows her eyes. 'You were covering yours and Strickland's arses and we both know it. *You* were at those same Long Service Awards drinks and you knew he'd been called, but *you* told him to finish his drink.'

The DCI's nostrils flare. He crosses his arms. 'I didn't know he'd been called to something so time-sensitive.'

'Didn't you? You were complicit, negligent even.'

Campbell jabs his finger towards Jennie. Fury in his eyes. 'How dare you suggest—'

'Imagine how awful it would be if the press knew the full story,' continues Jennie, raising her voice to be heard. 'Think how the community would react. Think how the top brass here would react.'

'Are you threatening me, Jennie?' Campbell splutters, red-faced and clearly furious.

Jennie puts her hands up. 'I'd never do that, *sir*. I'm just saying that the media trust me. Replacing me without proper explanation, with an incompetent misogynist, will inevitably result in a slew of difficult questions. It could seriously damage public confidence in this force, in you, even more.'

'You *are* trying to blackmail me.'

Jennie's tone is earnest. 'I care about the force, and this murder case. I want a great result for us and justice for the victim. I just want you to see that.'

The DCI shakes his head. 'Jesus, Jennie.'

Jennie glances out through the glass and wonders if the team are watching. Being in the office feels even more like being in a goldfish bowl than usual, especially as this time it feels like there's an invisible piranha in the bowl with her. 'Just let me do my job. Please, Dave. I can do this.'

She watches as her clearly conflicted boss wrestles with the decision. She hopes that she's done enough, said enough, to win him round.

'Fine.' The DCI fixes Jennie with a stern gaze. 'Stay on the case, but if you put one foot out of line, then you'll be off it for good.'

Jennie feels relief flood through her. 'Thank you, I—'

'Don't bloody thank me. I'm going to be watching every move you make,' Campbell continues, firmly. 'Everything has to come through me from now on, you understand – *everything*.'

As she leaves the DCI's office Jennie tries not to show how shaken she's feeling. That was far too close for comfort and there's no doubt she's trashed her relationship with Campbell. She replays the interview with Lottie Varney in her mind. Lottie dropped the bomb about Jennie taking the photograph of the darkroom crew, and then tilted her head to the side and smiled so sweetly, as if she was clueless about what she was doing. But something seems off. The sweetness and cluelessness could be bullshit, a smokescreen to make it appear that Lottie had outed her by accident. Jennie remembers the barbed words Lottie used to describe her: *she was almost like one of us.*

Bitch.

She *had* been one of them. She'd been more of one of them than Lottie by the end of term, too. Had Lottie held a grudge about that all these years? Had she blamed Jennie for encouraging Hannah's modelling ambitions? Was she harbouring resentment that Hannah had become Jennie's best friend rather than hers? Could it be true that Lottie was so devastated about Hannah wanting to move to London that she'd have done anything to stop her?

It's possible. Maybe. Jealousy is a powerful motivator, and Jennie's certainly investigated previous cases motivated by it. But would Lottie really have been capable of hurting Hannah? Lottie's tiny, petite; she couldn't hurt a fly, could she? It seems impossible that she could have snapped someone's neck.

As she reaches her desk and sits down, Jennie remembers something else. Back in early 1994, several months before they went on study leave, the darkroom crew were playing spin the bottle on a rainy Friday afternoon after school. Rob smuggled some Thunderbird into the basement under his prized *Flatliners* coat and declared they all had to have a drink.

Jennie hadn't really had much alcohol before; watching her mum's drinking had put her off. But she bowed to peer pressure that afternoon and gulped down half a beaker of the disgusting stuff as Hannah, Rob and Simon chanted, 'Drink, drink, drink!'

She felt weird pretty fast; warmer than usual, with her head all woozy. Sitting in a circle with her friends, with the bottle in the centre, everything seemed heightened: the burgundy of the sofa seemed richer, the overhead lights brighter, the smell of the alcohol and the closeness of Hannah beside her more intoxicating. They played a few spins of the bottle before it happened. Simon had to take off his trousers and wear them on his head. Lottie had to tell them if she'd ever shoplifted, and she told them about the time she stole a pair of sandals from the local River Island. Next spin, when the bottle pointed to Hannah, she chose a dare.

'Kiss someone for ten seconds,' says Rob, with a wolfish smile. 'Tongues are compulsory.'

A whoop goes up from the group. Lottie claps her hands together. Simon smiles rather smugly and leans across the middle of the circle, waiting for Hannah to kiss him.

She doesn't. Instead, Hannah turns to her left, to Jennie who is sitting beside her.

Jennie stares at her. Frowns.

'Hey,' says Hannah.

The group has fallen silent now.

Jennie isn't sure what's going on. Hannah's face is a bit fuzzy, as if someone's taken an eraser and rubbed gently around her edges. 'What's the—'

Hannah presses her mouth against Jennie's. Jennie freezes. Her lips stay closed. She doesn't know how to react. How to *feel*.

Undeterred, Hannah slips her arms around Jennie and pulls her closer. Jennie feels Hannah's fingers on the back of her neck. Hannah's tongue pushing between her lips. She yields to the pressure, opening her mouth a little, and Hannah's tongue is in her mouth.

The others cheer. Someone slaps Jennie on her back.

'You can stop, you've done ten seconds already,' says Lottie, somewhere behind her.

Rob and Simon tell Lottie to shut up.

Hannah doesn't stop. They're full-on snogging now. Proper tongue action. Jennie's never snogged anyone before. It's warm, and soft, and fuzzy, and weird.

And amazing.

It feels like forever and too soon when Hannah draws back, kissing Jennie on the tip of her nose as she releases her. 'You taste like strawberry,' murmurs Jennie, touching her fingers to her lips. Still reeling from what's just happened.

'You taste like Thunderbird,' says Hannah with a smile.

Rob lets out a long whistle. 'That was well hot,' he says, high-fiving Simon.

Hannah laughs. 'I thought you boys might like the show.'

'Just don't forget what a man tastes like,' says Simon, lunging across the circle to kiss Hannah, the bulge of his erection straining at his jeans.

Elliott catches her eye and gives a rueful shake of his head. Jennie shrugs as if to say, *What could I do?*

Rob starts campaigning for them to do it again, chanting and clapping. 'Snog. Snog. Snog.'

Jennie looks at Hannah and she's laughing. She pulls Jennie to her in a hug and that's the moment Jennie's gaze meets Lottie's.

It's Lottie's reaction that's burned into her memory. Lottie is sitting statue-still, glaring at Jennie. The jealousy she's feeling seems to have twisted her features into a caricature of herself.

Jennie shudders at the memory.

If looks could kill.

Chapter 20

Zuri clears her throat. Jennie looks up, pulled from the memory of spin the bottle with the darkroom crew all those years ago to see her DS looking at her over the partition between their desks. 'Yes?'

Zuri looks a little awkward. 'Robert Marwood arrived while you were in with the DCI. I've put him into interview room three.'

'Great, thanks,' replies Jennie, anger flaring through her. The only way Campbell could have known that she took the photograph of the darkroom crew, and that Lottie Varney put her hand on Jennie's during the interview that morning, was for Zuri to have told him. She's always had a good relationship with Zuri. She's a smart detective, committed and loyal to the job, and a good laugh when they've gone to the cinema or out for dinner together. It hurts that she's gone behind her back. Why didn't she talk to her if she was concerned?

Jennie shakes her head, swallowing down her emotion. Who's she kidding? She knows why Zuri did it. She's a by-the-book detective and she had a concern that her commanding officer might be compromised. Of course she did what the handbook told her to do – she informed the next in command. Jennie might have done it herself in a reversed situation. But it's still pissed her off.

Shit.

She's going to have to have a conversation with Zuri about it, but now isn't the time. Standing up, she looks across the open plan. 'Martin?'

DS Wright turns in his chair. 'Boss?'

'You can ride shotgun on the Rob Marwood interview. Come on,' says Jennie, gesturing for him to get up.

As a grin breaks out on Martin's face, Jennie sees a flicker of disappointment on Zuri's. She tries not to feel bad. She has to harden herself if she's going to make it through this investigation still in the lead. Zuri nearly got her thrown off the case, so it's safest for her to sit things out here in the office. Right now, Jennie needs someone she can rely on in the interview room, and whatever is going on between her detectives, Martin has never been anything but supportive.

Rob Marwood has changed a lot in the past thirty years. Back when they were at school, he was a tall, lanky teenager, full of nervous energy and constantly in motion. The sun-kissed man sitting at the chipped Formica table in interview room three right now looks every inch the medical consultant that Jennie knows him to be. His once long blond hair is cropped neatly, the hippie clothes he once favoured have been traded for a perfectly pressed pin-stripe Paul Smith suit and pale orange open neck shirt. His boyhood kinetic energy has been replaced by an air of professional calm.

His face lights up when he sees her and he gets up from the table, offering his hand. 'Jennie Whitmore, wow, it's so good to see you.'

She's slightly taken aback by his friendliness, but recovers fast and takes his hand, shaking it. 'Good to see you again, Mr Marwood.'

'Such awful circumstances,' Rob says, putting his other hand on top of hers and giving it a squeeze. 'But it's so nice to reconnect.'

Removing her hand from his grip, Jennie gestures for Rob to take a seat. 'This is my colleague, DS Wright, who will be joining us for the interview.'

'Good to meet you, DS Wright,' says Rob. His body language is open, his shoulders relaxed and his tone even and calm. He looks from Martin to Jennie. 'I'm here to help in any way I can. I would have come sooner but I only just flew home from holiday.'

'Where did you go?' asks Martin, conversationally as he and Jennie sit down opposite him.

'St Lucia,' says Rob, smiling. 'Was a bit warmer than it is here.'

'Very nice,' says Martin.

'Thanks for coming in to see us now you're back,' says Jennie, keen to get going on the interview. 'I understand you live in London now?'

'Yes, that's correct,' replies Rob, glancing at the recording machine on the end of the table. 'I have an apartment in Marylebone, although I'll be renting it out shortly as I'm due to change jobs.'

Jennie glances down at her notes. 'You're currently an anaesthesiologist at Chelsea and Westminster Hospital?'

'*Consultant* anaesthesiologist, yes,' corrects Rob with a touch of pompousness. 'But, as I said, I'm only back in the country briefly as I'm due to start a new clinical role in Dubai.'

'Congratulations,' says Jennie, making a note on the notepad in front of her. 'When are you leaving for Dubai?'

'Well, I...' Rob looks away. Fiddles with his cufflinks. 'We haven't tied down an exact date as yet but soon, within the next month.'

Jennie says nothing, just keeps her eyes on him.

He speaks to fill the silence as she'd hoped. 'It's nothing to worry about, there's just a few wrinkles that need ironing out beforehand, that's all.'

Jennie gets the impression he's trying to convince himself rather than her. He's definitely hiding something. 'We'll need to have up-to-date contact details for you during the investigation, so if you're going to be leaving the country it's important that—'

'I thought this was just a formality,' Rob frowns, his tone sounding more strained. 'I'm here as a witness, a friend of Hannah's?'

'That's right,' says Jennie, keeping her tone professional. 'But as the investigation is ongoing, we need to be able to contact you if any further questions arise.'

'Okay, yes, of course,' says Rob, nodding. He shifts his weight on the plastic chair as if suddenly uncomfortable.

Jennie narrows her gaze. There's something going on with Rob and she wants to know what. She pushes a little harder. 'Do you have an address in Dubai we can make a note of? Or your new employer's details perhaps?'

'That's not really ... I don't.' Rob stops himself. His composure slipping. 'Look, the contact details you've got at the moment are the best ones. The Dubai job, it's been put on pause, just temporarily, while a few things are cleared up.'

'Is that usual?' asks Jennie, her tone kind, encouraging.

'Not really,' says Rob, shaking his head. 'But ... look, you may as well know this, there's been a malpractice claim that I'm caught up in. It's nonsense, obviously, and I'll be able to clear my name in no time and then everything will be fine and I'll go out to Dubai and take up the new position.' His voice is becoming more animated, but his smile is unconvincing, the worried set of his brow and folded arms telling a different story to his words. 'It's all a silly misunderstanding.'

Jennie nods along. Rob's clearly agitated about the situation, but having discovered the details, she wants to move the conversation on. 'I'd like to turn your attention back to 1994 and Hannah Jennings. How would you describe your relationship with Hannah?'

Rob smiles and this time it looks genuine. 'Hannah? Well, she was like the twin sister I never had. We were the wild ones of our friendship group, kindred spirits. We both thrived on attention and adventure, daring each other to do more, to *be* more. She was an amazing girl.'

'Was there ever anything romantic between you?' asks Martin, just as Jennie had prepped him to before they'd gone into the interview.

'God no, that would have been a disaster. We were too alike for that, but we made great wingmen for each other.' Rob pauses. He smiles, as if remembering back to when he was with Hannah. 'She was attractive. I knew that, obviously. I wasn't immune to her charm, but I knew it'd be a bad idea. And anyway, Simon would've freaked out. He was such a bloody control freak.'

'Did you do drugs together?' asks Martin, ignoring the obvious follow-up question about Simon's jealousy in order to stick to the prearranged questions. 'You and Hannah?'

Jennie makes a mental note to ask more about Simon later.

Rob waves the question away. 'We smoked weed from time to time, but then we all did back then, didn't we?'

'Just weed?' asks Jennie.

Rob's eyes widen. He knows that Jennie never smoked more than weed with them. 'Sometimes Hannah and I might have experimented.'

'Might have?' Jennie asks.

Rob fidgets in his seat. 'It was a long time ago so ...'

'Think back,' says Jennie, her tone encouraging.

Rob's expression tells her he's at a loss as to how the information on drugs he took could be important. 'We tried a few other things, just the two of us. The others never really fancied it, but I've always been fascinated by the effects drugs have on us humans. Hannah shared my curiosity.'

'Did you take heroin?' asks Martin, clumsily. 'Did Hannah?'

Rob looks startled. 'Like I said, it was a long time ago, we experimented but in as far as to say whether we—'

'Did you?' asks Jennie, holding Rob's gaze. She's getting fed up with him dancing around the questions, not giving a straight answer.

He closes his eyes for a moment. Gives a brief nod.

Jennie doesn't take her eyes off him. 'Tell me what happened.'

Rob exhales hard. Opens his eyes. 'It was just the once, okay? Hannah had this thing about wanting to chase the dragon and

I, well, I was up for trying anything back then. All the pressure my parents were putting on me to get the best grades and into med school, I needed to blow off some steam. And the drugs, they helped.'

'Okay,' says Jennie, nodding for him to continue.

'It was about a month before she disappeared. Late on the Saturday night we went to the darkroom, just the two of us. Hannah had sneaked the key off Simon on their date earlier in the evening and after saying goodnight to him she'd gone to the school. She was waiting to let me in through the external basement door when I arrived. I could tell she'd had a drink, but she didn't tell me about the other stuff she'd taken until after we'd smoked the heroin.' He takes a breath and wipes the sheen of sweat from his upper lip. 'Things went wrong really fast. She had a bad trip, a bad reaction to something or the cocktail of stuff she'd taken didn't mix well, and she started convulsing, vomiting. Then, next thing I know, she'd passed out, and whatever I did I couldn't bring her round. I panicked. Didn't know what to do. So I grabbed her and rushed to A&E.'

'Who knew about this?'

'No one. I think the hospital tried to call Hannah's dad, but he was out at work and they discharged her before he'd got home. Hannah made me promise not to tell anyone, and I didn't.' Rob looks from Jennie to Martin. 'I never wanted to hurt her; it was just a bit of fun.' He looks back at Jennie. 'You can't believe I'd ever hurt Hannah?'

Jennie doesn't answer. She would never have put Rob down as a potential murder suspect, but he's changed a lot from the lanky, hippie teenager that she knew thirty years ago. He might look more polished, and it's clear that he's working hard to try to maintain the calm, professional persona he's cultivated, but the sweet soulfulness that she always associated with him has gone.

'Hannah's medical notes said she had marks on her neck when

she was brought into the A&E,' says Martin. 'What can you tell us about them?'

Rob stiffens. His eyes dart side-to-side. 'I don't know. It was a long time ago.'

'So you keep saying,' says Jennie.

'I...I tried loads of stuff to bring her round before I took her to hospital. At one point I thought she'd choked so I was whacking her on the back and making sure there wasn't an obstruction.' He avoids Jennie's gaze and looks across the interview room towards the closed door. 'Maybe I bruised her then, but I really don't know.'

He's lying, it's obvious. Jennie's tone is hard, no nonsense. 'Are you *sure* about that?'

Rob meets her gaze now. A muscle above his eye is twitching. 'Yes, totally sure.'

It's a lie. She can tell from the way he looks as if he wants to bolt from the room. But Jennie can also see that there's no way he's going to tell them the truth about those marks, not right now anyway.

'I don't know why you're so interested in Hannah overdosing. She made a full recovery and, like I said, we never did heroin again,' says Rob. 'The person you should be talking to is Duncan Edwards, that creepy art teacher. Have you interviewed him?'

'I'm afraid I can't disclose details on an active investigation,' says Jennie, irritated that Rob thinks he can direct the conversation away from himself. 'But why do you think we should speak to Mr Edwards?'

'I didn't see anything specific, but there were all these rumours about Hannah and him.' Rob leans closer to Jennie across the table. 'I know you were in a different group to us for art, but I was with Hannah and she was *always* first into his art class and last out.'

'Maybe she just liked art,' says Jennie, hoping Martin doesn't pick up on the familiarity of Rob's reference to her and the rest of the group.

'Maybe, but Duncan Edwards always seemed to be standing just a bit too close to her, or have his hand on her arm, or touching her somewhere.' Rob frowns. 'I never saw anything specific to say there was something going on between them; it was just a feeling.'

'Useful to know,' says Jennie, glancing at Martin, who is making a note of what Rob has just said. 'You mentioned that Simon Ackhurst, Hannah's boyfriend, could be controlling?'

Rob looks surprised to be asked the question, clearly having forgotten what he'd said about Simon earlier. 'Yeah, I mean, basically he was punching well above his weight with Hannah and he knew it. He wasn't dodgy or anything, but he was the captain of the football team and he had a reputation to protect, if you know what I mean? To be honest, I felt sorry for him, especially as he wasn't even getting laid.'

Jennie tries not to show her surprise; she'd always assumed Hannah was having sex with Simon. Hannah had told her she'd lost her virginity at fifteen and went on the pill just after that. The way Simon had always talked, it was as if they were at it every night. 'He hadn't slept with Hannah?'

'I know, weird right?' says Rob. 'They'd been together for ten months as well, but no, for all Simon's endless talk about sex, they weren't doing it. If Hannah was shagging someone, it definitely wasn't Simon. That's probably why whenever another guy started showing Hannah attention, he'd get a bit paranoid.'

'Did he get paranoid about anyone in particular?' asks Jennie.

'None of the kids, but he hated the rumours about Hannah and Mr Edwards. The rumour mill had been getting louder in the weeks leading up to her disappearance and I know she and Simon argued about it.'

Jennie remembers Hannah had been annoyed with Simon in the last week or so before she disappeared. She'd complained to

Jennie about him being clingy and how he'd floated the idea of them getting engaged more than once and then got into a huff when Hannah had told him there was no way she was going to get married. 'Was he ever violent with her?'

Rob looks shocked. 'Simon? God, no. He was all mouth.'

Jennie isn't so sure. Simon was a champion athlete. He was broad and powerful, and although Hannah might have been tall, she was delicate. Simon could easily have overpowered her. Did Simon confront her about the rumours, did the fight turn physical? Or did Edwards kill her?

'What were you doing the night Hannah disappeared?' asks Martin.

Rob nods, apparently happy to be off the topic of his friends fighting. 'I went to the cinema alone that night; I watched *Four Weddings and a Funeral*. I gave the police the ticket stub when they interviewed me back then. It should be in your file.'

Jennie frowns. It's not in the file, and there's no cinema ticket stub in the evidence catalogue either. With each discovery of sloppy investigation during the initial misper case she feels a rising anger at how they failed Hannah – losing evidence is unforgivable. But then she watches Rob; he's looking nervous again, fiddling with his cufflinks. 'Was that the first time you'd seen the film?'

'I … No, I'd seen it once already but, you know, it was such a riot when we all went that I wanted to see it again.' Rob smiles but, like earlier, the smile feels false.

Jennie makes a note on her pad to ask Naomi to double-check Rob's alibi. She knows he'd seen the film before – they'd all gone to see it a couple of weeks earlier, and Rob had been very vocal about how rubbish he thought it was.

As Martin closes the interview, Jennie feels her phone vibrate. Pulling it out, she reads the message from Zuri:

We've found Duncan Edwards.

Chapter 21

Duncan Edwards' address leads them to Essex and a high-rise building that's clearly seen better days. Parking the car on a nearby street, Jennie and Zuri get out and walk across the road to the block of flats. The atmosphere is frosty between them and they haven't spoken on the way over other than to prep for this interview. Jennie knows she needs to talk to Zuri about the photograph and her conversation with the DCI, but she wants to stay focused on the case right now, so she looks up at the building and tries to distract herself.

Built in the Sixties, the place is a blocky and brutalist pebble-dashed monstrosity. As they get closer Jennie sees that the intercom has been vandalised – the front panel has been ripped off and the electrical wires are spilling out like multicoloured spaghetti. She briefly wonders how they're going to get inside, before realising one of the glass front doors has been propped open with a red fire extinguisher.

Inside, the lift is out of order and so they take the urine-scented concrete stairs up to the seventh floor. As they push through the graffiti-tagged door onto the landing, a combination of loud dance music, children screeching, and what sounds like some kind of drilling assaults their ears.

'Jesus,' mutters Jennie. She turns to her DS. 'What flat is it?'

'713,' says Zuri, peering at the numbers on the doors closest to them. 'I think it's this way.'

They turn right along the corridor and follow it round. Gradually, the drilling noise fades, replaced by the sound of a crying baby from a nearby flat. 713 is at the far end of the corridor, next to a fire escape. The beige carpet tiles between Edwards' flat and its nearest neighbour are spotlessly hoovered and there is a smart-looking welcome mat outside the door. Jennie presses the buzzer and steps back, waiting beside Zuri.

A few seconds later, the door is opened on the security chain and a cautious male voice comes from behind the door. 'Yes?'

'Duncan Edwards?' asks Zuri, craning her neck to try to see the person the voice belongs to.

'Who wants to know?' The man's voice has a slight tremor to it.

'It's the police, Mr Edwards,' replies Jennie. 'We're investigating the murder of Hannah Jennings. Can we come in?'

'I need you to show me some ID.'

'No problem.' Jennie takes out her warrant card and holds it up to the peephole in the door, then Zuri does the same. 'Now can you let us in?'

There's no answer, but she hears the sound of the chain being removed. When the door opens, the man standing there looks nothing like the attractive teacher pictured in the original case file. This man looks withered and grey, aged beyond his years.

'Duncan Edwards?' asks Jennie.

The man's expression is wary. 'You lot fucked up my life before, and now she's been found, you're back to finish me off?'

'We need to ask you some questions,' says Jennie. She wonders if her old art teacher will recognise her. He must have read her name on the ID she showed him.

'How bloody marvellous.' Duncan Edwards shakes his head and steps back, opening the door wider. He shows no signs of recognition.

The studio flat smells of pot noodle and mildew, and the cramped space seems barely large enough for the three of them. Edwards sits awkwardly on his unmade bed, Jennie perches on the only seat – a battered green leather armchair – and Zuri leans against the small fridge in the corner.

Edwards eyes Jennie with undisguised hostility. 'What do you want to know, then?'

Normally, Jennie would try to build some rapport with a subject before going for the weightier questions, but given Duncan Edwards' behaviour she doubts any amount of soft pedalling is going to help. 'Were you having a relationship with Hannah Jennings?'

'No, I wasn't.' Edwards crosses his arms. 'Like I told you lot back when she first disappeared, Hannah and I had a professional student-teacher relationship, nothing more. I was in a relationship with a grown-up woman. I didn't want anything more.'

'But there were rumours that there was more to your relationship with Hannah than just a professional one?' asks Jennie.

'Yes, there were,' says Edwards, scratching at his straggly beard. 'Those bloody kids were always starting some kind of drama or other.'

'You're saying there wasn't any substance to them?' presses Jennie.

'There *wasn't* any substance,' says Edwards, irate. 'I was barely twenty-three when I was teaching at White Cross Academy – only a few years older than the students – so they thought I was fair game. It was like a sport to some of those girls – love notes tucked into their homework, topless polaroids left in my desk drawer, offers of staying behind to help "tidy up". It was full on harassment.'

'And Hannah was like that?' asks Zuri.

'No. Hannah *never* pulled any of that shit. She was a good student, that was it. I encouraged her painting. She had talent. Like I told the officers back when she first disappeared, there was never any funny business.'

Jennie isn't sure she believes Edwards. He's too twitchy. 'You said you were in a relationship at the time?'

Edwards exhales loudly. 'We were engaged. We'd been together nearly three years when Hannah went missing, but with all the press attention, and the way people would come after us, me, in the street ... let's just say she ended things pretty fast.' He glares at Jennie. 'Even though I wasn't guilty of anything.'

Jennie has read about the relationship in the original investigation file, but she needs confirmation. 'Can you tell us who you were in a relationship with?'

Edwards frowns. 'Angela Totley. It should be in your files. I had to repeat it to your lot often enough when you hounded me before.'

Miss Totley had been one of the English teachers at White Cross Academy. 'And have you seen her since?'

'Yeah, right, like she'd want anything to do with me,' says Edwards, bitterly. The springs creak as he shuffles back on the bed. 'I wasn't guilty of anything but ever since the papers printed my picture back in 1994, I've been treated as if I am. I mean, I wasn't even a bloody suspect, but that didn't matter, did it? No one cares about the bloody truth.'

'So you haven't seen her?' asks Zuri.

'No. She made it very clear she didn't want anything more to do with me, so I've stayed away. I always hoped Hannah would come forward one day, alive and well, and maybe then I'd be able to rekindle something with Angela.' He laughs bitterly. 'That's never going to happen now, is it?'

Jennie and Zuri say nothing.

'Yeah, I'm a lost bloody cause, and it's *all* because of you lot. Do you know I was top of my class in teaching training? I got a bloody first-class degree as well. I should have been a head of year or even a headteacher by now. Instead, I'm stuck in this shithole tutoring morons online.' He looks at Jennie, his hands clenching into fists. 'You lot fucked me over, screwed my career and buggered the only relationship I ever cared about. And now you're here dredging it all up again.'

'Hannah Jennings is dead.' Jennie holds his gaze, fed up with his self-pitying bullshit. 'I'm sure as one of her former teachers, you're as keen as we are to find the person responsible.'

'Well, yes.' Edwards unclenches his fists. Looks away, out through the grubby window. 'I am sorry she's dead. She was a good student, like I said.'

Jennie sees no hint of compassion in Edwards' expression, just a man wallowing in his own bitterness. 'Can you tell me where you were on the night Hannah Jennings went missing?'

'I was at home, with my fiancée, having dinner,' replies Edwards, his voice getting louder, angrier.

'And Angela Totley will confirm that?' asks Jennie as Zuri scribbles notes onto her scratchpad.

'I can't confirm anything my ex-fiancée, who I haven't seen in over twenty years, will say. How could I?' shouts Edwards. Cursing loudly, he gets to his feet signalling that the interview is done. 'All I know for sure is that I never touched Hannah Jennings.'

They leave Duncan Edwards, descend the uncared-for communal stairs to the ground floor. The stench of urine is almost unbearable, and Jennie can understand how hard it must be for Edwards, having fallen so far from the leafy, picturesque town of White Cross to this rundown, concrete-covered environment. No wonder he's bitter. But even so, his lack of sympathy for Hannah's death shocks her. Surely, if he was truly innocent, he'd express greater sadness?

As they exit through the propped-open foyer door, Jennie turns to Zuri and nods back towards the stairs. 'That man really creeps me out.'

'Yeah, he's a creep, but I'm not sure he's guilty of anything more,' replies Zuri.

Jennie grimaces. Her intuition tells her Edwards is dodgy, but they've got nothing concrete from the interview. It's so frustrating. The harder she digs, the murkier things become. 'He's hiding something.'

'Maybe, says Zuri, thoughtfully. 'But he's not the only one. Rob

Marwood withheld a hell of a lot of information from the first investigation. Elliott Naylor did too.'

Jennie nods. Zuri's clearly still gunning for the darkroom crew but she has a valid point. Although Jennie isn't totally convinced, she can feel doubt starting to niggle at her resolve. She wonders if schoolyard loyalty has blinded her to the truth.

Has she been looking in the wrong place all along?

Chapter 22

Elliott

Elliott tries to stay present as the midwife takes them through into the private examination room for their thirty-two-week scan. He and Luke have wanted to have kids for so long and now it's finally happening. They've paid to go private every step of the way, not caring about the cost; uppermost in their minds are the outcome and the safety of their child and Belinda. And they're so close to the birth now, the longest wait is almost over. He should feel joy, excitement, even wonder, but that's not at all how it feels. Instead, as he watches the midwife take Belinda's blood pressure, Elliott feels oddly removed, as if he's not in the moment at all. This is meant to be the best time of his life, but since Hannah was found, everything has seemed suddenly and irreparably out of kilter.

'So that's all fine,' says the midwife, smiling as she removes the blood-pressure cuff from Belinda's arm. 'Let's take a look at baby, shall we?'

'Great,' says Belinda, pushing her curly blonde hair off her face as she moves back onto the bed. She looks at Elliott and Luke. 'You ready to see how she's doing?'

Elliott nods, smiling at Belinda as she lies back.

Luke takes Elliott's hand in his left hand and Belinda's hand in his right. 'I'm so nervous.'

'It'll be fine,' says Elliott, patting his husband's hand. They've been together almost ten years and there's nothing they don't know about each other, almost nothing anyway. If anything, Luke has yearned for a child even more than Elliott. 'It's just a formality, just to make sure we're totally prepared for the birth.'

'I know, I know,' says Luke. 'I just want everything to be perfect.'

The midwife squirts gel onto Belinda's stomach and starts the ultrasound. Luke grips Elliott's hand tighter, his expression a mix of excitement and worry. Elliott envies his husband, wishes he felt something in this moment other than numb.

As the midwife talks them through what they're seeing on-screen – the baby's growth, her heartbeat, and the estimate of her current weight – Elliott finds himself zoning out. Lottie had texted him earlier to tell him about the candlelit vigil she's organised in the park this evening. He'd said he didn't know if he could make it, but Lottie had kicked off – calling him and crying down the phone that he had to be there. She said it wouldn't be right if he didn't come; that he'd be letting Hannah down. And in the end, she'd guilt-tripped him into saying he'd be there.

He regrets it now. God knows how he's going to get away.

There's also the fact the police have asked him to go in for a formal interview. Lottie mentioned they'd interviewed her and that she'd had a message from Rob saying he was going in to see them earlier today, so it seems as if it's routine, but he doesn't get why they need to talk to him again; they've already questioned him once. It's strange, but Jennie must have a reason. She's always been smart.

Luke squeezes his hand hard, and Elliott looks up, pulled back into the maternity room. Belinda is wiping the gel off her stomach. The midwife is tapping something onto her computer.

'That's great news, isn't it?' says Luke, his eyes shining, and his voice overly bright.

Elliott, wrong-footed but trying to cover it, nods vigorously as he forces a smile. 'Yes, absolutely. The best.'

They order a celebratory supper at *Carrot!*, a trendy vegan organic place that Belinda is keen to try out. It's all huge multi-pane industrial-style windows, stripped white oak floorboards, pale oak banquet seating with powder-blue cushions, and slate-grey feature walls with hanging macrame plant holders and trailing green foliage. It's a bit overly bright for Elliott's liking, but he doesn't say anything and nods along as Luke and Belinda get increasingly animated over the modern art canvases on the back wall, depicting stylised vegetables, and the candy-coloured chairs and matching crockery.

They order the hummus sharing plate to start, followed by avocado salads and a side order of sweet potato fries to share. But as Belinda and Luke chatter about the baby, Elliott feels as if he's watching the scene from afar, like some weird out-of-body experience.

'So I think we've settled on her name,' says Luke, looking towards Elliott. 'Can I tell Belinda?'

'You *have* to tell me,' says Belinda, laughing as she removes her napkin from across the lap of the floral maxi dress she's wearing.

'Sure, of course,' replies Elliott. He knows he should sound more excited, and it hurts him to see the fleetingly concerned look that Luke gives him, but he feels so flat, so weird.

'It's Martha,' says Luke, his voice sounding a little nervous as he says out loud the name they'd agreed on. He runs his hand through his blond hair, twiddling the front up into a quiff. 'Do you approve?'

Belinda reaches out and clutches Luke's hand. 'Oh, that's so darling.'

'Isn't it?' says Luke, grinning, the relief clear on his face.

'It's perfect. Absolutely perfect,' says Belinda, rubbing her belly. 'Little Martha.'

Luke looks at Elliott and he nods. It is the perfect name.

Still smiling, Belinda gets up from the table. 'Now, if you'll just excuse me for a moment. Nature calls, because little Martha insists on sitting right on my bladder.'

As Belinda heads to the loos, Elliott takes a gulp of his wine and tries to figure out how he's going to mange to leave here in half an hour in order to get to the park vigil on time. Lottie was adamant he shouldn't be late, but the service in *Carrot!* is super slow, and he doubts they'll even have their mains by then.

'What the hell is wrong with you?'

Luke's tone cuts through Elliott's thoughts, jerking him back into the restaurant. 'Nothing, I'm just—'

'Don't give me that crap, you've been on another planet the whole day.' Luke glares at him, accusingly. 'You were super rude to the midwife, and you're barely acknowledging Belinda. I mean, after all she's doing for us, surely you could force yourself to engage?'

'Yes, I ... I'm sorry, I've just got a lot of my mind at the moment.' Elliott hates to upset Luke, and he can see from the way his husband's eyes are watery and his lower lip quivers that he's *really* upset. 'I'm here now. I promise.'

Luke frowns. 'Are you, though?'

'Of course,' says Elliott, but even as he says it, his own voice sounds fake to him. 'One hundred per cent.'

Luke takes a breath. 'Look, I have no idea what's going on with you, whether it's cold feet, or some kind of regret that we're not twenty-five and partying, or what. But whatever it is, you need to snap the hell out of it. We're finally going to be parents. The least you can do is act as if you bloody well *care*.'

Chapter 23

It's really quite something. As the sun sinks below the hills and darkness takes hold, hundreds of candles illuminate the park. Jennie padlocks her bike to the park railings and walks across the grass towards the bandstand. It's amazing how many people have turned out to be part of the vigil. Some are a similar age to her, so perhaps they went to the school and remember Hannah. Some are older, parents of kids who attended the school perhaps. But many are younger, people who would've barely been born when Hannah went missing.

There are a few uniformed officers hanging back, keeping an eye on things, and over to the far side of the crowd there look to be a few journalist types. The mood is sombre and peaceful.

Secured to the rail around the bandstand, a huge poster of Hannah looks down on the gathered crowd. Flowers and teddy bears have been laid around the bottom of the poster. There are so many roses, hundreds of them; pinks and whites and yellows. As Jennie watches, a woman in a black maxi dress and silver flip-flops kneels down in front of the poster and places a bouquet of white lilies on the grass. As the woman turns away, Jennie catches a proper look at her tear-stained face and realises with a jolt that it's Becky Mead, one of her sixth-form nemeses. Despite the situation, she can't help smiling to herself: Hannah would've loved all these people coming out here for her, especially the mean girls.

Hannah.

Jennie blinks hard and swallows down the emotion welling up inside her. She always gets emotional in crowds – parades, gigs, anything that involves large groups of people in a heightened state always affects her, and this is worse because it emphasises even more that Hannah really is gone.

'Thank you all for coming.' Lottie Varney's voice crackles over the tannoy.

Jennie looks up and sees her standing at the top of the band-stand steps, loudspeaker in hand. Rob Marwood is standing over on the other side of the steps, his head bowed. A stocky-looking guy with a receding hairline is standing beside Rob, and there's something really familiar about him. She watches him for a few moments before realising it's Hannah's old boyfriend, Simon Ackhurst. The years have not been kind to him.

'Hannah Jennings was my best friend,' continues Lottie from the bandstand, turning to look at the huge poster of Hannah. 'She was kind and beautiful and smart. She loved eating cheese toasties, listening to Duran Duran, and watching her favourite show, Byker Grove. She wanted to be a fashion model and she had her whole life ahead of her.' Lottie pauses.

The gathered crowd waits. All eyes are on Lottie, while Lottie herself watches a latecomer make his way through the crowd to the front.

Jennie turns to look at him too, watching as Elliott Naylor stops on the opposite side of the steps from Rob and Simon. He looks flustered as he takes a candle from a woman who is handing them out to the crowd. Once it's lit he looks up at Lottie, who gives him a small nod and continues with her speech.

'Hannah was just eighteen when she went missing. That was thirty years ago. And all that time we believed – the police led us to believe – that she had run away.' Lottie looks around the gathered crowd, pausing as her gaze finds Jennie and giving a sad smile. 'But she hadn't run anywhere. She had died, as she had lived, right here in White Cross. Where we all live. Where our children live. A place we think we are safe. But someone killed my beautiful, funny, kind friend and buried her in the basement of the school. They snuffed out her light when it should have shone so brightly.' Lottie's voice cracks. 'Her light should still have been shining now. But they murdered my best friend.'

The crowd seems to be hanging on Lottie's every word. As she speaks, the press move closer to the bandstand and a few of them start taking photographs of Lottie. She dabs daintily at her eyes with a tissue, making sure not to ruin her make-up. Jennie wonders if her actions look as rehearsed to the crowd as they do to her.

'The police investigation into Hannah's disappearance has been reopened. If you remember anything from around the time she went missing, please, please get in touch with them and report it.' Lottie's voice becomes more impassioned. 'We *have* to find the person who killed Hannah. We *cannot* let her death go unpunished. Please. Help me find the truth about how she died. We must get justice for Hannah.'

The crowd claps. Jennie hears someone crying a little way behind her. As Duran Duran's 'Ordinary World' plays over the speakers, more people step forward to lay flowers beneath the poster of Hannah. There's a group of teenagers a few metres away holding pictures of Hannah and crying. An elderly lady, who Jennie recognises as one of the school dinner ladies back in her day, walks past carrying a stuffed teddy bear to put with the flowers beneath Hannah's poster. There's no sign of Paul Jennings or his new wife.

It feels utterly surreal.

Jennie watches Lottie walk down the steps from the bandstand to join Rob and Simon. She hugs Rob, and nods hello to Simon. Elliott walks over to them, and the darkroom crew are reunited, in part at least.

Stepping back to make space for a pink-haired woman in a wheelchair on her way to lay flowers at the foot of the bandstand, Jennie looks back across the park and sees even more people have joined the vigil. As 'Ordinary World' fades and gives way to another Duran Duran hit, 'Come Undone', a memory flits across Jennie's mind's eye. Hannah dancing as the song played on the CD player in the darkroom, her twirling body silhouetted in the red light. A sharp pang of grief slashes across her heart like a knife.

Pushing the memory away, Jennie looks back towards the bandstand. Elliott and Lottie have moved closer to the flowers, cards and cuddly toys and are talking with the pink-haired woman. Rob and Simon are still beside the steps but the atmosphere between them appears to have changed. Rob looks pale and shaky as he speaks to Simon, his hands gesticulating wildly. Simon doesn't reply, instead shaking his head and taking a step back, his lips pursed into a hard, angry line. Rob reaches out, putting his hand on Simon's arm. For a moment it looks as if the tension is broken, then Simon says something and Rob throws down his candle and turns away.

Jennie watches Rob storm off, bemused. What the *hell* was that all about?

Chapter 24

Jennie flinches as a fox scurries across the lane ahead of her. She feels hyper-alert cycling home tonight, the close call with the car a few nights ago still vivid in her memory. At least it's not raining, although the heavy cloud has hidden the moon, making her route seem darker than usual. Her mind wanders back to the vigil at the park and the argument she witnessed between Rob Marwood and Simon Ackhurst. Rob has only been back in town a day, and she didn't have the impression he sees Simon very often. She wonders what they were arguing about. Whatever it was, there was a real heat between them.

As she cycles along the main road, her phone rings in her jacket pocket, making her jump. She lets it ring out, then flinches again a few moments later as it beeps and vibrates telling her a text has arrived. Whoever it is seems very keen to get hold of her.

Concerned that it might be one of her team, Jennie pulls into the side of the road and steps up onto the kerb. She pulls out her phone and reads the notifications on the screen.

1 missed call.
1 text message: Jennie, it's Rob, I got your number from Lottie. We need to talk. Meet me at our old party spot up on White Cross.

As she's reading the message another one pops onto the screen, also from Rob's number: Jennie, come quickly. Please.

She frowns. Today was the first time she's seen Rob in years, and there's no reason for him to want to speak to her other than if it's about Hannah. She was sure Rob was hiding something in his interview, and Zuri intuited the same. At the vigil he was clearly agitated.

Pulling a U-turn across the road, Jennie pedals quickly back along Main Street towards the school and the white cross on the hillside beyond.

It takes almost ten minutes to reach the bottom of the path that leads up through the woods to the chalk landmark. Chaining her bike to the kissing gate, she closes the bike lock and hurries through the gate and up the narrow trail. It's dark under the trees, really dark. She pulls her phone from her pocket and switches on the torch app, quickening her steps.

There's a rustle from the undergrowth to her left and Jennie's breath catches in her throat. Overhead the leaves rustle in the breeze. In the distance she hears the call of an owl. Suddenly she feels very isolated, vulnerable.

Jennie looks at her phone. There are no new messages from Rob.

Could Rob have been the person lurking in her front garden last night, watching her from the shadows? She remembers him as a fun-seeking wild teenager, but the man she met today was completely different; far more guarded and clearly stressed at being under investigation over a claim of death by malpractice. It's been thirty years since she really knew Rob Marwood. People can change a lot in that time.

She keeps walking, her fear escalating minute by minute. She's alone in the darkness. No one knows she's come here and there's no one waiting for her at home.

Is coming here a stupid mistake?

Rob admitted to meeting Hannah after hours in the school, just the two of them. He said they only did heroin the one time, but what if he was lying? Could there have been another bad trip or overdose? Was Rob the one who killed and buried Hannah? Did he realise in the interview that Jennie was suspicious of him? What would he do if he had?

Am I walking into a trap?

The breeze whistles through the trees. The branches creak as they sway in the wind, heightening her anxiety. Jennie presses on, half expecting Rob to jump out at her at any moment.

She's close to the top of the hill now, maybe just a hundred metres from the summit. It's too late to turn back. The creaking is getting louder, more rhythmic.

The path opens up into the clearing where she took the photographs of Hannah all those years ago. A rabbit sprints across the path in front of her, illuminated by the beam of her phone's torch, and Jennie's stomach flips, then she laughs at the ridiculousness of being afraid of a bunny.

You're fine.

Then there's another creak. Louder this time, and directly in front of her. Using the torch, Jennie scans the path up ahead. Her breath catches in her throat. She stops, unable to comprehend what she's seeing as she raises the beam of light from the ground ahead and unsteadily upward.

An old crate, fallen onto its side.

Brown brogues.

Orange and blue socks.

Pin-striped Paul Smith trousers.

Rob?

Jennie rushes forward. She grabs Rob's legs, trying to take his weight, to put slack in the rope that's around his neck, but she can't. He's too heavy and she stumbles, losing her grip. Desperate, she climbs the tree. It's a big gnarly oak, the trunk twisted and ancient. She scrambles up and along the branch to the rope.

Her heart is pounding in her chest. Her fingers scrabble at the rope, trying to undo the knot, but it's stuck firm. She puts her phone on the branch and yanks at the rope. The branch creaks. The rope slowly rotates, the torchlight illuminating Rob's face.

Oh God.

Jennie tugs at the knot, desperate to release him. Her actions become more frantic. She accidentally catches the end of the phone with her hand, and it falls from the branch to the ground with a soft thud. There's no light on the rope now. It's impossible to see what she's doing but she can't give up. She can't. She can't.

Jennie keeps wrestling with the rope. Battling to release the tension.

'Come on, come on,' she says, yanking at the end of the rope. Tears of frustration prick her eyes. Then, finally she feels the knot loosen. The rope slips through.

The release is sudden. The drop brutal.

Leaping down from the tree, Jennie hurries to Rob's prone form. Gripping his shoulder, she turns him over then gropes about in the dirt to find her phone before shining its torch beam on his face.

Eyes open. Mouth wide. Blue-tinged lips. Rob Marwood looks dead.

Jennie checks for a pulse and uses her other hand to dial 999. There's only one bar of signal, but thankfully, the call connects. She puts the phone on speaker and blows two breaths into Rob's mouth. She can't find a pulse. Is she too late? She can't be. She has to know what he wanted to tell her.

Questions swirl in her mind. Did he try to take his own life? Did someone follow him into the woods and attempt to kill him? If he was going to take his life, why did he want to meet her so urgently?

'What is your emergency?' the call handler's voice sounds distant and tinny on the other end of the line.

'This is Detective Inspector Jennie Whitmore,' she says, starting chest compressions. 'I need an ambulance sent to the clearing on the main path at the top of White Cross Hill, use my position to co-ordinate. There's been an incident. The man has no pulse. I've started CPR.'

'Are you in danger?' asks the call handler.

'No, I …' That's when Jennie sees the note, still gripped in Rob's right hand. She angles the torchlight closer, peering forward to read what it says.

For a moment it feels as if everything stops.

It's hard to find peace when you've got blood on your hands. I'm sorry.

Day Five

Chapter 25

Jennie hears the creak of the rope. She sees Rob's brown brogues swinging in the breeze.

She wakes with a jolt, but the memory from last night keeps playing in her mind's eye. How she kept doing CPR until the paramedics arrived and told her to stop. The sympathetic expression on their faces as they told her Rob was gone. How she told Zuri and the officers attending the scene what had happened, and she showed them the text Rob had sent her. That she cursed herself for not getting to him faster. Angry at herself for always having to cycle. For never having learnt to drive.

Sitting up, Jennie checks the time on her phone and sees that it's almost seven o'clock. She feels groggy after going to bed late and then lying there for hours trying to get to sleep. When she finally drifted off, she woke up time after time, spooked by every tiny sound on the street outside.

Walking through to the bathroom, Jennie turns on the ancient, limescale-scarred shower and twists the temperature gauge all the way around to cold. She steps onto the avocado shower tray and stands under the water, trying to revive herself with the arctic blast. It does help to clear her head a little, but as she switches the water to warm and sets about washing her hair, the sense of unease doesn't leave her.

She feels disturbed, and confused, by Rob's death. She doesn't understand why he called and texted her, wanting to meet so urgently, if he was planning to take his own life. His text had said he wanted to talk. If that was true, why didn't he wait for her? It makes no sense.

Unless he just wanted her to find him?

That could be true, but why her? He'd stayed in contact with Elliott and Lottie; why didn't he call them instead? Did they fall out as part of the argument Rob was having with Simon at the vigil? Was the argument related to Hannah's death?

Jennie rinses the conditioner from her hair as the questions flood her mind. It's not just Rob's death that's put her on edge, it's the weird things that have been happening to her. First the car that was following her home, then the shadowy figure watching her from the front garden. She doesn't know who's behind them. But they started after Hannah's body was discovered; there's a strong chance that they're connected to the case.

Towelling herself dry, Jennie walks back to the bedroom to get ready for work. The suit she wore yesterday needs dry cleaning; the trousers have dirt and leaf mould over them from the time she spent trying to bring Rob back. So from the rickety orange pine wardrobe she takes her other black suit, identical to the first one, along with a pale blue shirt. As she dresses, Jennie tries to make sense of what's happened in the last few days, but her tired mind is sluggish and unresponsive.

Hammering on the front door makes Jennie jump.

Her heart races as she hurries to the window and, staying low so that whoever it is can't see her, pushes the curtain aside, looking down into the front garden. She sees no one. That's weird. Really weird. There was definite knocking. She didn't imagine it.

Jennie flinches as there's more pounding on the door. Her heartbeat accelerates.

There *is* someone there.

Rushing down the stairs, she stops at the bottom step, peering at the front door. Through the frosted upper panel of the door, Jennie sees the outline of a person. A man, she thinks. Adrenaline is pulsing through her: her body's automatic fear reaction prompting her into flight or fight.

'Who is it?' Jennie calls, trying to inject as much authority into her voice as she can.

There's no answer, but another burst of quickfire knocking pummels the door.

What is this person's problem?

Picking up the heavy lamp from the hall table, Jennie approaches the front door. With her heart bouncing in her chest, she unlocks the door but keeps the chain in place, opening the door just a few inches. 'Yes?'

The delivery driver on the doorstep smiles disarmingly. He gestures at a large cardboard box on the top step.

'Oh, thanks,' says Jennie. Her heart rate starts to steady, but she's still on high alert as she glances past the driver to check the garden. There's no one else there.

'Can you sign?' the delivery guy's voice is overly loud.

Jennie looks back at him. He's twentysomething, with a good tan and wearing white earbuds. 'Sure.'

He leans closer and holds out a handheld device for her to sign on the touchscreen. As she does, Jennie can hear the music blaring from his headphones.

Taking her parcel, Jennie closes the door and carries the box into the kitchen. There's nothing on the label to identify the sender.

Who the hell sent this?

She puts it on the pine table and grabs a knife from the dish rack, slicing open the tape. Her heart rate accelerates again. She feels suddenly nauseous.

What's inside?

As she opens the box, she remembers. Smiling, she shakes her head. It's the photo-developing kit and chemicals she ordered. She'd totally forgotten they were due to be delivered today.

Putting down the knife, she lays her hands on the top of the box and takes a couple of deep breaths, trying to calm her nerves. She needs to get a grip, not freak out over every tiny thing. If whoever is watching her is trying to distract her from the investigation, then she refuses to give them the satisfaction. She's going to find the truth, whatever it takes.

Grabbing her cycle helmet and her bike, Jennie heads out, pulling the door firmly shut behind her.

Chapter 26

Her oversized *Friends* mug isn't here. She's checked all three shelves, the sink and dishwasher, but there's no sign of it. Jennie curses under her breath. She'd left it on the draining board yesterday evening, and now it's gone. Bloody people just helping themselves to other people's stuff. It's not on – they're police officers for God's sake!

'You all right?' asks Martin, coming into the staff kitchen and switching on the kettle.

'Someone's pinched my mug,' replies Jennie. She looks around the kitchen again. It's small and basic with budget cabinets, a stainless-steel sink and a granite-effect laminate countertop. There are a few dirty mugs in the sink but definitely no sign of her *Friends* mug.

'Yeah, happened to me a couple of weeks ago but it turned up again,' says Martin. 'It's probably some rookie uniform who didn't realise it's not part of the communal stuff.'

I doubt that's true, thinks Jennie. The communal mugs are plain white, and hers is very clearly not. She goes back to the dishwasher, double-checking her mug isn't hiding in the jumble of used chinaware and cutlery. It isn't.

Martin takes two mugs out of the cupboard and spoons coffee into them. He adds milk to one, then fills both with boiling water. He hands the one without milk to Jennie. 'Here you go.'

'Thanks,' says Jennie.

He waits a fraction longer than she expects before letting go of the mug. 'Are you okay, boss?'

No, I'm wondering where the hell my mug is.

'I'm fine, I just—'

'It can't have been easy last night, finding the body.' Martin lets go of the mug and steps back, leaning against the counter. 'They said you had to cut him down?'

Jennie meets her DS's gaze. He looks sympathetic, like he'd be a good listener if she told him her concerns, her fears. It's tempting, but she doesn't. She's the boss here; she can't go around burdening the team with what she's got going on, she *has* to stay professional. 'We should get to the incident room: the DCI wanted a full briefing.'

Not waiting for a response, Jennie turns and strides along the corridor to the incident room. The space is already crowded. Naomi and Steven are sitting over near the whiteboard. Zuri is in her usual spot at the front, and the DCI has taken the seat Jennie would usually have. He gives her a curt nod, reinforcing the fact that she's not been forgiven for forcing him into keeping her as lead on the case. She turns her attention to the new faces in the room. There are a few uniforms standing towards the back who Jennie recognises as the first responders last night. She smiles and says hello.

Not able to be in her usual spot, Jennie sits down beside Zuri. There's a seat free next to her, but Martin continues towards the back of the room and takes a seat in front of the uniforms. He looks irritated and Jennie wonders if it's because she didn't open up to him or if it's because she's sitting with Zuri. Whichever it is, she has no time for games or petty squabbles today.

She gives Zuri a nod to get started. 'What have we got?'

Zuri looks from Jennie to the DCI, seemingly mindful of the hierarchy and the tension in the room. 'Robert Marwood's death has been ruled a suicide. The cause of death was asphyxiation. There were no defensive or self-inflicted wounds other than those caused by hanging. Hassan called it in first thing this morning.'

'Okay,' says Jennie, thoughtfully. 'What about the scene?'

'DI Strickland and his team caught the case; they were up last night,' says Zuri, glancing towards the DCI.

Campbell clears his throat. 'I thought you and your team had enough on your plate with the Hannah Jennings case. There's a lot of public interest in finding her killer. I didn't want you to be spread too thin.'

Bloody Strickland! The last thing she needs is him poking his nose into her case and her relationship with Rob Marwood. She wonders if putting Strickland on Rob Marwood's death is the DCI's way of getting another DI close to the Hannah Jennings case by stealth. 'What did they—'

'We agree with Hassan's conclusion,' says Detective Inspector Strickland as he walks into the room with more than a hint of swagger. 'There was no sign of foul play in or around the site the body was found. The only footprints were Rob Marwood's, DI Whitmore's and the attending paramedics. We found no signs of a struggle. It's a tragic incident, but there was no crime.'

'With respect, I'd like to take a look at the evidence myself,' says Jennie, doing her best to control her irritation. 'Robert Marwood was a witness and potential suspect in the Hannah Jennings case. He was—'

'A mate of yours?' asks DI Strickland, raising his eyebrows. Rather than sit on one of the chairs he perches against the table at the front beside the DCI. 'My team have done their job, DI Whitmore. Hassan and his CSIs have done theirs. We all agree, Robert Marwood took his own life.'

Jennie bridles at DI Strickland's condescending tone. They've always been rivals, ever since Jennie got promotion ahead of him to DS and then DI, and she's never appreciated his sexist attitude towards his female colleagues. After his mishandling of the attempted abductions, she would've thought DI Strickland would have reflected on his practice and made some changes, but it seems he's just as arrogant as ever. She looks at the DCI. 'Do *you* agree, sir?'

'Having reviewed the evidence, I agree with your conclusion,' says Campbell, his expression neutral. 'The thing yet to be decided is whether Robert Marwood was Hannah Jennings' killer. I understand you were interested in him?'

Shit.

'He was one of a number of people we were talking to,' says Jennie. 'But we hadn't reached any definite conclusion.'

'The note he was holding is an admission of guilt though, surely?' counters Zuri, referring to her notebook. 'I had our handwriting expert take a look and they've confirmed that the writing on the note is a match with several other samples of Robert Marwood's handwriting.' She looks from Jennie to the DCI. 'Surely it's obvious that Marwood killed Hannah, and that's what the note meant. It was a confession of sorts.'

Jennie frowns. That doesn't sit right with her. 'No. I don't think it's that clear-cut. Rob's career was in tatters; we heard about that from him in his interview earlier yesterday – the malpractice claim obviously had him rattled. The note could have been referring to the patient who died under his care. My view is we need to continue our investigation until we're totally sure. At the moment, the evidence against Rob is tenuous at best.'

'I agree,' says DCI Campbell. 'You need to keep on with the investigation until you can prove without doubt that Robert Marwood, or someone else, killed Hannah Jennings. We have to be watertight on this.'

As Zuri opens her mouth to speak, the phone on the table beside the DCI rings. Answering the call, he nods as the person calling tells him something, then thanks them and hangs up. He looks at Jennie. 'Elliott Naylor has arrived for his interview. I said you'd be right down.'

The mood is sombre. Jennie and Martin sit opposite Elliott Naylor in the small, boxy space of interview room two. Jennie watches as her old friend runs his hand through his hair, the anguish he's feeling etched deep in the lines on his face.

'I just can't believe he's gone. It was so sudden. First Hannah, now Rob.' Elliott shakes his head, his eyes watery. 'I never knew. He kept it all bottled up. I just wish he'd asked for help, you know?'

Jennie nods. Her tone is sympathetic. 'Tell me what happened at the vigil last night.'

Elliott jerks his head up, surprised. 'What do you mean?'

'I was there,' says Jennie, with a gentleness that she doesn't feel. She wants to say, *I was there but none of you noticed me, it was as if I didn't exist, just as it has been since Hannah disappeared.* But she doesn't. Instead, she says, 'I saw Simon and Rob arguing after Lottie's speech.'

Elliott says nothing for a moment, then he sighs. 'Yeah, they were arguing about Hannah. They *always* used to argue about Hannah, that's why Rob never kept in touch with him. Last night Simon started going off on one about how we should have done more when she disappeared. Rob told him that we did all we could, but Simon wouldn't let it go. He kept banging on and in the end, Rob couldn't take it any more, so he left.'

It's plausible, but to Jennie the argument between the men had looked more personal. Maybe there had been more to Rob and Hannah's relationship than Rob had let on, and maybe Simon had always suspected that, causing a rift between them. Or maybe it was survivor's guilt – that Hannah died and he didn't prevent it. That, mingling with the guilt and pressure of the malpractice claim, could possibly have pushed an already highly stressed Rob to take his own life. Or perhaps, as Zuri believed, Rob *had* been the one who murdered Hannah.

The problem is, with Rob dead it's going to be hard to know for sure. Jennie decides to change tack and move the questioning back to focus on Elliott. 'When we last spoke, you made a change from the statement you gave in 1994: you told us that you'd seen Hannah on the night she disappeared, and left her in the darkroom in the basement of White Cross Academy with her father. You told us that her dad was in an angry and agitated state, and that you were afraid of him.'

'That's right,' says Elliott.

'After you'd left Hannah in the basement that night, did you make any attempt to contact her?'

'I … no.' Elliott's voice sounds strained.

'Just to confirm, you *didn't* try to make contact with Hannah Jennings to check on her wellbeing at any time after leaving her alone with her father in the school darkroom?'

'I was worried about her, but I didn't want to intrude. So I, I didn't call her or anything.' Elliott hangs his head, guilt-ridden. 'I wished afterwards that I had. I wish I hadn't left her that night …'

Jennie narrows her gaze. Elliott was one of Hannah's closest friends, surely if he was that worried about her he'd have called? It makes no sense. As she watches him slump forward, his head in his hands, Jennie isn't sure what to think. He had been one of *her* closest friends too, but he'd moved on very quickly the summer Hannah disappeared. Now, learning he withheld information from the police back in 1994, and did not bother to check in on Hannah after leaving her in the basement with her violent and angry dad, she wonders if she really knew him at all. The Elliott she thought she'd known was kind, thoughtful and empathetic, but his actions around the time Hannah disappeared seem to paint a different picture. Surely if he was that afraid of Hannah's dad, it would have been even *more* reason to tell the police what he'd seen, especially after she'd gone missing?

She shifts in her seat, fighting the nagging feeling that Elliott is keeping things from her. *Something's not right here.*

Opening the file on the table in front of her, Jennie removes the copies of Elliott's bank statements which Naomi has marked up. 'You make a monthly payment to Simon Ackhurst of a thousand pounds.' Jennie taps her finger against one of the payments high-lighted. 'You've been paying him for almost thirty years. Why?'

Elliott glances at the bank statement then looks back at Jennie. 'I'm just helping out an old friend who's fallen on hard times. Is that a crime?'

Jennie watches Elliott. His tone is friendly enough, but his body language has changed – he's sitting up straight now, his spine is rigid, and his arms are crossed. 'Not a crime, no, but unusual perhaps.'

Elliott shrugs. 'I don't know what to tell you. I'm a generous guy.'

He's definitely hiding something. Jennie glances at Martin, but he's sitting back and clearly happy to let Jennie do all the questioning. She regrets not having Zuri in on the interview; she's a great detective, and they make a good tag team. Martin never seems to be proactive about asking questions; she always has to prompt him beforehand. And for this interview, there wasn't time.

Jennie decides to change tack again. 'How were things between you and Hannah in the weeks before she went missing?'

'They were fine,' replies Elliott.

'Is that right?' says Jennie. 'Because we have a witness statement saying that the two of you were arguing a lot in those last few weeks.'

Surprise flits across Elliott's face before he quickly changes his expression to appear unbothered.

'So, what were you arguing about, Elliott?' says Jennie, her tone firmer now, pushing him for an answer.

Elliott grimaces, reluctant. He glances at the audio recorder. 'It was a personal thing.'

'I don't doubt that,' says Jennie. She softens her tone a little. 'But I need to know. For the investigation.'

Exhaling hard, Elliott nods. 'Look, if I'm honest, mine and Hannah's relationship was a bit strained. It had been for a while, for months rather than weeks.'

It's news to her, but Jennie tries not to let her surprise show. 'Why?'

'Earlier in the year, around Valentine's Day, she outed me to a boy I was crushing on, Mark Fredricks. Let's just say that Mark didn't take it well. He came and found me after school and told me I was repulsive and a bunch of other foul things. Then he punched me. A lot.'

'I never...' Jennie fights back the urge to ask Elliott why he hadn't told her. Martin's giving her side-eye as it is. She can't afford for him to catch wind that she and Elliott were proper friends at school. She clears her throat. 'I imagine that might have caused a rift between you.'

'Yeah.'

Jennie keeps her eyes on Elliott's. He's holding something back, she can sense it. 'Was that hard?'

'You could say.' Elliott takes a breath. 'I didn't handle it well. I'd never had the courage to tell anyone I fancied how I felt. I was too afraid I'd be rejected, or ridiculed.'

Jennie nods. Keeps her gaze on Elliott.

He shakes his head. 'I couldn't believe Hannah just casually told this guy.'

'Did you talk to her about it?' says Jennie. She ignores Martin's confused look, knowing he doesn't get why she's pursuing this line of questioning.

'No.'

'Because of what happened with Mark?'

'Yes, because of what happened.' Elliott sounds angry now. He clenches his fists. 'I'd fancied Mark for months and when he found out he clearly thought me utterly abhorrent and beat the crap out of me. Can you imagine how that feels?'

'I can't even...' Instinctively, she reaches out to put her hand on Elliott's arm, needing him to know she would have been there for him if he'd have told her. 'I wish I'd—'

'It broke me, Jen.' His voice cracks. 'I... I didn't think I could go on.'

Jennie's breath catches in her throat. Elliott's never let her in like this before. His hurt is still so raw it's as if she can feel it too. 'How did you?'

'I...' Elliott closes his eyes. His voice is barely a whisper. 'I tried to end things.'

Jennie's too stunned to speak. *How didn't I know? Elliott was my closest friend after Hannah, yet I was blind to his anguish. What does that say about our friendship? About me?* 'Jesus, Elliott, that's so... I'm so sorry. I never knew. I—'

'Most people didn't.' Elliott's voice is flat, as if the emotion of telling her has overwhelmed him. 'I was off school for a few weeks afterwards; my parents told our form tutor I had flu.'

'I remember that,' says Jennie, thinking back to the time and finding nothing to make her suspect that he'd been away for a different reason. 'Did you speak to Hannah when you returned?'

'Only when I had to. The worst thing was that she asked me why I hadn't confided in her. She told me she would've supported me during my time of crisis. That she'd have understood.' Elliott shakes his head, angrily. 'She didn't get that *she* had been the cause of my utter humiliation. I said a lot of things to her that I'm not proud of, but I was upset. I'd have forgiven her in time, but back then it was still so raw.' He looks at Jennie.

She nods her head, trying to think of what next to say. Her head is spinning with everything Elliott's told her. It's so much to process, but she wants him to know she would have been there for him. If only he'd told her. 'I totally get that.'

'That's why I didn't call to check on her,' continues Elliott. 'It's why I didn't stay in the darkroom even though her dad was so angry and she looked afraid. If I'm honest, I didn't want to be around her. She was still my friend, but I just didn't like her very much.'

Jennie struggles to get her emotions in check. She can feel Elliott's anguish, and can only imagine the awful turmoil he must have been in back when it all happened, but she can't understand how she had been oblivious to it all. The investigation has brought out so many revelations about her friendship group and their individual relationships with Hannah that she feels as if she wasn't really present at all that last year of sixth form. Rob and Hannah taking hard drugs together; Elliott and Hannah falling out after Hannah caused a chain of events that led Elliott to attempt to take his own life; Lottie's continual insistence that she was Hannah's best friend... It's a real headfuck.

When the interview is over, and they've seen Elliott out, Jennie turns to Martin. 'What did you think?'

'Hannah Jennings sounds like a real piece of work,' says Martin, dismissively. 'Naylor was just a kid and he was dealing with a lot of shit. I'm not surprised they fell out, but I don't think there was any more to it than that.'

Jennie nods, but she isn't so sure. Pushing away the residual feelings from their childhood friendship, she tries to consider objectively what they've learned from Elliott's interview: the payments to Simon his "old friend", the falling out with Hannah, and the fact that he never checked in on Hannah to see if she was okay after being so worried about leaving her with her dad in the school basement. An occasion Hannah's dad vehemently denies.

She hates to think that any of her school friends could have been involved in Hannah's death, but can't help wondering whether Elliott was so humiliated, so hurt by Hannah, that he confronted her about what she'd done. Today, Jennie has seen the anger he still feels about what happened all those years ago. Back then it would have been so much stronger. Did he confront her and did things get out of hand, turn violent?

Jennie's jaw clenches. Elliott was one of her best friends; one of the good guys. Before this investigation she would've sworn on her life that he'd never do anyone harm. It makes her sick to her stomach to think it, but has she been blinkered to the truth?

Could Elliott be responsible for Hannah's death?

Chapter 27

Duncan Edwards' ex-fiancée, Angela Totley, lives in a new-build house in Milton Keynes. She was surprised to see Jennie and Zuri on her doorstep when she answered the door, but she invited them in, if a little hesitantly. Now they're sitting, each with a mug of Earl Grey, in a front room tastefully decorated in various shades of white and off-white. Jennie's mouth is dry, but she's reluctant to take a sip. Earl Grey always tastes like used dishwater.

'Thank you for agreeing to talk with us today,' says Jennie. On the baby grand piano behind the sofa where Angela is sitting, a clutch of silver-framed photographs shows Angela and a man who Jennie assumes is her husband posing with two blonde girls, chronicling the years from babyhood to graduation. The family group look happy and glamorous; a far cry from Duncan Edwards and his lonely studio flat. 'As I mentioned earlier, we're investigating the murder of Hannah Jennings.'

Angela Totley nods. A petite, stylish brunette in her late fifties, she looks every inch the top private school headmistress that she now is. 'I'm happy to help. I assume you want to ask me some questions about Duncan Edwards?'

'We do,' says Jennie, a little surprised at how direct Angela is being. 'And also to get your sense of Hannah Jennings herself.'

Angela frowns. 'Now, I would have thought you could answer that question for yourself, Jennifer?'

Heat spreads across Jennie's cheeks, as if she's a naughty schoolgirl who has been caught out. It's clear Angela Totley recognises her. And although Jennie had always been a well-behaved pupil she'd never especially clicked with the rather prim English teacher. Jennie injects a stronger air of authority into her tone. She's not one of Miss Totley's pupils now. 'Of course, but we're looking for other people's perspectives.'

'Understood,' replies Angela, stiffly. 'It's hard for me to have an objective view on Hannah Jennings. I didn't know her particularly well – as you know, she wasn't in my class for English – but she seemed like an energetic child who was well liked by teachers and her peers.'

There's something about the way Angela talks about Hannah that makes Jennie think there's more to her reticence than purely not having been one of Hannah's teachers. But she parks the feeling for now, not wanting to push the witness too much before they've discussed her fiancé.

'You were engaged to Duncan Edwards at the time that Hannah Jennings went missing, is that right?'

'Yes, that's correct,' says Angela. She takes a dainty sip of her Earl Grey. 'Duncan and I had been together several years. We were living together at that time, and had been due to get married the following summer.'

'But that didn't happen?' interjects Zuri.

'No. It did not.' Angela picks up her mug of Earl Grey again and takes another sip. 'I broke off our engagement about a month after the investigation into Hannah's disappearance concluded she had run away.'

'And why was that?' asks Zuri, making a note on her scratchpad.

'I didn't want to marry him any more.' Angela Totley's tone implies that's as much as she's willing to say.

'Why?' asks Jennie.

Angela says nothing but it's clear from her expression that she's struggling to contain her emotions. 'As I said, I ended our relationship shortly after the investigation was closed. I left the White Cross Academy, took up a position as head of English at Campbell Park High in the new school year, and I haven't seen him since.'

Jennie watches the previously composed woman start to tear

up. There's a lot more going on here than they'd first supposed. She glances at Zuri.

'Have you had *any* contact with Duncan Edwards since your split?' asks Zuri, gently.

At first Angela doesn't reply. She puts her mug down on the side table, then nods. 'He has tried to contact me.'

'When?' asks Jennie, leaning forward in her chair.

'All the time,' says Angela, starting to speak faster. 'At first it was the odd email or text, but I blocked his number and email address and that stopped. Then, it was Friends Reunited. Even all these years later, any platform I join, I get a friend request or a new follow from him. I decline and block, of course, but then he puts together a fake account for a friend of a friend and I don't realise. He'll comment on every photo I put up, every thought I share.' She shudders, tearful now. 'Then he bombards me with DMs: Facebook, Twitter, Instagram. He comments on my Strava runs. This year he followed me on Threads. As soon as I block him in one place, he finds another. And it doesn't stop, *he* won't give up. He's been cyberstalking me for nearly thirty years.'

'Have you reported him?' asks Zuri.

'What good would that do?' says Angela, sighing. 'You're all so overstretched, and he hasn't actually *done* anything in real life.'

'From what you've said he's exhibiting obsessive behaviour.' She wonders if Duncan Edwards harboured a similar fixation for Hannah. He clearly has form for it. 'Thirty years is a long time to sustain an obsession.'

'He never wanted to accept that we were over,' says Angela, sadly. 'I think it stemmed from the fact that he knew it was all his fault. At first, he probably believed he could make it up to me. Then when he realised I wasn't going to forgive him, it was as if he couldn't let me go entirely. It's sad, really. I pity him.'

'You don't think he's dangerous?' asks Jennie. She's finding it hard to get a read on Angela; one moment she's distressed over how Duncan has stalked her, the next she's waving away their concerns and saying not to worry.

'Duncan?' Angela laughs. 'He's harmless. A fool, and a relentless one perhaps, but harmless none the less. He'd never hurt me, and I'm sure he didn't hurt Hannah Jennings, if that's what you're thinking. Although I'm sure there were plenty of others who'd want to.'

Jennie frowns, not understanding. 'Why would other people want to hurt her?'

Angela holds her gaze for a moment. 'Because Hannah Jennings was a dirty little slut.'

Jennie raises her eyebrows. She can't stop the shock registering on her face. Angela Totley started off prim, became emotional, and is now being provocative. Although her accusations are vague and more than a little evasive, there's something very personal about the way she's talking about Hannah.

Jennie pushes her a bit harder. 'You mentioned earlier that it was hard for you to have an objective view on Hannah. Why was that?'

'Well, like I told you, she wasn't a student of mine, so I didn't really know her,' says Angela, starchily, taking another sip of tea.

Jennie holds her gaze. There's something more; she just knows it. 'Is that all? Because referring to her as a "dirty slut" sounds like a pretty strong view.'

Angela bites her lower lip. Puts her tea mug down with a bang. 'Look. Okay. I didn't like Hannah Jennings. Actually, if you must know, I hated her. That little slut was the reason I broke off my engagement to Duncan. It was why I had to get another job at a different school. The reason I couldn't bear to stay in White Cross.'

Jennie feels her jaw clench. Her teeth start to ache.

'Why did you hate Hannah?' asks Zuri, her voice calm and sympathetic.

'Because I saw them together, her and Duncan, the day she

went missing. That little bitch was kissing him. Groping him right there at his desk in the art room after school, as if she had no shame, no morals. I just couldn't…' Angela pauses. Takes a breath. 'Duncan was kissing her back. When I saw that, I knew our relationship was over.'

So the rumours *were* true. Jennie wishes Hannah had told her the truth about Duncan Edwards. She'd never confirmed or denied the rumours, and Jennie had just assumed they were fiction not fact. She knows better now. 'There's no mention of that in the statement you gave during the first investigation. Why is that?'

Angela shakes her head and looks contrite. 'Because I was really embarrassed. Duncan pleaded with me not to tell the police. He said they were already looking at him as a suspect and if I told them about him and Hannah kissing just before she disappeared it would put the final nail in his coffin.'

'So you protected him, even though he'd cheated on you and could have been responsible for Hannah going missing?' says Zuri, clearly unimpressed.

'I protected him because I knew there was *no way* he was responsible for Hannah's disappearance,' counters Angela. She looks at Jennie.

'Duncan left Hannah and chased after me. We went home, arguing, in the same car, and continued to argue for the rest of the night. It was like a warzone in our apartment. The worst night of my life. Duncan insisted Hannah had provoked him, that she'd kissed him, and that he was about to push her off when I walked in. We yelled and cried and threw stuff, but neither of us left until the next morning, when we drove to school together and taught lessons for the whole day. I was with him the whole time.'

Angela fixes Jennie with a hard stare before she concludes, 'Duncan couldn't have had anything to do with Hannah Jennings going missing.'

Chapter 28

'I don't like her.' Jennie knows she sounds unprofessional, but can't resist sharing her personal opinion as they drive back to White Cross. 'She withheld information relevant to the case in 1994, and she would've done it again today if we hadn't pressured her.'

'Just because you don't like her, it doesn't make her a murderer,' says Zuri, evenly, as she indicates right and takes them around yet another roundabout on their route out of Milton Keynes.

'I know that,' says Jennie, glancing out of the window as they pass Stadium MK. 'But it makes me suspicious not just of Edwards, but of her too.'

Zuri says nothing, concentrating on the unfamiliar road layout as they pass a huge Asda and IKEA superstore and cross more roundabouts, taking them out towards Bletchley and the A5 beyond.

Pulling out her phone, Jennie messages Martin, telling him to bring in Duncan Edwards and seize his computer and phone. 'I'm having Edwards brought in. He totally bullshitted us about his relationship with Hannah. We need to let him know we're onto him and push him harder.'

'No matter how much of a dick he is, he's got an alibi,' says Zuri. 'He can't be Hannah's killer.'

'Not necessarily. Angela Totley might have given Edwards an alibi for the time Hannah went missing, but she's also got one hell of a reason for wanting Hannah gone. They could have been in on it together.'

Zuri shakes her head. 'I don't see it.'

'But it *has* to be Edwards,' says Jennie, not wanting to think

about what the alternative means. 'He could have killed her because—'

'There's something off about the darkroom crew,' says Zuri
firmly as she takes the turn off another roundabout onto the
A5. 'Rob Marwood might have been ruled a suicide but that
doesn't mean he or one of the others can't be guilty. Elliott Naylor
certainly seemed to get more defensive in his latest interview.'

Even though she has her own nagging suspicions, Jennie doesn't
like Zuri suggesting her old schoolfriends are in the frame for
Hannah's murder. She bristles. 'Never go behind my back again.'

For a moment Zuri looks confused, then she blushes deeply as
she realises what Jennie's referring to. But her expression remains
serious. 'I didn't. I was updating the whiteboard in the incident
room. The DCI saw me in there and asked for a catch-up.'

'So you told him I took a picture of the darkroom crew and
made out like it was a huge deal?' says Jennie. 'I took pictures
of a lot of people at that school. My A level art project was a
photography collection.'

'I didn't tell him it was anything,' says Zuri, frowning. 'But I
couldn't *not* tell him.'

Jennie shakes her head. She's not especially close to any of the
team, but she considers Zuri a friend as well as a colleague. In
addition to their film dates, they've had dinner from time to time
when one of them needed a sympathetic listener. Zuri had been
really kind when Jennie's mum died. So telling the DCI about the
photo feels like a betrayal, even though Jennie knows that Zuri
was just doing her job as DS. 'I thought we were friends. If you
had a problem, you should have talked to me first.'

Zuri stays silent. She takes a turn off the A5 onto the road that
will take them all the way back to White Cross.

'If you have a problem, tell *me* about it, okay?' says Jennie,
frustrated.

'Fine,' says Zuri. 'I don't have a problem with you personally,
Jennie, but I'm sorry, I do have a problem with you leading this

case. You clearly knew the victim and it's having an impact. It's a conflict of interest.'

'Yes, I did know her. I was at the same school, in the same year. The DCI knew that, and I told you all in the initial briefing,' says Jennie, trying to get Zuri back on-side. She hates feeling estranged from her. She hates it even more that she has to be so economical with the truth.

Zuri glances at her. There's frustration on her face but concern too. 'You've not been yourself since we started this investigation.'

'I'm just a bit tired from trying to sort out my mum's place,' counters Jennie.

'No, it's more than that. Your focus is off and it's screwing up the case. You're hell-bent on Paul Jennings or Duncan Edwards being the killer when there are far more discrepancies in the statements made by Hannah's mates. I don't get why you're acting so blinkered. It's like I care way more than you do.'

No you don't.

Jennie looks away, staring out of the window at the fields flashing past as she struggles to hold back the emotion that's threatening to overwhelm her. In her mind's eye she sees Hannah's remains half-buried in the mud in the school basement, Rob's body swinging from the rope in White Cross woods, then Hannah twirling in the same woodland clearing, alive and happy with everything to live for.

Zuri's got great instincts, but she's wrong about one thing. She doesn't care more than her about this case. Not by a long way.

Not about Hannah.

Chapter 29

'No!' Voice raised, Duncan Edwards thumps his fist down onto the Formica table in interview room one. 'I told you I never touched Hannah, and I've never harassed Angela.'

His solicitor, a neatly groomed man in a black suit and glasses, leans towards Duncan and tells him something that Jennie can't hear but assumes is along the lines of 'keep it together'. Jennie waits to see what Edwards says next.

'For the last thirty years I've been misunderstood and unfairly maligned.' Duncan Edwards looks at Jennie, his eyes pleading. 'I *never* stalked Angela.'

So that's the way it's going to be.

'Your browsing history tells a different story.' She pushes the printed sheets of paper towards him one by one. 'The yellow highlighter shows all the times in the last three months you visited Angela Totley's Facebook page; the green highlighter shows your visits to her school's staff page on their website; and the pink highlighter shows the attempts you've made to view and contact her other social media accounts.'

Edwards shakes his head. He glances towards the high window above Jennie's head as if he's sizing it up as a means of escape. 'I didn't… you can't prove that—'

'This is proof, Mr Edwards. And if you give us a little bit longer, we can go further back through the years. The techs tell me this is just the tip of the iceberg.' Jennie puts another page on top of the rest. 'As well as the social media stuff I've mentioned, these are the emails you've sent to Angela Totley's email address during the last three months. As you can see, there are more than fifty of them. I have printouts of each individual email if you'd like me to—'

'No, don't,' says Edwards, holding up his hands. 'I get it, but I wasn't stalking her.'

'Under the Protection from Harassment Act 1997, the offence of stalking includes contacting, or attempting to contact, a person, and monitoring a person's use of the internet including email,' says Zuri, firmly. 'Angela Totley described multiple attempts made by you to contact her. Attempts which caused her to take action to block your number and social media accounts and to change her own.'

'I was just looking out for her,' says Edwards, shaking his head. 'You've got this all wrong.'

'Look at all the times you've attempted to contact her, or viewed her social media in the past few months,' says Jennie, pushing the highlighted sheets closer to him. 'Do you not think that looks obsessive?'

'I wasn't stalking or harassing her. Honestly, I just wanted to feel close to her,' says Edwards, dropping his head into his hands. 'I love Angela.'

'Like you loved Hannah?' asks Jennie.

Edwards head snaps up. 'I *never* said I loved Hannah. She was just a student. A young girl.'

'She was,' says Jennie. She takes out another batch of printouts detailing Edwards' browsing history from the folder and pushes them across the table. 'Like all the young girls on these sites that you've visited.'

Edwards' face falls. He looks from Jennie and Zuri to his brief. The solicitor leans closer to him and whispers something. Edwards shakes his head vigorously.

Jennie knows she needs to push him harder. She needs to get Edwards on the ropes, to make him admit his relationship with Hannah. She reads from the printout. 'There seems to be a theme here – www.mysugardaddy.com, www.fuckmyteen.com, www.youngnsweet.com. Shall I go on?'

Edwards pales. 'No. I—'

'There are sixteen different websites here, Mr Edwards, all catering for those whose preference is young females,' continues Jennie. 'Your porn site history shows the same preference – teenagers with older men.'

'You clearly have a strong sexual interest in teenage girls, Mr Edwards,' says Zuri, barely able to hide her disgust.

'I like to watch these women – yes, okay, I admit that. But that's it.'

'Girls,' says Jennie, unable to disguise the disgust she feels towards Edwards. 'Some of the girls on these sites are barely sixteen, Mr Edwards. They're children.'

He shakes his head. 'They know what they're doing.'

Anger flares inside her and she swallows it back down. She has to stay focused on the end goal here, getting Edwards to admit his affair with Hannah. 'Hannah was the same age as a lot of the girls on these websites, wasn't she?'

Edwards stares back at her. Doesn't reply. His brief looks po-faced.

'The rumours about you and Hannah were rife at the school. You told us so yourself when we last spoke. You said, and I quote, that the kids were always creating "some kind of drama". Are you sure that's all it was?'

'Very sure,' says Edwards, crossing his arms.

'That's interesting, because we have a witness who saw you and Hannah Jennings kissing,' says Zuri, her tone professional. 'We know that you touched her.'

'They're lying,' says Edwards, his eyes darting side-to-side.

'We don't think so,' says Jennie. The smell of stale sweat mixed with cheap vinegary aftershave is coming off Edwards in waves. 'Did you fixate on Hannah just like you have on Angela?'

Edwards shakes his head. 'No, I never fixated on—'

'Did Hannah end things with you?' says Jennie, refusing to let him off the hook. 'Did you lose your temper and kill her?'

'For God's sake *I* was the one trying to end it!' shouts Edwards, banging his palms down onto the table. Ignoring a warning look from his solicitor, he continues, 'She was all over me and the rumours were flying around the whole bloody school about us having a fling. I told her it had to end.'

'So, for the record, you now admit that you *did* have a relationship with your student, Hannah Jennings?'

Edwards exhales hard. 'I'm not sure you'd call it a relationship as such, but things did get a bit heavy a few times.'

'Define heavy, Mr Edwards,' says Jennie, holding his gaze.

He looks away, keeps his eyes downcast as he speaks. 'We kissed. There was a bit of fooling about.'

'Did you have sexual intercourse?' asks Zuri. 'Was there any kind of penetration?'

Edwards curses under his breath. He glances at his solicitor but the man just shakes his head. Edwards' voice is lower when he replies, 'Yes.'

'How often?' says Zuri, leaning forward, keeping up the pressure on him.

'A few times,' says Edwards. 'Six, maybe seven times over a number of months.'

Jennie tries not to let the revelation derail her line of questioning. She wishes Hannah had confided in her; she thought they'd told each other everything. But it seems her thing with Duncan Edwards wasn't just a one-off; it had continued for months. 'But you wanted it to stop?'

'Yes. *She* instigated the whole thing, not me,' says Edwards, wearily. 'Hannah was more of a fantasy I got to act out; it was never anything real. I was happy with Angela and I wanted to marry her. I wasn't looking for more.'

Hannah was most definitely real, thinks Jennie, and given Edwards' browsing history and obvious hard spot for teenage girls, she doubts he resisted. He's just sorry he got caught, that's all. 'When did you end it?'

'I was trying to end it,' says Edwards, grimacing. 'By June, when the upper sixth were due to go on study leave, the rumours were gaining momentum. Sheila, the headmistress, had caught wind of them and called me in to explain myself. It was excruciating. I thought I was going to lose my job, or Angela, or both.'

'So what happened?' prompts Jennie, unable to feel any sympathy for the man.

'The day she disappeared, just after I'd finished teaching my last class of the day, Hannah came to see me. She had that look on her face and I knew what she wanted.' Edwards pauses. Shakes his head. 'I can't believe I'm telling you this. You're just looking for an excuse to pin this on me, and now...'

'Telling us what, Mr Edwards?' says Zuri, looking up from the notes she's taking.

Edwards blows out hard.

Enough of his delaying tactics.

Jennie's voice is firm. 'Tell us what happened.'

'She came straight up to me and kissed me, right there as I was standing at the desk. Starting rubbing me through my trousers. She had this wild look in her eye and kept saying she wanted me to fuck her right there in the classroom and that it was my "last chance". I said no, it was too risky, but she didn't care – said it didn't matter any more if we got caught. It was crazy; anyone could have seen us. The way she was acting, totally demob happy... it freaked me out. I knew I had to stop it, whatever it was we were doing, right then. So I told her it had to end and I asked her to tell people the rumours were false.'

Edwards' self-righteous tone infuriates Jennie. Blaming Hannah when *he* was supposed to be a responsible adult and her teacher! But she tries to hide her irritation. She needs to hear this, even if she despises the man. 'And how did she react?'

'She just smiled and shook her head at me.' Edwards balls his hands into fists. There's anger in his tone now. 'Do you know what she said? She said no. And then she laughed at me while I pleaded

196

with her to deny the rumours. She said, "But that wouldn't be true, would it?" Then, as I begged her to change her mind, she said, "Goodbye, Mr Edwards," and kissed me again. That's when Angela came in and saw us and my whole bloody life was ruined.'

Chapter 30

'He was shagging a pupil and he lied about it,' says Jennie, looking around the team, and the DCI, who are gathered in the incident room listening to her briefing on the Edwards interview. 'In my opinion, Duncan Edwards is a liar, and he's still holding on to a lot of anger about what happened. We know he saw Hannah on the day she disappeared, and we know she refused to quash the rumours. He had motive, and as a teacher, he had access to the school basement.'

'But he has an alibi and Angela Totley doesn't have cause to lie for him,' says Zuri.

'She lied for him in the first investigation,' counters Jennie.

'Yes, but they had a relationship then; they don't now,' says Zuri, flicking through her notes. 'Also, he saw Hannah much earlier in the afternoon. We have multiple witnesses who saw her after that time.'

Martin's frowning. 'Yeah, but that doesn't mean anything, Edwards could have sought Hannah out later, desperate to get her to keep schtum about the affair.'

'Good point, Martin. We need to check that out,' replies Jennie. It seems a reach for Duncan Edwards and Angela Totley to be in on Hannah's murder together, but she doesn't want to rule it out. 'So where are we with everything else?'

Martin clears his throat. He looks rather put out. 'The forensics are back. There isn't much, given the age and condition of the samples sent, but they did find a high concentration of hydrochloric acid on the remnants of the victim's shirt.'

'It's likely she got the acid on her when she was developing pictures, isn't it?' says Zuri. 'It's used as part of the process.'

The rest of the team nod, agreeing with Zuri. Jennie stays silent as Naomi writes the forensics on the whiteboard. They used hydrochloric acid, and a bunch of other chemicals, in their photograph development processes in the basement darkroom, but it was only really she and Elliott who processed their own film. The others mainly just hung out, especially Hannah. She was always in front of the camera, not behind it. There's no reason for acid to have been on her shirt.

When she's finished writing, Naomi turns to Jennie. 'I looked into the other school clubs that used the basement area. There were three of them – chess club, darts club and, on occasion, the drama club when they needed extra rehearsal space. They all used the bigger room between the darkroom and the boiler room, but none were given their own key.'

'Okay,' says Jennie. She hadn't even realised White Cross Academy had a darts club.

'I also followed up on Rob Marwood's alibi,' continues Naomi. '*Four Weddings and a Funeral* was scheduled to play at the White Cross Cinema that day, but their records show there was a problem with the projector in the main screening room. All the showings had to be cancelled while the engineers figured out the problem. They didn't reopen until the following afternoon.'

'So Marwood's alibi was false?' says Zuri.

'Looks that way,' replies Naomi.

Jennie feels a burst of triumph that her hunch had been right, followed by the crushing realisation that one of her old friends had lied about his whereabouts. She frowns. 'That potentially puts Rob Marwood's suicide in a different light.'

Zuri nods. 'He lied about where he was. It's possible he's our killer.'

Jennie knows her DS is right. It's possible Rob did have something to do with Hannah's death; she can't discount it. 'What else do we have?'

'I spoke to the headmistress,' says Steve, reading from his

notes. 'Sheila Heseltine retired over ten years ago and now lives in Australia. She confirmed the school secretary's story about the drainage guys not having access to the basement until one of the school staff unlocked it to let them in. She also confirmed that Duncan Edwards was pushed out after Hannah went missing. He was told that a disciplinary investigation was about to be started into his conduct, and apparently he jumped before he was fired. Mrs Heseltine said she'd told the police in the first investigation about her suspicions that he'd been having a relationship with Hannah.'

'Okay, that's helpful corroboration,' says Jennie, waiting for Naomi to finish writing up the notes. 'So let's look at each of our suspects and discount or identify them as needing more investigation.' She moves across to the whiteboard and reads from the suspect list in order. 'Hannah's dad, Paul Jennings – thoughts?'

'He doesn't have an alibi after he was fired from his job and forced to leave early, and we have witness sightings of him arguing at home and on the street outside with Hannah, and later finding her in the school basement,' says Naomi.

Paul Jennings might have turned his life around since Hannah disappeared, but there's no denying he was an angry, violent man back then, and he showed them a few glimpses of his old self during the last interview. She suspects he inflicted the injuries Hannah had sustained, and doesn't doubt that if she hadn't left the house that night, he would have done more damage. But Jennie's not sure about the basement sighting. 'Do we believe Elliott Naylor? He didn't tell the police about Hannah or her dad during the original investigation. Something seems off to me.'

'Agreed,' says Zuri, nodding. 'I think Naylor's hiding something.'

'So Paul Jennings is still a possible, but looking less likely as our killer,' says Jennie. She turns back to the whiteboard. 'Next is the janitor, Tom Blake?'

'Blake has an alibi,' says Martin, sitting up a little in his chair. 'I spoke to him, and checked out what he told me. He was playing football, a local league thing, that night. There's a write-up in the local paper that mentions the two goals he scored and has his picture as part of the winning team. Several of his teammates, and the owner of the local pub where the team celebrated after the game, have confirmed his whereabouts.'

'Okay, so the janitor is in the clear,' says Jennie, as Naomi puts a line through Tom Blake's name. 'The drainage guys are next. They've already alibied out and we have multiple people confirming they didn't have a key to access the basement out of hours, so they're also clear.'

Naomi crosses out their names.

'Next, we have the photographer from the modelling gig Hannah had booked.' says Jennie.

'He alibied out,' says Steve.

Naomi crosses the photographer's name from the list.

'Duncan Edwards?' asks Jennie.

'He had motive and access to the basement,' says Naomi.

'But also an alibi,' says Steve.

'He's guilty of being a seedy, repugnant liar of a man,' says Zuri, her dislike for Edwards obvious in her expression. 'But there's no concrete evidence suggesting he murdered Hannah.'

'I'm with Naomi on this,' says Jennie, putting a question mark beside Duncan Edwards. 'Yes, Angela Totley gave him an alibi, but I don't trust either of them. They both withheld information in the original investigation and Edwards clearly has a thing for teenage girls. I don't want to drop him as a suspect just yet.'

At the back of the room, DCI Campbell nods. 'Agreed. Keep Edwards and Totley in the frame for now, we can circle back to them if needs be.'

'Will do, sir,' says Jennie, deferentially, knowing she needs to keep the DCI onside. She looks at the next name on the list. Feels her stomach flip. 'So, what do we think about Lottie Varney?'

Martin mutters something Jennie doesn't quite catch. 'What's that Martin?'

He shakes his head. 'Nothing, boss. She just seems high maintenance, that's all.'

'Yeah,' says Jennie. Bloody Lottie telling Zuri *she* was the person who took the photo. 'Any other thoughts?'

'She seemed deeply insecure,' says Zuri, thoughtfully. 'And although she put a lot of effort into painting herself as the loyal best friend, it was clear she and Hannah were arguing a lot around the time that Hannah went missing. But there's no evidence she was involved.'

Jennie wishes she could tell the team that she knows Lottie's alibi is bullshit, but if she does, she'll have to admit why she knows that for sure. 'So she's no longer a suspect, okay.' *Not officially, anyway.* 'Next up is Elliott Naylor.'

Naomi draws a line through Lottie's name.

'Like I said earlier, he's hiding something,' says Zuri, consulting her notebook. 'If his sighting of Hannah in the basement is true then he's one of the last people to see her alive.'

Steve raises his hand. 'The hydrochloric acid found on the shirt puts Hannah in the darkroom that day.'

'It puts her in the darkroom at some point, but not necessarily that day,' says Zuri. 'She could have worn the shirt in the darkroom before and spilt acid on it, but not washed it yet.'

'Is that really likely?' says Martin, raising his eyebrows. 'I mean, if you get a load of acid on your shirt, you're going wash it quickly, aren't you?'

'We can't be sure either way,' says Jennie. 'But we know that when we interviewed Elliott Naylor, he changed his story from what he told the first investigation back in 1994.'

'I think he should stay on the list,' says Zuri. 'He's hiding something.'

Martin shakes his head.

Much as Jennie hates to think that Elliott could have had

something to do with Hannah's death, she's inclined to agree with Zuri. She glances to the back of the room at the DCI. He nods. 'Okay, let's keep him on the list for now, and see if we can find out what he's hiding. We also need to push him on the money he's been paying Simon Ackhurst all these years. It seems weird to me. Speaking of Simon Ackhurst, we need to talk to him as a matter of urgency.'

'We've got his address, boss,' says Martin. 'He lives in a house-boat on a permanent mooring on the canal.'

'Great; we'll visit him as our next priority.' She looks at the last name on the list. 'Rob Marwood?'

'Well, he's dead obviously,' says Martin, smirking as he plays for laughs.

Jennie shakes her head. She knows that dark humour is part of the deal in the police, but Rob's death still feels raw. He'd been a friend once.

The DCI grimaces. No one says anything. The mood in the room remains serious.

Martin looks unusually self-conscious. 'Sorry, it's too soon, I guess.'

'Anyone else, thoughts?' asks Jennie. 'We know his alibi was faked, and he was in a highly anxious state of mind before he died. What else?'

'The note,' says Zuri, her tone determined. 'I still believe it was a confession to killing Hannah.'

At the back of the room, DCI Campbell is running his hand across his jaw. Jennie gets the impression her boss might be sway-ing more towards Zuri's theory that Rob is their murderer.

Personally she's not so sure. 'If he killed Hannah, where did it happen? Elliott has said he was in the darkroom all along. If Rob and Hannah had been there, he would have seen them.'

Zuri nods, thoughtfully. 'True. I think we should have another go at questioning Naylor. He knows more than he's letting on, I'm sure of it.'

'Agreed. Can you set that up?' asks Jennie. Jennie looks at her DCs. 'Naomi, Steve, follow up with all Duncan Edwards' employers since he left White Cross. Find out if there's been any complaints about his conduct with students or female colleagues. He might not be our prime suspect any more, but we need to cross all the t's and dot all the i's on him.'

'On it,' says Naomi, making a note of the actions on the white board.

'Fine,' says Steve, looking up at the clock on the end wall.

Jennie glances at her watch. It's almost six, but she isn't ready to call it a day yet. At the moment, they have more questions than answers. Frustrated, she rubs her temples, trying to ease the tension headache that's brewing behind her eyes. She needs a clear mind, has to be at her best.

It's time to be reunited with the final surviving member of the darkroom crew.

Chapter 31

Simon Ackhurst's narrowboat is moored a quarter of a mile along the tow path from the Flotilla pub and restaurant. Martin parks in the pub car park and they walk past the busy beer garden – the smell of pub grub making Jennie's stomach growl – and out along the gravel path. It doesn't take them long to find Ackhurst's mooring. It's a beautiful spot. The grassy bank is dotted with wildflowers and clover, and the willow trees that curve across the water from the other side of the canal provide some shade from the warm evening sun. She can hear the birds singing in the trees, and a little further along the canal a family of swans are gliding gracefully through the water.

'This is all right, isn't it?' says Martin, echoing her thoughts. 'Private spot, close to a pub. Perfect.'

'Yeah,' says Jennie. She looks at the navy narrowboat with gold-trimmed windows and a few tubs of white and red geraniums on the bow. 'Nice boat.'

Stepping onto the boat, Martin goes down the steps and knocks on the wooden door.

It opens almost straightaway and a tanned, broad-shouldered man with thinning blond hair steps out wearing board shorts, a baggy pink T-shirt and sliders. 'DS Wright?'

'That's me,' says Martin. 'Thanks for meeting with us at such short notice. This is my boss, DI Jennie Whitmore.'

'Jennie?' says Simon, putting his hand up to shield his eyes from the sun. 'Bloody hell, you haven't changed a bit.'

She knows he's lying, but then he always was one to try to charm the girls. 'Likewise.' He probably knows she's lying, too.

'Come in, come in,' says Ackhurst, moving into the boat and

gesturing for them to follow. 'It's been forever, Jennie. Must be, what, at least thirty years?'

Jennie nods. 'Thirty years, yeah. Since school.'

'And now you're a detective, that's so cool,' says Simon, enthusiastically. 'I'm glad things have worked out well for you.'

Jennie just smiles. Life has worked out nothing like she thought it would. From what she's read of Simon's rap sheet she guesses the same for him. He was the school's top athlete, and the guy all the fifth-formers and a lot of the sixth form were crushing on; destined for big things in the sporting world. But none of it happened after he went off the rails when Hannah disappeared. 'As you know, Hannah Jennings' remains were found buried in the basement of the old White Cross Academy. We're investigating her murder, and as one of her close friends, we'd like to ask you a few questions.'

'Of course, of course,' says Simon, gesturing for them to sit down on the bench seat. Behind him on the stovetop a kettle starts to whistle. 'Can I get you a drink? Tea, alcohol-free beer?'

'We're fine, thanks,' says Jennie. Her tone is professional, firm; Simon needs to realise this isn't a social call. She takes a seat. The boat is bigger than she'd expected – and more homely, with its pine-clad walls, paintings of local landscapes and check curtains. There's an armchair next to the small log burner and bench seats either side of a narrow table.

As Martin sits beside her, Simon moves the armchair so it faces the bench and takes a seat. 'So how can I help?'

'Why don't you start by telling us about your relationship with Hannah Jennings?' says Jennie. The slight movement of the floor beneath her feet is a bit disconcerting, it's years since she's been on any kind of boat.

'Erm, sure,' says Simon, slightly wrongfooted, perhaps because he'd expected Jennie to just go on what she knew of the relationship. 'I started dating Hannah when we were kids really, seventeen years old and no clue about life. We'd known each other since we were small. It started off at junior school with me pulling her pigtails and her thinking boys were gross, then we became mates at the academy, and it ended up with us becoming an item in sixth form. But you know that bit.'

Jennie nods, acknowledging that she did know that. She glances at Martin but the reference seems to have gone over his head. 'Obviously we were both in the last year of sixth form together, but it's important we get your perspective on what happened around the time Hannah went missing. Can you talk us through what you were doing the day she disappeared?'

'Sure,' says Simon. His voice sounds a little strained now. His face turning slightly paler beneath his tan. 'Hannah said she needed to study for her drama exam later in the week, so we agreed we'd get together after that. I was at home most of the day, I slept until just after lunch, did a bit of studying for my chemistry exam, then did my usual workout at the gym around three o'clock for an hour or so. After that I went to work. I worked the night shift, packing in the warehouse at EDT Logistics, and got home just before eight in the morning and went to bed.'

What Simon is saying matches the statement he gave the police back in 1994, but there's no evidence in the file that his alibi had been checked and confirmed. Jennie tries not to let her irritation show. What else did they forget to do back then? She keeps her voice even; it's not Simon's fault the first investigation was so sloppy. 'So, just to clarify, you didn't see Hannah at any point that day or night?'

'No.'

'But things were good between you? Any arguments?' asks Jennie.

'We were good,' says Simon, sadly. 'She was the love of my life. I bloody worshipped her. You know, she was super focused on becoming a model, and I was totally behind her doing it. There was a lot of talk in the papers back when she disappeared about how she was going to move to London and all that rubbish, but she wasn't. We'd talked about it and she was going to stay in White Cross and commute. Nothing was going to come between us.'

Simon's deluded, thinks Jennie. Even if she hadn't said exactly when she was leaving, Hannah had made no secret of the fact she wanted to leave White Cross and move to London. Had he really believed she wouldn't go, or was this a self-protection mechanism, allowing him to pretend their relationship had been more important to Hannah than he knew it really had been? Jennie knows she needs to explore this. 'Did you know about the rumours that Hannah was seeing a teacher?'

'Of course I'd heard those bloody rumours, they were all over school,' says Simon, his upper lip curling into a snarl. 'Mr Edwards was always perving over Hannah – it was disgusting. It was totally obvious why there were rumours. The bloke was a complete lech.'

'Was there any truth in them?' asks Jennie.

'No,' says Simon, quickly. 'Hannah wouldn't touch that pervy bastard.'

'So the rumours saying she was sleeping with him were wrong?' says Martin.

'Totally, mate,' says Simon. 'The only person she was shagging was me.'

Interested in the more casual way he replies to her DS, Jennie nods as if agreeing with Simon. Thinking it might encourage him to open up more, she glances at Martin and gives a small nod, staying silent to let him ask the next question.

Martin consults his scratchpad. 'Can you tell us what happened in your life after Hannah disappeared?'

'It screwed me up, mate.' Simon runs his hand through his thinning blond hair, looking troubled. 'Her just being gone like that, it messed with my head. I buggered up my exams and dropped out of the football team, and just couldn't get my shit together. It was the not knowing, yeah? The wondering where she was and when would she come back. It made me angry, adrift, and I kind of lost the plot.'

'In what way?' asks Martin.

'Grief and rage got the better of me. I turned to drink, drugs – anything that'd numb the feeling of helplessness.' Simon shakes his head. 'It was bad, mate. I did a lot of things I'm not proud of – I was done for GBH, theft… But I got lucky inside – was given help and got clean. In a weird way, prison was the best thing that could've happened to me. It helped me get my shit together. When I came out, I trained as a counsellor. Now I run my charity and help young offenders who've lost their way like I did.'

'Very admirable,' says Martin, smiling.

'Lucky, I'd say,' says Simon. 'I could easily have gone another way, but the help I got saved me. Now I'm just trying to pay it forward.'

Jennie resists getting sucked into the love-in that seems to be developing between Simon and Martin. 'What about the payments Elliott Naylor makes to you? A thousand pounds every month since he started work after university?'

Simon looks shifty. 'Look, I'd rather not say if that's okay? It's Elliott's story to tell.'

'But I'm asking *you*,' says Jennie, narrowing her gaze. 'Are you blackmailing him?'

'Dear God, no, far from it,' says Simon, looking horrified.

'It'd be good if you could tell us what the money is for,' says Martin, conversationally. 'Just so we can eliminate you as a suspect.'

'A suspect? Really?' Simon looks shocked but recovers quickly. 'Okay, fine. If you really have to know, I guess you'd call it a gratitude payment.'

'For what?' asks Jennie.

'Because I saved his life.' Simon looks torn, as if he doesn't really want to tell them more. 'Look, okay, some stuff happened earlier in the year before Hannah disappeared. Elliott had a thing for this guy. He never told him, but the guy found out and beat the shit out of him. Elliott hit a real low and tried to take his own life. It was awful. I found him passed out on pills, covered in vomit, and I thought he was dead … I was really bloody shit-scared. Totally panicked. But I managed to call an ambulance and get him help.' He pauses. Takes a breath. Then looks back at Jennie. 'When I was coming out of the worst time in my life, things were going well for Elliott and he wanted to help me out, like I'd helped him. So he started donating a monthly amount into my account. He's never wanted to stop.'

Again, Jennie feels the pang of sadness that Elliott hadn't felt he could confide in her. She thought they'd been close, but it seems even Simon, who Elliott had seemed to tolerate rather than like when they were at school, knew more personal things about him than she had. Why did none of her friends tell her? Why didn't Hannah?

Pushing her feelings aside, Jennie concentrates on Simon. She doesn't get the sense that he's lying, but it seems a stretch that Elliott would be so grateful for something that happened thirty years ago – even something as major as saving his life – that he'd pay out a grand a month forever. After all, he's recently finished an expensive renovation on his home and the costs of having a baby through surrogacy can't be cheap. Surely there's more to it? 'Did Hannah tell Elliott's crush that he fancied him?'

Simon purses his lips. 'I heard that, yeah. But it seemed out of character for her.'

'Could she have done it while she was high?' asks Jennie.

'I don't know what you—'

'We know Hannah and Rob sometimes met up to do drugs together,' says Jennie, pausing as the boat rocks again and her stomach lurches. 'There was an incident four weeks before she disappeared, an overdose or bad reaction – we have the A&E record.'

'Yeah, shit. Hannah was … experimental, okay? And you know that Rob was totally obsessed with that film *Flatliners*. He thought he was bloody Kiefer Sutherland or some bollocks like that, and kept banging on about how we needed to try and reach a higher level of consciousness. It wasn't my thing: a bit of weed, yes fine, but not the hard stuff. Hannah was into it, though. Her and Rob used to chase the dragon, take acid, poppers and whatever other mad shit Rob got hold of. She used to treat that stuff like it was candy.' Simon shakes his head. 'Problem is, after each high she wanted to do more, push it further, and bloody Rob was always willing to go along with whatever she wanted, searching for the ultimate high.'

'Like what?' asks Jennie, sensing there's more that Simon knows.

There's a look of disgust on Simon's face. 'They used to play with neck ligatures. Rob said they were experimenting, trying to see if starving themselves of oxygen while on drugs gave them an even greater high. He used to call it a homage to *Flatliners*, but that was bullshit. He was a kinky fuck without the balls to tell Hannah how he really felt about her. And it was only ever Hannah who got choked out.'

How did I never know this? Why didn't Hannah tell me? I thought we told each other everything. I told her everything.

Jennie takes a breath, struggling to keep focused on the interview. The more questions she asks the more she learns about the secret life Hannah led. She pushes down the hurt.

Martin glances at Jennie and she can guess what he's thinking. The A&E record of Hannah's overdose documented marks around her neck. It could be that ligatures were involved that time, even though Rob hadn't mentioned it. If Rob's note really was a confession to causing Hannah's death, had it been a drug-fuelled experiment that went wrong?

Jennie looks at Simon. No longer looking relaxed, he's visibly tense now, his posture stiff. He's told her new information about Rob, but he's also revealed something about himself, because it's clear he's feeling jealousy and anger towards Rob. She thinks back to the argument between Simon and Rob at the candlelit vigil; it doesn't look like there is any love lost between the two of them then, yet they've been friends for years. 'Is that why you argued with Rob at the vigil?'

'No, I …' Simon shakes his head. 'Look, I don't like speaking ill of the dead and all that, but Rob was always a bit of an arsehole. We never really got on. He looked down on me, especially after I went to prison. And at the vigil, with Hannah's picture right there… knowing the stuff he used to do with her… it made me almost lose my shit.'

'How do you know about Rob and Hannah's drug-taking?' asks Martin. 'Were you there?'

'No, mate, I smoked weed, like any other teenager, but nothing heavier than that,' says Simon. 'I had a key for the darkroom. If they wanted to use it, they had to ask me for the key. I turned up once while they were there, curious about what they were getting up to. I saw for myself the state they were in.'

'When was this?' asks Jennie. Out of the boat's window she sees a red and black narrowboat pass by along the canal, a Jack Russell terrier sitting on the stern, watching the water intently.

'Couple of months before Hannah disappeared,' says Simon. 'After that I used to ask Hannah about her trips. She wanted to try the ligature thing when we had sex, but I said no. I wasn't into that shit.'

It's the second time Simon's talked about sex with Hannah. Jennie makes a mental note to circle back to it. 'Who had the key on the night Hannah disappeared?'

Simon thinks for a moment. 'Must have been Elliott. He was in the darkroom developing pictures that day.'

'And when did he give it back to you?' asks Jennie.

'I'm not sure, probably the next afternoon. Like I said, I was at work and then went to bed, so the earliest would have been the next day.'

Jennie frowns. If Elliott had left Hannah and her dad in the basement darkroom, what had he done with the key? Did he leave the place unlocked? She makes a mental note to ask Elliott when they interview him again. Then changes tack. 'Do you think Rob killed Hannah?'

'Shit, I...' Simon runs his hand through his hair again. 'Rob wasn't a bad guy; I don't think he'd ever mean to hurt a person. I mean, he was a doctor, yeah? He wanted to save lives.'

Jennie nods. It's interesting that Simon's dodged answering directly with a yes or no. It's also curious that he's never once expressed sadness or shock that Rob took his own life.

Simon clears his throat. 'Look, it's obvious Mr Edwards killed Hannah. He was totally fixated on her, and there was no way she wanted anything to do with him. I reckon he killed her because he couldn't handle the rejection.'

Jennie looks at Simon's bunched fists and how his face is now flushed and the veins raised on his forehead, and thinks he's working too hard to throw Edwards under the bus. There's definitely jealousy in play, but the more she listens and observes him, the more she thinks that it's on the part of Simon. 'Did you use protection when you had sex?'

Simon sits more upright in his armchair, the leather creaking as he moves. 'Yeah, we used rubbers. Neither of us wanted a kid, obviously.'

'That's very diligent of you,' says Jennie, injecting an air of surprise into her tone.

'What do you mean?' says Simon, frowning.

'Well, considering Hannah was already on the pill, you really doubled down. Although it was probably wise if you were worried she was sleeping with Mr Edwards too; condoms give far more protection against STDs.'

'Hannah wasn't on the pill, and she would never have slept with that old perv,' says Simon. 'She didn't—'

'*You* never actually slept with her, did you?' says Jennie, pushing him harder. He clearly has no idea that Hannah was on the pill.

For all his big talk, Jennie doubts he ever got close to sleeping with her friend. 'You were still a virgin.'

'I bloody well wasn't,' says Simon, his cheeks reddening, and his voice getting louder. 'I'd done it with loads of girls.'

'The thing is, we've heard it from multiple sources that you and Hannah hadn't slept together.' Jennie looks at Simon sympathetically, her voice kind. 'There's no shame in it, Simon. It's just we know Hannah was sexually active, and we need to find out who she *was* sleeping with.'

Simon presses his fists into his thighs as if trying to stop himself from losing his temper and leans closer to Jennie, his eyes fixed on hers. 'She couldn't get enough of my dick. Morning, noon and night she always wanted *me* up her.'

Jennie tastes the bitterness on her tongue and fights the urge to heave. As she looks at Simon, his laddie bravado failing to cover the resentment he's harbouring, she struggles to disguise how disgusting she finds him. But she knows she's right; he'd felt emasculated and jealous, and maybe enough anger to push him over the edge and kill Hannah.

She holds Simon's gaze. Feels the rage coming off him in waves. *Is he Hannah's killer?*

Chapter 32

It's getting late by the time they get back to the station, so Jennie takes Martin up on his kind offer to put her bike in his boot and give her a lift home. The light is going as they arrive outside her place and although she's perfectly capable of removing her bike, Martin jumps out to help her retrieve it from the car. Thanking him, Jennie slings her rucksack over her shoulder, and wheels the bike up the garden path towards the front door.

Martin trots after her. 'You all right, boss?'

'Yeah,' says Jennie. But she isn't, and she knows she's been quieter than usual, dwelling on the interview. 'He pissed me off, that's all.'

'What, Ackhurst?' says Martin.

'All that bravado bullshit, going on about shagging and Hannah begging for it...' She shakes her head.

Martin nods, his expression sympathetic. 'It was disrespectful.'

'Exactly.' Jennie knows she's particularly sensitive to the way her murdered friend is spoken about, but even if she hadn't known the victim personally, she'd still have been disgusted by Simon's words. He was supposed to have cared for Hannah.

'It must be hard investigating the death of someone you knew,' says Martin, as if reading her thoughts.

Jennie nods, resisting the urge to minimise her friendship with Hannah. She knows that she should, but it feels as if she's disrespecting Hannah by denying their relationship. 'Yes.'

'If it means anything, I think the way you handled Ackhurst was really impressive,' says Martin. 'A man like that has no respect for women, but you were such a pro in the way you conducted yourself and the interview.'

Jennie smiles. It's the first positive feedback she's had from a member of the team on her handling of the case. She thinks about Zuri's criticisms of her leadership during this investigation – that she's too close to the people involved, and that she's not casting the net wide enough – and wonders if Martin or the others have had the same concerns. 'Thanks, that means a lot.'

Martin holds her gaze. 'Don't worry about DS Otueome. She'll see you're right in time.'

Jennie's not sure if he means about Rob Marwood, or Duncan Edwards, or the way she's led the investigation, but it's nice to hear anyway. They've reached her front door. Key in hand, she turns to face Martin. 'Thanks, I hope so.'

Martin moves closer. 'You're doing a great job.'

'I wonder if I am sometimes,' says Jennie.

'It must be lonely at the top,' says Martin, his expression kind, understanding.

Jennie nods. 'Thanks for the lift. See you tomorrow.'

Martin doesn't reply. Holding her gaze with an intensity she's never seen from him before, he leans in and brushes his lips against hers.

It's unexpected, unwanted.

Surprised, Jennie steps back, her elbow knocking against the front door. 'Martin, I—'

He lunges forward, crushing his mouth against hers, pressing his body against her. She tries to move away but his hand grips the back of her neck, clamping her to him. His tongue is in her mouth. His teeth clashing against hers. She feels as if she can't breathe.

Jennie struggles, trying to get free, but there's no space, she's up against the door. Using all her strength, she puts her hands on his chest and shoves him away hard. 'What the hell, Wright?'

Martin looks put out, confused. 'What's the matter? You've been giving me the come-on for weeks.'

'No, I…'

'Come on, you want it really,' says Martin, reaching for her waist, his fingers digging into her flesh. 'Don't be a bloody tease.'

Jennie slaps his hands away, but he grabs for her, pinching her right breast and snatching at her belt, trying to yank her to him.

'Get off.' She shoves him again. Her voice is firmer, louder, this time. 'Leave. Now.'

Martin scowls. His face is red. The muscles in his neck are bulging. He shakes his head, furious, and moves towards her. Jennie pulls her phone from her pocket, holding it up as if she's going to film him. Martin stops when he sees it, seemingly thinking better of whatever he was about to do. He turns and hurries down the steps, back towards his car.

With shaking hands, Jennie unlocks her front door and pushes it open. She looks over her shoulder before she goes inside, double-checking that Martin really is leaving.

He sneers at her from the front gate, his expression full of hate. 'Fucking frigid bitch.'

Chapter 33

Lottie

With Queen and Adam Lambert's live album playing over the kitchen sound system, Lottie leans on the marble countertop and scrolls through the news on her phone, reading article after article about the murder of Hannah Jennings and the suicide of Rob Marwood. There are so many of them. Some are straight facts, some go for the more human-interest story, talking about Hannah's modelling dreams and showing pictures of her distraught father. Others, particularly the online news outlets, have gone for more investigative pieces, posing questions about whether Rob murdered Hannah and why. Some show graphical timelines of the night Hannah went missing. Others speculate over the guilt or otherwise of her teacher, Duncan Edwards.

Lottie can hardly bear it. It was awful back in 1994 when Hannah disappeared, and now to have it all dragged up again... it's too much. And Jennie still hasn't answered her texts. Lottie's messaged her every day asking if they've made any progress on the case, but she hasn't heard back. It's not right. Friends help friends, right? Surely they must be getting closer to the truth by now?

A burning smell pulls her from her thoughts.

Dammit.

Hurrying to the grill, she pulls out the slightly smoking flatbreads and switches the extractor fan onto maximum speed. Tipping the least charred flatbreads onto a plate, she carries them and a bowl of chopped salad over to the long oak dining table.

'Dinner's ready,' she calls as she passes the doorway.

Back in the kitchen, Lottie opens the oven and removes the

pasta bake. The Le Creuset baking tray is so hot that she can feel it through her White Company oven gloves. Biting her lip, she speeds across to the table and sets the pasta down on the central mat before the heat becomes unbearable.

She hears the thunder of feet on the stairs. Her two blonde-haired, ruddy-cheeked girls appear at speed. Katelyn is already in her favourite Barbie pyjamas. Octavia's still wearing her dirt-stained jodhpurs and polo shirt from her after-school riding lesson. The pair rush to the table like locusts and immediately grab for the flatbread, jostling over which piece is bigger.

'Octavia, darling, at least wash your hands first,' says Lottie as she heads to the doorway again. She raises her voice. 'Anthony, dinner's ready.'

Lottie waits by the door, listening for any sign of movement upstairs. Hears nothing.

Oh for God's sake. It's like this every day.

Hurrying to the stairs she climbs them to the twist and calls again. 'It's dinner, Anthony. Come on, it's getting cold.'

Moments later she hears the click of her son's bedroom door opening, and so heads back down to the kitchen. The girls have helped themselves to pasta and are eating as they gabble away to each other. Lottie tries to listen in to the conversation but she's not exactly sure what they're talking about; something about a demi-pirouette – so dressage or ballet perhaps?

The sound of the back door opening makes Lottie jump.

'Hey, kiddos,' says her husband, Nathan, as he comes in from the integrated garage. He drops his car keys in the walnut bowl on the end of the island and his briefcase on the floor.

Lottie smiles. 'You're just in time for dinner.'

'Great,' says Nathan, although his tone doesn't imply he's pleased about it.

As he walks towards her, Lottie thinks he's going to give her a hug, or maybe a kiss. Her stomach clenches. It's been such a long time since he touched her. But instead, he leans across the counter and presses mute on the iPad music app, cutting off the music in the middle of 'Who Wants To Live Forever'. Nathan sighs. 'You know I can't think with that awful row going on.'

'Dad,' says Anthony joyfully as he comes into the kitchen.

Nathan grins. 'Hello, mate.'

'Can I get a Pepsi MAX?' Anthony asks, hopeful.

'No, darling.' Lottie speaks at the exact moment Nathan agrees. 'Mineral water only with dinner; you know the rule.'

'It's not fair,' says Anthony, glaring at her. He stomps across to the American-style fridge and presses his glass against the ice-maker, then carries it back to the table and sloshes San Pellegrino over the cubes.

As Nathan and the kids settle down to eat, Lottie goes back to the grill pan to see if she can rescue any of the more burnt flatbreads. One is a complete write-off, but the other is only a little singed. As the kids animatedly tell Nathan about their day, Lottie cuts off the worst of the burnt bits and pops the bread onto a side plate.

She sets the plate down next to the empty spot at the table and looks at Nathan. 'Do you fancy some wine?'

'I'm in the middle of a conversation here,' replies Nathan, wearily, but pushes his glass towards her.

Suppressing a sigh, Lottie carries his glass and her own across to the wine fridge and selects her favourite dry white. She pours them both a generous measure, then returns the bottle to the fridge. Nathan detests wine that's anything other than perfectly chilled. As she walks back to the table she tunes into the conversation.

'...And so my trainer says me and Harley can do our first one-day event in the autumn if I keep working hard,' says Octavia, shovelling more pasta into her mouth. 'We concentrated on the dressage today – you know it's my weakest phase – but Piggy said that I'm more of a six now than a five, and Harley's canter is almost a seven.'

'Brilliant,' says Nathan. 'You're really putting the work in. I'm proud of you.'

'Yes, well done, darling. I'm very proud too,' says Lottie as she sits down.

Anthony rolls his eyes as he scrapes his plate clean. He sets down his fork with a clatter. 'Can I be excused?'

'No, it's family time, you need to wait until we're all finished,' says Lottie, helping herself to a small scoop of pasta bake and a larger helping of salad.

'So unfair,' says Anthony, grabbing the last flatbread and chewing it moodily.

Nathan finishes his last mouthful of pasta and stands up. He looks at Anthony. 'You can leave the table now, bud.'

'Thanks, Dad,' says Anthony, leaping up from his seat and rushing back upstairs to his Xbox, half-eaten flatbread in hand.

'But I haven't finished,' says Lottie, hating the whine to her voice.

'I've got a Zoom call.' Nathan barely looks at her as he gets up, leaving his empty plate on the table but taking his wine with him. '*Some* of us have to work.'

As Nathan retreats to his man cave in the converted attic, Lottie knows she's unlikely to see him again tonight. They had been in love once – at least she thinks that they had – but the feeling and the memory are long gone. Now she always feels like the least important person in the room.

'Finished,' chimes Octavia.

'Finished,' parrots Katelyn as she chews her last mouthful.

'Well done, girls,' says Lottie, trying to inject her voice with a brightness that she doesn't feel as the girls run back upstairs to play.

Finishing her wine, Lottie stands up and carries her glass back into the kitchen for a refill. This time she fills it to the brim. Leaning across the counter to the iPad, she unmutes the sound system. Music fills the kitchen as Queen and Adam Lambert sing about how *the show must go on*.

Lottie takes a big gulp of her wine.

Why is life so bloody hard?

And why does she have this anxiety, this growing sense of dread, that things are only going to get much harder?

Chapter 34

It's hopeless.

Jennie lies in bed in the darkness of the guest bedroom, thoughts of Martin kissing her repeating in her mind over and again. The way he pushed her against the door, trapping her. How he gripped the back of her neck, forcing her mouth to his. The feel of his tongue thrusting into her mouth, uninvited.

What the hell was he thinking? Why did he think I wanted that?

He said she'd been giving him the come-on, but she's sure she hadn't given any indication of wanting anything more than a professional relationship. There's never been anything like that between them. Although, thinking back, years ago when he'd first joined the station he had made a joke about asking her on a date. But it was just a joke. They'd all laughed. Him kissing her makes zero sense. He made out he was a devoted family man, always talking about his kids and his wife. Was it all bullshit? It must be.

Even though she knows she didn't lead him on, Jennie feels the doubt starting to crowd her thinking. Had she been too friendly? Too interested in his life, in him? Had she looked at him as if she wanted more?

No.

Bullshit.

She's certain she did nothing wrong. All the same she feels grubby, guilty almost. Complicit in his attempted infidelity. A witness to a predatory side of Martin that she's never before seen or had any inkling of.

Picking up her phone from the bedside table, she checks the time. It's almost midnight, but sleep has eluded her for over an hour and there's no way she's going to get to sleep anytime soon.

Throwing off the duvet, she gets out of bed and pulls on her old jogging bottoms and sweatshirt. If she's awake, then she may as well do something.

Jennie pads along the threadbare orange-and-brown-swirled Seventies carpet of the hallway and into her childhood bedroom. Picking up her old Nikon SLR camera, she carries it down the stairs to the kitchen where the photo developing supplies delivered this morning still sit in their box on the table.

She needs something to take her mind off what happened with Martin. And the ritual of the development process always used to feel like a meditation to her; it never failed to quiet her thoughts, even when her mum was at her worst and the grief for her father threatened to become overwhelming.

Jennie always used to listen to Radiohead when she was working in the darkroom. She finds their album *Pablo Honey* on Spotify and sets it to play on repeat, then opens the window to give some ventilation before unpacking the supplies and laying them out on the kitchen table. The supplies are basic compared to the set-up they'd had in the basement darkroom; there's no red light here. But they should do the job.

Ready.

The film is half-used. She clicks through until the film reaches its end and the Nikon automatically rewinds it, ready for developing. Jennie removes the film and sets the camera to one side. The first step is tricky. Carefully, with Radiohead urging her on, she migrates her film to the changing bag. She grabs the other equipment she needs for this stage and puts it into the bag as well, then zips it up, ensuring the bag is fully light-safe.

Next, she pushes her hands through the armholes in the bag and locates the film canister, using her can opener to prise one end off. It's harder than she remembers, but then she's out of practice and it all has to be done by feel. Removing the film, and taking care only to touch the edges, she cuts off the blank tongue of film at the beginning of the roll, then unwinds the film and cuts it off from the spindle.

Careful not to put fingerprints on the film, Jennie attaches the film onto one of the reels. Holding her breath, she gradually slides the film onto the reel. It's been years since she last did this, and her rustiness makes her hesitant; she doesn't want to make a mistake.

Exhaling as she completes the process, Jennie finds the canister pipe and loads the film, using a spacer reel to ensure the film stays in position. Then she lifts the reels into the canister. Once the canister is light-safe, Jennie sets to work mixing her chemicals, preparing her developer, fixer and stop bath. She makes sure the distilled water is at the right temperature, keen to ensure the negatives don't have mineral spots.

Jennie works through the steps to the rhythm of the music, as if in a trance: developer, stop bath, fixer. When the steps are complete, she carefully removes the film from the developing canister and pulls the film off the reel, carefully using a sponge to absorb some excess water. Using film clips, she pins the negatives to the string she's rigged up, then sets about tidying the equipment.

She realises quickly that there's something wrong. The negatives are too washed out and over-exposed to be able to make out what the pictures are supposed to be.

Jennie swears under her breath. It could be the age of the film, or that it's been sitting in the camera all these years; or it could be that she's messed up the process. She needs an intensifier to try to bring out more detail. Searching through the rest of the supplies box, she finds a small bottle of hydrochloric acid. She remembers using it a few times in the darkroom at White Cross Academy – it was Elliott's intensifier of choice.

Carefully, Jennie runs through the process with the acid, hoping as she works that it will rescue her pictures. She's relieved when the negatives turn out better once she's finished, the clarity and grain of the images much improved. She can see the pictures are of people, but the negatives are too small to see enough detail and make out who they are.

Jennie should let the negatives air for a few more hours until they're completely dry, she knows that, but she doesn't want to wait. Cutting the negatives into strips, she slides them into negative sleeves. She could continue the analogue process and print her own photographs – she's got the kit to do it. But the manual process will take a while and she's impatient to see the pictures, so she decides to try a digital shortcut.

Picking up the negative sleeves, she walks out of the kitchen to the cluttered front room. Her laptop is on the sofa and her printer is set up on the console table at the side of the room. She's pretty sure it has a scanner function, although she's never used it before.

Switching on the printer, she flicks through the menus until she finds what she's looking for. There is a scanning function. It's only black and white, and will be far lower quality than a proper film scanner, but for now it will do to satisfy her curiosity.

Pressing first one and then the other sleeve of negatives onto the glass, Jennie scans them in turn and sends the results to her laptop. Carefully, she removes the negative sleeves from the printer, then walks around to the sofa to collect her laptop and goes back to the kitchen.

She yawns as she walks, tiredness starting to catch up with her. Then puts the laptop on the kitchen table before rehanging the negatives to let them dry more. Yawning again, she makes a coffee to try to perk herself up. She's determined to go through the pictures before she lets sleep take her.

Opening the laptop, she finds the files and opens the photographs one by one. There are seven images. The first four she recognises as pictures she took on the same day that she'd taken the group photo of the darkroom crew on the sofa; it's the image used by Lottie on the Facebook group that had caused Jennie all the angst with her DCI. She must have changed the roll of film just after taking the picture, although she doesn't remember.

The images are unposed, reportage style. There's Elliott hanging up photos on the washing line in the darkroom, still diligently wearing his safety glasses and gloves; there's Lottie applying her lipstick, Coral Delight, in a handheld mirror; there's Simon, the basement key on a leather string around his neck, looking like he's in the middle of a heated debate with Rob; and finally, there's Hannah, watching the two boys with wry amusement.

Jennie smiles. It had been the last day they'd all been together in the darkroom together. These were the last pictures she took of her friends. Excited to see the rest of the photos, she clicks on the thumbnail images of the remaining three pictures she scanned and waits for them to appear on the screen.

Jesus.

Jennie watches as the picture files open on her laptop. One, two, three.

What the hell?

No way did she take these shots.

As adrenaline chases her tiredness away, she stares at the image now on the screen. It shows Hannah, wearing a black vest top, denim hotpants and her favourite Celtic knot belt buckle, in the darkroom. She's preening for the camera, but her smile seems different, distorted somehow, and the look in her eyes as she peers over the top of her mirrored shades is almost manic. Jennie has never seen her friend look like this.

There's a person reflected in the mirrored shades. Zooming in, Jennie's breath catches in her throat as she realises who it is. It's Rob, bare-chested and barefooted. He has the same wild look on his face and Jennie's camera in his hand.

Jennie knows she wasn't there when this was taken. For one thing, she'd *never* have allowed Rob to use her camera. And for another, she never saw him without a shirt on. Was this one of the times Hannah and Rob had met up to get high? From their expressions it certainly looks like it could be.

She clicks onto the next picture. It's blurred and taken at an angle, as if the person holding the camera hadn't meant to take it, but on the table beside the burgundy sofa she can make out bottles of alcohol – Thunderbird and vodka – and what looks like some smaller objects that Jennie can't help but presume are drugs.

Jennie feels her heart rate accelerate.

When was this picture taken? Could this have been the night Hannah disappeared? Did Hannah and Rob get high, and something go wrong again, but this time Hannah died? Is Zuri's theory that Rob is the killer, even if accidentally, correct? Is that why Rob lied about his alibi?

Is that why Hannah never arrived at the bus stop?

As Radiohead's 'Creep' plays on her phone, Jennie clicks onto the final picture.

What the . . . ?

Although not perfect, the focus is better in this one and she easily identifies the people in the shot. Simon, wearing only his boxer shorts and a headband that makes his blond hair stick up at weird angles, is leaning over Lottie, who's lying on the sofa, and he's trying to pour vodka from the bottle into her mouth. Elliott is developing negatives in the darkroom behind them, while Hannah looks as if she's dancing in the space between the sofa and Elliott. Jennie guesses Rob was taking the photo.

The five of them were having a party without her.

Standing up, Jennie moves across to where the negatives are drying and unclips them from the string line. She checks the time stamp on them. Feels the hairs on the back of her neck stand on end.

The last three photographs are date-stamped 06-06-94 and the time taken ranges from 21:49 to 21:57. Hannah disappeared on Thursday 9 June, 1994. All these photos were taken earlier in the week Hannah disappeared.

Jennie feels a stab of jealousy. They were partying without her. Hadn't she been part of the crew? Why had they excluded her?

As she turns back towards the laptop, preoccupied, Jennie

knocks the open bottle of hydrochloric acid with her arm. It tips and she has to move fast to stop it from emptying onto the floor. As she grabs the tipping bottle, some acid splashes onto her hand.

Shit.

Rushing to the sink, Jennie runs the cold water and holds her hand under it, watching as an angry red burn appears on her skin.

Fighting back tears, she wonders if she really knew her so-called friends at all. The more she has discovered through the investigation, the more it's seemed the answer to the question is no, especially now. The final, soul-crushing lyrics of 'Creep' have never felt truer. She didn't belong there.

Turning off the tap, Jennie looks at the burn on her hand. It hurts, but it's not so bad that she needs medical attention. Instead, she gets a tube of aloe vera from the cupboard and covers the blistered patch of skin.

Trying to push away the feelings of rejection and exclusion, Jennie switches off the music app. She needs to think about what she's discovered and how it might relate to Hannah's disappearance. The house is dead-of-night quiet now, eerily so, but she welcomes the silence. Thoughts about each of her old school friends are ricocheting through her mind. She needs to order them, to try to take her emotions out of it and be objective, logical.

Rob was with Hannah in the photos. He admitted the pair of them were the wildest of the group, far wilder than Jennie ever realised at the time. He was obsessed with *Flatliners*, which she'd already known, and Simon had told them Rob was always experimenting to try to achieve the next level of consciousness. They had the medical records to prove that Hannah had an accidental overdose while taking drugs with Rob, and Rob had admitted it. He'd said it was a one-off, but the photos Jennie has just found prove that was a lie.

Simon had said Rob and Hannah experimented using neck ligatures to further heighten their drug-induced highs. Given the marks on Hannah's neck documented in her medical records during the visit with Rob four weeks before her death, Jennie's inclined to believe him. Rob told them he was at the cinema when Hannah went missing, but they now know that must have been a lie. Was he in the basement, hiding her body instead? Jennie shakes her head. She has so many questions for Rob, but she can't ask him now he's dead.

As she thinks, Jennie begins to tidy up the developing kit. She screws the bottle cap back onto the hydrochloric acid, and places it into the kit box, then starts to dismantle and wash the canister, taking care not to splash water on her burn.

Simon had the basement key. He seemed to be lying in the interview and trying to push Duncan Edwards into the spotlight. Perhaps to hide his own guilt? If any of the group were in the darkroom after hours, he'd have to have known – he would've had to let them in or lend them the key. Or had he arranged to meet Hannah the night she went missing? Was he angry and jealous that she still wouldn't have sex with him but was rumoured to be in an inappropriate relationship with Edwards? Was it a crime of passion? Did he kill her in a murderous, jealous rage?

One by one, Jennie dries each part of the canister and puts them into the kit box. She thinks about Elliott, once her best friend after Hannah, and how Simon told them the monthly payments from Elliott are because he feels beholden to Simon for saving his life. Would he be that loyal even if Simon had done something awful like commit murder? Elliott certainly seemed to have been holding back in the interview, and she now knows he is perfectly capable of keeping secrets: he never told her about the trauma he'd been through during the early part of 1994. Was saying Paul Jennings was at the school that night a tactic to divert police attention elsewhere?

As she puts the rest of the chemical bottles back into the kit box, Jennie's thoughts move to Lottie. They were never the best of friends, but Lottie seemed over-friendly towards her when they met at the reunion on White Cross Hill. Since Hannah's body was discovered, Lottie has contacted her multiple times. She seems desperate, always wanting to know what's happening with the investigation. Is it because she's anxious for Hannah to get justice, or is something more sinister going on? Could it be that Lottie knows what really happened to Hannah and is trying to find out if the police are close to discovering the truth? Was she there when Hannah died; is that why her alibi for the night she disappeared is fake? Could that have been Lottie's motivation for dropping Jennie in it with the photo revelation?

Jennie rubs her forehead. She's exhausted now. Folding up the light-safe bag, Jennie places it on top of the kit box and closes the lid. She glances at the cuckoo clock on the wall: it's almost three-thirty in the morning. She has to get some sleep, or she'll be useless tomorrow.

Switching off the lights, Jennie climbs the stairs. She's starting to believe at least one of her friends could have been responsible for Hannah's death, and it's messing with her head. But she's close to the truth now, she can feel it.

She can't screw this up.

She just can't.

Day Six

Chapter 35

'This is very uncomfortable for me.'

Jennie is sitting opposite DCI Campbell in his office. She feels groggy and sleep-deprived. Furious, too, but she knows she has to stay calm if she's to get through telling her boss. It's early, and Martin hasn't arrived yet, which she's thankful for. The last thing she needs is him watching through the glass wall as she tells the DCI what happened last night. It's bad enough having to come to Campbell with this anyway, especially since the last time they spoke properly she'd virtually blackmailed him to keep her on the case.

'Take your time, I'm listening,' says Campbell, putting his pen down on the desk and taking a quick sip of coffee. There's an edge to his tone that didn't used to be there in their interactions. 'But I've only got ten minutes max before the weekly stats meeting.'

Jennie knows how much he hates the crime statistics meetings. She takes a breath. 'Last night DS Wright and myself interviewed one of the suspects, Simon Ackhurst, at his narrowboat home on the canal.'

'Did he give you some kind of trouble?' asks the DCI.

'Not Ackhurst, no.' Jennie clears her throat. Feels the nerves fluttering in her stomach. 'After the interview it was getting late, and DS Wright offered to give me and my bike a lift home. I was tired and so I accepted.'

Campbell nods. 'Okay.'

'After helping me get my bike out of the car, DS Wright escorted me to my front door. I thought it a little strange, but we were discussing the case and debriefing on the interview so it kind of made sense. What happened next didn't. DS Wright grabbed me around the back of my neck and kissed me. When I asked him what he was doing and told him no, he lunged for me again. I had to physically push him away, twice, and he wasn't pleased.' Jennie pauses as her voice starts getting higher pitched.

The DCI is shaking his head, his lips pursed into a thin line as he makes some notes on the Moleskine notepad beside his computer.

Jennie can't tell what he's thinking or how he's going to react. She's never had to report anything like this to him before, and that it's a member of her own team who sexually harassed her seems to make it all the more awkward. She keeps her tone professional. Keeps to the facts. 'DS Wright told me I had been leading him on, which I assure you I had not. He also said I was a frigid bitch.'

The DCI waits a moment before he speaks.

Jennie's aware of movement through the glass in the open-plan office space. She shudders, but doesn't turn to see who it is. It feels as if they're watching her.

'I'm sorry that happened to you, but I want to commend you for coming and telling me. Obviously, I take any allegation of inappropriate conduct very seriously, so I'm going to look into this.'

Jennie bristles at his use of the word 'allegation'. It happened. Martin needs to be dealt with. But rather than express this as strongly as she feels it, she bites her tongue, fearing that if she makes too much fuss, the DCI might feel the case could be compromised and pull her and the team off it. So, instead, she asks, 'So you'll be speaking to DS Wright?'

'I will,' says the DCI as he starts typing a two-fingered email. 'Just as soon as I've spoken to HR for their view.'

Jennie sits for a moment, watching as he types. She thinks he's taking it seriously, but he hasn't asked her how she is, or how she feels about working with DS Wright. 'Do I need to write a formal statement?'

He looks up at her, frowning. 'Yes, probably. I'll come back to you after I've talked to HR.'

'Okay.' Jennie gets up to leave. She feels weird, wrong-footed. The nagging fear returns: that she did lead Martin on, that she is somehow to blame for what happened last night. The guilt is like a heavy weight on her chest. But she doesn't say anything. Doesn't want to cause a fuss. So she leaves the DCI to his email and walks out of his office.

The open-plan area is busier now. Jennie sees Martin is at his desk, talking to someone on the phone. He turns away from her as she walks between the desks to her own, an action that both irritates her and makes her feel relieved. She isn't up for another confrontation right now.

'Elliott Naylor's arrived,' says Zuri as Jennie sits down at her desk opposite.

'Great,' says Jennie, smiling gratefully at her DS. 'Thanks.'

As she reaches for the file in front of her, Jennie has the feeling she's being watched again. Looking up, she sees Martin is glaring at her. The hatred in his eyes is unmissable.

Shivering, Jennie feels suddenly cold.

I need to get out of here.

Jennie looks at Zuri over the desk divider. 'Shall we go and get started with Naylor then?'

Not waiting for her to reply, Jennie stands and grabs a file from her desk. Turning, she strides towards the stairs, desperate to be out of the open-plan and the close proximity to Martin.

At least in the interview suite, she'll be safe.

Chapter 36

Elliott Naylor looks awful. There are dark circles beneath his bloodshot eyes and dandruff flaking along his hairline. His solicitor, Geraldine Metcalf, a sophisticated thirtysomething woman in a smart black suit and cream blouse, sits beside him. Her poise and good posture are in stark contrast to the way Elliott is hunched over the Formica table.

Zuri completes the pre-interview formalities, then hands over to Jennie once the tape is running. The set-up is more formal than for the previous conversations they've had with Elliott, and intentionally so. They have to get the truth this time.

Jennie looks at Elliott. She tries not to think about how he and the others were meeting up without her, excluding her and using her beloved Nikon SLR camera without her knowledge. She squashes down the emotion that's threatening to bubble to the surface. Stays calm, professional. 'Thanks for coming in again to talk to us.'

Elliott frowns. 'Look, I know what this is about, Jennie. You're fixated on the money I give to Simon each month, right? You seem to think there's something sinister about it, but there really isn't. It is just a mate helping out another mate.'

It's interesting that he's raised the money. She hasn't mentioned it to him other than during their last interview, and that hardly qualifies as fixated. 'We've only asked you on one occasion about the money you give to Mr Ackhurst each month, as far as I understand.'

'But you asked Simon about it too, didn't you? He told me last night when we got together with Lottie to raise a glass in memory of Hannah and Rob.' Elliott's eyes become watery. He clasps his hands together on the table. 'I can't believe they're both gone, can you?'

Jennie wants to remind him that she's the one asking the questions here, not him, but he looks so upset that she doesn't have the heart. She can't believe they're gone either, but they are, and she needs to find out why. 'So, you discussed it with Simon?'

Zuri glances at her. Jennie knows she's deviating from the plan they'd agreed, but she's following Elliott's lead. They need to know more about the dynamic between the two men and the payments.

'Yeah,' says Elliott, nodding. 'Like I said, the three of us met up last night. Simon said you'd been over to the boat asking him questions about Hannah and about the money. I just want to clear up any confusion.'

'Well, good,' says Jennie. She tries to stay focused on the interview, but the fact that the three of them met up without her is galling. She couldn't have met them anyway: they're suspects and she's leading the investigation. But it still hurts. 'Last time we met, you told us that the reason you make the payments to Simon Ackhurst is because you're a generous guy and you're helping out an old friend; do you stand by that statement?'

'I do,' says Elliott, glancing at his solicitor. He waits for her to give him a small nod before continuing. 'There is more to it, though. When we last spoke, I told you that I'd attempted to take my own life.' He pauses, looking at Jennie for confirmation.

'You did,' says Jennie.

'Well, the reason my attempt failed is that Simon found me. He alerted my parents and the emergency services. If he hadn't got me help, I'd have died. I owe him my life.' Elliott's voice cracks with emotion. 'That's why, once I was earning proper money after university, and when Simon came out of jail, I started giving him some money each month. His life hadn't gone the way he'd wanted, but he'd faced his demons and was trying to make a real go of things. I wanted to help him, and I've carried on helping him ever since.'

His story tallies with what Simon had said. More facts that she never knew about her friends. More reasons to make her feel as if she was never really a proper member of the darkroom crew. It seems she was always an outsider, even though she never realised at the time.

'Why continue the payments?' asks Zuri.

'Why not?' Elliott asks, an air of exasperation in his voice. 'I was grateful at the time, and I'm grateful now.'

Jennie's not used to seeing Elliott getting riled up, but he's not as calm as he's been before. When she knew him back in school, he was always the steady one of the group, logical and considerate. She understands why he started making the payments to Simon; she just isn't convinced he's been honest about why he's continued them for so long.

'By our calculations, you've given Simon Ackhurst just over three hundred and twenty thousand pounds,' says Zuri, undeterred. 'That's a lot of money.'

Elliott shrugs. 'I'd say my life is worth it.'

Realising they're not getting any further forward on the payments, Jennie decides to change tack. 'Paul Jennings denies being at the school at any time of the day or night on the date Hannah disappeared.'

'Well, he would, wouldn't he?' says Elliott. His tone is light, but there's no mistaking the tension in his jaw.

'Are you certain that you saw him on the day she went missing?' asks Jennie.

'Absolutely,' says Elliott.

Zuri glances at Jennie, frowning.

Jennie knows why; she sees it too. There's doubt in Elliott's eyes, and fear. He's lying. Her stomach lurches. She has to push him, she knows that, but if she does it'll kill whatever is left of their childhood friendship.

Zuri's gaze intensifies. The pause is becoming prolonged, awkward.

Jennie tries to harden her heart and use the hurt she's feeling about him excluding her to fuel her courage. She feels sick, really sick, but she pushes it down. She has to. 'Are you sure? Perhaps instead it was Simon who turned up at the basement that evening? We know he was angry about the rumours that Hannah was sleeping with Mr Edwards. Did he confront her? Did his jealousy get the better of him? Did he attack Hannah and kill her, then bury her body?'

'No,' says Elliott, loudly. 'Simon would never—'

'Did you help him cover up what he did?' says Jennie.

Elliott shakes his head. 'I wouldn't—'

'Or did all the resentment you'd been harbouring about her exposing you bubble to the surface?' says Jennie, challenging him further. 'Did *you* kill Hannah?'

'No, I'd—'

'Did Simon help you cover up what *you'd* done?' continues Jennie, pointing at Elliott. 'Is that why you've been paying him all these years?'

'No. That's not true. It's not true.' Tears stream down Elliott's face. He looks at her, horrified. 'Why would you say that, Jen? Why?'

Elliott's raw emotion, and the anguish on his face, makes it feel as if her heart is about to shatter, but she can't stop pushing. She *has* to know the truth.

'You're harassing my client,' says the solicitor. 'Any more of this and we'll leave the interview.'

'The interview's finished when I say so,' snaps Jennie. She narrows her gaze at Elliott. 'You're a killer, aren't you? A liar and a manipulator. You're lying to us, to me.'

'Jennie, please,' whimpers Elliott. 'Stop—'

'You make people think you're their friend and then you use them and discard them.' Jennie's heart is pounding. Her voice is getting louder. She slams her hands down on the table, making Elliott flinch. 'Did you discard Hannah? Did you kill her? Admit it, Elliott. Tell me what you did. Tell me that you killed her and that you pay Simon to keep quiet. Tell me the—'

'Enough!' bellows Elliott's solicitor, angry and red-faced as she begins to stand. 'We're going.'

Jennie holds up her hands. She nods at Zuri, indicating for her to continue the interview. The expression on her DS's face tells her she went too far, but that's bullshit.

I didn't go far enough.

As Zuri persuades Elliott's solicitor to stay, and continues the questioning in a less confrontational manner, Jennie watches Elliott. There's a haunted look on his face, but that's not what has caught her attention.

Clearly unsettled, he's clasping and unclasping his hands together on the desk as he talks, and as he does so Jennie looks at the marks on his hands that she'd assumed were eczema. She glances at her own hand; at the red, blistered acid burn. The mark, although fresher, is not dissimilar to Elliott's. She looks up, and their eyes meet. Next moment, Elliott swiftly removes his hands from the table and puts them in his pockets out of sight.

They don't get anything else of use from the interview. Elliott's solicitor is on them like a hawk for any questions that could be perceived as out of line, and Elliott himself becomes increasingly withdrawn, sitting back in his seat with his head bowed, avoiding eye contact. They call it a day after another half an hour and watch as Elliott and his brief walk away towards the exit, the solicitor speaking to him in urgent, hushed tones.

When the pair leave through the double doors at the end of the corridor, Jennie turns and heads towards the stairs, still thinking about the acid and the marks on Elliott's hands. Zuri goes with her.

'What happened in there?' asks Zuri. 'You totally blindsided me.'

'Sorry, I felt he was holding out on us and I wanted to push him more,' says Jennie.

'You certainly did that.' Zuri frowns. 'Did you know him well at school?'

Jennie tenses, but tries not to show her discomfort at the question. She turns into the stairwell, stepping slightly ahead of her DS so she doesn't have to make eye contact as she replies, 'As well as anyone.'

'Please don't fob me off,' says Zuri. 'Just how many of our suspects were you close with?'

Shit.

'Look I knew him, okay? We were friends almost thirty years ago, but I haven't seen him since school,' replies Jennie, trying to keep her tone light. 'I guess he was trying to appeal to my sense of nostalgia to get me to back off but, the thing is, I don't remember my time at White Cross Academy especially fondly, so it was never going to work.'

As they reach the top of the stairs Zuri turns and holds Jennie's gaze for a long moment, then shakes her head. 'For the record, I think you're right that he's holding something back. Any hypothesis on what?'

'Nothing concrete,' says Jennie, trying not to think about the anguish on Elliott's face as she accused him of murder. 'But something isn't adding up. I've got a hunch, but nothing behind it. I want to check a couple of things, then let's debrief properly.'

'All right.' Zuri pauses, her hand on the door into the open-plan team office. 'Are you okay, Jennie? I don't mean to pry, and I'm not judging you, really, but you seem kind of detached. We usually share theories *before* we check them. Are you freezing me out?'

'I'm fine, just a bit tired,' says Jennie, annoyed that Zuri is back to this again. 'You don't need to worry about me or the investigation. Like I told you when you asked before, I'm fully committed to it.'

Zuri does look worried though. Maybe her explanation of why she went so far berating Elliott didn't reassure her DS as much as she hoped.

Jennie exhales hard. She can't bloody win – people either think she doesn't care enough about the case or that she's overdoing it. She knows her emotions are all over the place and, as much as she wants to believe Zuri is wrong, she also realises she's probably acting differently from usual. But she's trying, she really is.

Knowing she needs to keep Zuri onside and can't afford to get defensive, Jennie softens her voice and forces a smile. 'I'm fine, really, but thanks for asking; I appreciate it. When this case is over, let's go to that nice Italian and eat pasta and drink all the wine.'

Zuri smiles, but there's still concern behind her eyes. 'Sounds good.'

They enter the open-plan area. As they walk towards the desks, Jennie sees through the glass wall that sitting in the DCI's office are Martin and a stern-faced woman she recognises as being from HR. The DCI looks like he's in full flow. Not wanting to get too close, she diverts across to where Naomi is sitting.

Naomi and Steve have desks opposite each other and you couldn't get two more different spaces. Steve's is all old takeaway coffee cups, chocolate wrappers and piles of paperwork, whereas Naomi's is spotless and paperless aside from the file she's currently working with.

Naomi looks up as Jennie approaches. 'How was the interview with Naylor?'

'Not hugely illuminating,' says Jennie, stopping beside Naomi. 'But there are a few things I'd like you to check on.'

'Sure,' says Naomi, reaching for her notebook and pen.

'Can you double-check Simon Ackhurst's alibi, and then go through the photography club inventory for the month Hannah went missing and look for any orders of chemicals, specifically hydrochloric acid?'

Naomi jots down the actions onto her pad. 'No problem.'

'Thanks,' says Jennie. She glances towards the DCI's office and her stomach flips. Inside, Martin is jumping to his feet. From his aggressive pointing, and the way he's leaning over the desk towards Campbell and the HR woman, Jennie can see Martin's furious. She can guess why.

As he turns towards the door Jennie stiffens. After going through what happened with the DCI earlier, and the difficult interview with Elliott, she can't face having to deal with Martin right now.

I need to get out of here.

Chapter 37

Jennie takes the back road out of White Cross town and powers up the long, steep drag of Monument Hill. There's no one around: it's just her, the bike and the tarmac. Every pedal stroke, each pound of her racing heart, makes her feel calmer. More grounded. Focused.

The corn crops in the fields on either side of the road have been baked gold by the sun; they sway in the light breeze as if dancing to a song only they can hear. In the distance, she hears a combine working in one of the fields. It sounds as if the harvest has begun.

Her thoughts go back to the interview with Elliott. Perhaps Zuri is right: maybe she did push it a little too far. All the pent-up emotions she's trying to hold in overspilled, and her anger got directed at him. It's just that there's been so much to process. The shock of Hannah's murder. The gut-wrenching realisation that she might not have abandoned their joint plan to leave town, but had been killed before they could meet. The hurt of discovering Hannah hadn't shared everything with her as she'd thought. The pain of learning she'd been excluded from the darkroom crew's parties. The weird encounter with the car following her a few days ago, and then seeing someone lurking in her front garden watching the house. It's been a lot.

Jennie pedals on. Her breathing becomes heavier. Sweat forms on her forehead and her upper lip. She's relieved when the top of the hill comes into sight.

She feels bad about pushing Elliott, but that's the residual affection from their childhood friendship colouring her judgement. He *was* being evasive, and the more she thinks about the marks on his palms and fingers, the more she believes that they're not due to eczema but something more like her acid burn. She doubts he'd tell her the truth about them though, even if she asked. She's alienated him now, that's for sure.

She reaches the crest of the hill and loops through the woodland past the Glade pub, looking as charmingly characterful as ever with its Tudor exterior of white plaster and black beams, the frontage bedecked with brightly coloured flowers in hanging baskets and tubs. A few groups of walkers sit at the picnic benches outside enjoying lunch in the sun. On another day Jennie would feel tempted to join them. But not today.

At the crossroads, she takes a left onto White Cross Lane. It's a narrow, single-track road with high banks flanked by the forest on either side. The grass on the banks stands lofty and seeding. Cow parsley and hemlock have woven themselves between the grasses, standing even taller.

This route down is the steepest in the Chilterns. As Jennie starts her descent, the wind whistling past and the brief sense of freedom lift her spirits. She won't let this case, and the bastard who killed Hannah, beat her. She won't let Martin's behaviour drive her away from *her* team. She's going to find the truth and bring the murderer to justice.

Jennie's halfway down the hill when she hears the growl of an engine behind her. She glances over her shoulder but there's nothing. The noise is getting louder, though. The car can't be far away. She keeps tight against the verge as she steers the bike through the zig-zagging bends. The lane is at its narrowest here, barely room for a car and no space for easy overtaking.

As she rounds the final bend and the lane starts to straighten up, Jennie exhales. An engine roars behind her and she glances over her shoulder again. She sees a blue car speeding around the corner towards her.

The road is still narrow. The car needs to slow down.

It keeps coming, accelerating.

Jennie's heart starts to race. She can see the spot up ahead where the lane gets wider. Crouching over the handlebars she pedals faster, trying to reach it.

There's not enough time. The car's on her. There's nowhere for her to go.

She feels a hard jolt as the car rams the back wheel of her bike, then she's falling, tumbling in a mess of flesh and metal, smacking down onto the tarmac.

The breath is knocked out of her. She tastes blood in her mouth.

She can't open her eyes. Can't move her legs.

Her body feels as if it's on fire.

Jennie hears the squeal of brakes, then the sound of a car door slamming shut.

Then there's only darkness.

Chapter 38

Beeping.

That's the first thing she hears when she wakes. Then she feels the pain.

Slowly, Jennie opens her eyes. They feel sore, gritty. The right side of her face throbs and the rest of her body feels worse. With every inhale it's as if something sharp is being jabbed between her ribs.

She lies still, keeping her breathing as shallow as she can. The hospital room is bright white – too bright. The beeping comes from a machine on her left connected to her by the heart monitor clipped to her index finger. She seems to be wearing a hospital gown.

Raising her head for a better look, Jennie is immediately assaulted by a strong bout of nausea. On the chair beside the trolley bed, she catches a brief glimpse of her clothes, phone, and cycle helmet. The helmet's bashed in along one side and the helmet cam looks completely mangled. She tries to raise her head higher to get a better look, but the movement makes the hospital room start to spin around her. Black spots dance across her vision.

Jesus.

Resting her head back on the pillow, she waits for the urge to vomit to pass.

There's a burst of noise as the door opens and a busy-looking nurse hurries in wearing blue scrubs, her black hair in a long plait. 'You'll want to lie still for a while. You took quite a whack to the head. There's no skull fracture but you've got a bad concussion.'

'What happened?' says Jennie. Her throat feels scratchy. Her voice sounds weaker than usual. 'Where am I?'

'You're in Moreton Hospital A&E. You fell off your bike,' says the nurse as she checks the heart rate monitor, then indicates for Jennie to raise her arm so she can put on a blood-pressure cuff.

As Jennie raises her arm, pain shoots from her elbow to her shoulder. She winces.

I didn't fall.

'A car hit me,' says Jennie.

The nurse frowns. 'You should tell the police then. The paramedics said a couple of lycra-clad road warriors found you and called it in.'

I am the police.

The nurse finishes the blood-pressure check and makes a couple of notes on the chart. 'I'll be back in half an hour for your next set of obs.'

'When can I go?' asks Jennie.

'Not for a while. We need to do half-hourly checks for the next few hours. Then you'll get discharged if everything's okay.'

Jennie frowns.

The nurse's expression is grave. 'Look, you're lucky to be alive. That helmet saved you from the blow you took to the head, but your brain has still had a major shake-up. On top of that, a couple of your ribs are cracked and you've got some nasty road rash on your face and arm. You need to rest.'

Jennie waits for the nurse to leave the room before she tries to sit up again. Her memory of what happened is hazy, but she knows it wasn't an accident. The car hit her on purpose – she's sure of it.

She manages to sit upright without vomiting. Waiting until the room has stopped spinning, Jennie leans over to the chair and grabs her phone. The movement causes the nausea to rise again, but she pushes through it. She has to know exactly what happened.

The screen is cracked but the phone is still working. Jennie navigates to the helmet camera app and taps on the footage of her most recent ride. She fast-forwards through the footage, letting it play from the moment she turns onto White Cross Lane.

The footage shows her whizzing down the hill. The audio sounds blustery with the occasional burst of birdsong. A few minutes later, she hears the sound of an engine and the view switches quickly as she looks over her shoulder, but there's nothing behind her. Twenty seconds later, the engine noise is louder. The view swivels again, and this time there's a blue car approaching at speed. Jennie hears her breathing get louder as she pedals. Next moment the view blurs as the camera rotates, catching unfocused glimpses of the car, her bike, the grass bank and the trees, before slamming down against the road.

The camera lens fractures. Jennie hears herself groan.

From the view, the camera seems to be lying sideways on the tarmac. The cracked lens makes it harder to see, but Jennie can just make out the tyres of a car a few metres away. The engine is still running.

Moments later, she hears a car door slam and footsteps approaching. The person's feet come into view and halt in front of the camera. They're wearing black Doc Martens with blue and claret laces. Jennie gasps.

What the . . . ?

I know those shoes.

She watches the last few moments of footage, reliving the pain at what he did to her as she sees it play out on the screen. The rage builds inside her.

Bastard.

You won't get away with this.

Pushing herself up to standing, Jennie dresses as fast as she can. She blinks hard to stop the room from spinning. She's still shaky, her stomach lurching at every movement, but she fights the nausea and keeps going.

How hadn't she known he'd be capable of this?

Bugger the doctor wanting her to have half-hourly observations.

She can't wait around here another minute. Not when *he's* out there. Not when he's done *this*.

He could've killed her.

Maybe he thought he had.

Grabbing her bashed-up helmet from the chair, Jennie walks on shaky legs to the door and peers out. The place is heaving, patients in every bay, nurses and doctors hurrying between them. If she can make it out of A&E unseen, she should be able to grab a taxi from the rank outside.

Jennie takes a deep breath. Forces down the ever-present nausea. And opens the door.

There's no time to waste.

Chapter 39

Twenty minutes later, Jennie hurries through the open-plan space towards DCI Campbell's office. She keeps her gaze fixed straight ahead – she feels less sick that way – and ignores the shocked and concerned expressions on Zuri's, Naomi's and Steve's faces.

Zuri calls after her, but Jennie keeps walking. She *has* to tell her boss what's happened. She raises her good arm in a rather pathetic attempt at a wave. 'I'm okay.'

She walks into Campbell's office without knocking and collapses into the visitor's chair opposite him.

The DCI looks up, initially surprised to see her, then hostile. Then his expression becomes increasingly horrified as he takes in the damage to her face and body. 'Jennie, bloody hell. Shouldn't you be at the hospital?'

For a moment she can't speak as she swallows down another wave of nausea. Instead, she takes her phone from her pocket and opens the helmet camera app. Setting the phone down in front of the DCI she taps play on the footage. 'You need to see this.'

As Campbell watches the video he becomes increasingly grim-faced. The action plays out. DS Martin Wright's car hitting her bike. Jennie smacking down onto the tarmac. Martin's distinctive Doc Marten shoes with the claret and blue laces approaching her as she lies prone on the road. His voice is clearly audible as he spits the word 'bitch' before kicking her twice in the stomach and ribs.

'Bloody hell.' The DCI grimaces as he watches the footage. 'That sick bastard.'

Jennie's gaze flits back to the open plan, checking to see if Martin has appeared, but there's no sign of him. The more she's here, the more on edge she's feeling. Emotions ricochet inside her, anger and fear in equal measure, but she doesn't let that deter her. 'He tried to kill me, and it wasn't the first time. There was an incident a few days ago when I was riding home when I realised a car was kerb-crawling behind me, and then a couple of days ago I saw someone in the shadows in my front garden, watching the house. I think both times were Martin too.'

Campbell looks appalled. 'Can you forward this video to me? I'm going to put a call into Professional Standards and instigate criminal proceedings right away. I'll see to it that Martin Wright never works another day in law enforcement.'

'Thank you, sir,' says Jennie, relief flooding through her. She glances towards the open-plan again. 'Is he here?'

'No, not now. After you briefed me on his conduct this morning, I pulled him in and suspended him pending a disciplinary investigation. Let's just say it didn't go well. He was ranting and raving about injustice, and I had to get him escorted out. He hasn't been seen since.' The DCI shakes his head. 'I'm sorry I didn't see how infatuated he was with you. We only searched his desk after he'd left. If I'd done it while he was still here, I'd like to think we could have averted this.' His gestures towards the helmet cam footage freeze-framed on Jennie's phone.

Jennie frowns. 'I don't understand?'

'We think DS Wright had been fixated on you for some time. When we searched his desk, we found stuff belonging to you.' Campbell reaches down and picks up a cardboard archive box from the floor. Putting it on the desk, he slides it across to Jennie.

Lifting the lid, Jennie sees her silver pen, the oversized *Friends* coffee mug, a green scarf that went missing a couple of months ago, her pink stapler and her spare pair of cycling sunglasses. She stares at her lost belongings. Feels suddenly cold.

What the hell?

'I never realised *he'd* taken my stuff,' says Jennie, her voice shaky.

'I thought with the stress of mum dying and trying to clear the house, I'd got more forgetful or something. But it was him?'

'None of us realised,' says the DCI, the regret clear in his tone. 'DS Wright managed to keep his obsession under the radar for months.'

Jennie nods, trying to hold back the emotion threatening to burst out. She's trying to stay professional, appear fit to work the case, but it's a struggle. Her own DS, a man she's worked with day in, day out for months, is her stalker. He tried to kill her.

'I know we haven't always seen eye-to-eye,' says the DCI, solemnly. 'But if I'd realised what Martin was doing, what he was thinking, I would've taken immediate action. We can't have someone like that here. We can't have people doing what he did. You're a valued member of my team and I'm sorry this happened, I really am.'

Jennie meets his gaze. Given the fights they've had over Hannah's case, she's still wary. But he looks genuine, the concern and empathy clear in his expression. 'Thanks, sir.'

He frowns as if sensing her reticence. 'You're a good detective, Jennie, and your instincts are spot on.'

Jennie exhales, suddenly exhausted. She thinks of Zuri. 'I wish all the team agreed.'

'Well, you certainly have the respect of DS Otueome,' says the DCI. 'She overheard DS Wright ranting about the injustice of his suspension as he was being escorted from the office and came to speak with me. It appears not only had Wright sexually harassed several female colleagues, including her, he was also the instigator of a WhatsApp group in which several male officers share compromising images and disgusting views on women. It appears DC Williams had been added to the group without his permission, but had left it immediately. He told DS Otueome he'd been disturbed by what he'd seen.'

Why didn't Zuri and Steve tell me?

'Why didn't they report it at the time?' asks Jennie.

'It seems they felt they'd become targets if they did. I believe several of the men in the WhatsApp group are higher-ranking officers. It's all in the hands of HR now though. There's no place for people, and views, like that here.'

'I'm so sorry they had to go through that,' Jennie says, sadly. She feels battle-weary and as if she's let her team down. 'I wish I could have done something to help them.'

'DS Otueome spoke very highly of you,' says the DCI.

Zuri had my back. A good colleague. A proper friend.

As the realisation hits home, Jennie fights the urge to cry. 'She's an impressive detective. She'll have your job one day.'

The DCI smiles. 'I don't doubt that, but not just yet.'

Chapter 40

Once he's off the phone with Professional Standards, the DCI calls Jennie and Zuri into the incident room. As they follow him inside, Jennie senses that something important is afoot. She's relieved she was able to persuade him to let her stay at work rather than go off on sick leave, even if it's not good HR procedure. A few painkillers have sorted her headache, and the nausea seems to have abated. It's the road-rash on her face and lacerations to her arm that are the most distracting.

They gather around the whiteboard. Jennie stares at the pictures of Hannah, Paul Jennings, Duncan Edwards, and the rest of the darkroom crew staring down at them.

'I'm not going to sugar coat this,' says the DCI. 'I'm being put under a hell of a lot of pressure to get this case closed. The media frenzy shows no signs of stopping, I'm being bombarded with endless press questions and the community is becoming more angry every day that goes by without an arrest.'

'But it's only been five days,' says Zuri. 'Surely the brass can give us longer?'

Campbell blows out hard. 'They can, but they'd prefer not to. We already had accusations of institutional misogyny being bandied about after the mishandled abduction case, but with what's come to light today – the attack on Jennie, the suspension of DS Wright and the prolonged campaign of misogyny and deeply disturbing misconduct by him and several others within our ranks – we're going to see some really ugly press headlines once the media catch wind of it. I know you all want to do right by the victim and so do I. And we sure as hell need a win for the community and a good news story for us. So, what do you think, do we have our killer?'

Jennie grimaces. Hannah deserves better than a bodged job of a misper investigation and a murder case cut short. 'We have several possible suspects, but we're not done yet.'

'Several? Who's top of your list?' asks the DCI.

Jennie looks at Zuri. The frustrated expression on her DS's face mirrors how Jennie feels. Still, she nods. 'Okay. We narrowed our suspects down to Hannah's father, the teacher Duncan Edwards, and Hannah's four childhood friends, including the boyfriend.' Moving closer to the board, Jennie taps her finger on Edwards' picture. 'The teacher was our top suspect, but we've been unable to break his alibi. Edwards and his ex-fiancée alibied each other. Naomi and Steven have spoken to a few of their ex-colleagues and neighbours, but so far their story holds up. The ex-fiancée had motive too; I think they could have colluded to murder Hannah together, but we're still looking for evidence to prove it. We had a good look at Hannah's father, but although he was violent towards her and was a shitty dad, we don't think he's in the frame for her death.'

'So Rob Marwood is our prime suspect,' says Zuri, gesturing to Rob's image on the board. 'He and Hannah had a history of doing drugs together and experimentation in oxygen deprivation, and we know he lied about his alibi – he wasn't watching the film he claimed at the cinema the night Hannah died, because the projector was broken and the cinema couldn't open. We can't ask him why he lied, but it's a reasonable supposition that Hannah's body being found and years of crippling guilt about her death, combined with the stress of the medical malpractice case against him, is what pushed him to take his own life. As I've said before, I believe the note he wrote was his confession to killing his friend.'

The DCI nods thoughtfully.

'Rob supplied Hannah with drugs regularly,' says Jennie, continuing from where Zuri left off. 'And he'd taken her to A&E a month before her death when she accidentally overdosed. They found marks on her neck which we've determined were consistent with erotic asphyxiation. One hypothesis is that Hannah's death was an experiment into "higher consciousness" that went wrong.'

'The tox report on Robert Marwood shows he had high levels of fentanyl and alcohol in his system at the time he died,' says Zuri. 'Further digging into his financials has turned up payments to two exclusive and highly confidential rehab clinics in the past year and a number of other occasions dating back twenty years, but it seems the rehab never stuck. He was clearly deeply troubled by something that happened in his past.'

'I'm inclined to agree,' says Campbell. He gestures to the remaining three members of the darkroom crew. 'What about the other friends and the boyfriend?'

'Nothing concrete,' says Zuri.

'But we do have some suspicions,' Jennie adds. 'If we can have a few more days to—'

'I'm sorry,' says the DCI. 'But given what you've told me I think we've got our killer. Robert Marwood basically confessed to the murder of Hannah Jennings in his suicide note. We might not know exactly what happened, or whether it was intentional, but as he lied about his alibi, the drug-taking and the erotic asphyxiation, I think we have enough to conclude he *was* responsible for Hannah's death.'

'I agree,' says Zuri. She looks at Jennie apologetically. 'I also agree that in an ideal world we'd have been able to put the charge to Robert Marwood, and dig deeper into his faked alibi and what happened that night. But we can't.'

Jennie lets out a heavy breath. She's knows even if she fights this she won't win, but she's far from convinced they're making the right call. And so, although she nods along as the DCI tells them to officially close the case and prepare a press statement, she's already planning her next move.

*

Back at her desk, Jennie finds a Post-it note from Naomi stuck on her keyboard. As she reads the two updates on the note, adrenaline floods her body. Whatever the DCI thinks, now Jennie knows she's right. There *is* more to uncover. The case *isn't* over.

Suddenly she feels exhilarated, vindicated, the exhaustion of a few moments ago forgotten.

Simon Ackhurst's alibi was fake, just as she'd suspected. He didn't show up for work on the night Hannah disappeared and had been docked wages for his absence.

Why did he lie?

According to the school's historical records, Elliott, on behalf of the photography club, had signed for a delivery of supplies, which included a bottle of hydrochloric acid, on the day Hannah disappeared. The next order for a bottle of hydrochloric acid was made two days later.

As everything starts to slot together in her mind, Jennie pulls out her battered phone and sends three texts. Grabbing her coat, she takes the developed photographs from last night out of the buff folder on her desk and leaves the office. The case might be closed, but it isn't over for her. Not yet. Not until she knows the whole truth and is sure she's got justice for Hannah.

There's no time to lose.

Chapter 41

As the cab pulls away Jennie stands on the pavement, peering through the rusted iron gateposts at the old White Cross Academy building. The site seems deserted; there are no builders or rubbernecks today. Only birdsong and occasional road noise disturb the silence. Behind the school, the Chiltern Forest stretches up the hillside, its green foliage framing the whiteness of the 85-foot-high chalk cross. Two of her friends died here, leaving so many unanswered questions. Now it's time to get answers.

She walks onto the site, along the weed-lined pathway to the tall wooden fence that shields the main site from view, and heads through the gate. Staring up at the once grand stately home with its boarded windows, collapsing gutters and crumbling stonework, she feels a strange affinity with the place: in the wake of the bike crash, her own facade is as crumbling and badly damaged now.

The police tape that formed the outer cordon is still up, and Jennie sends a quick text before ducking under it and striding across the yellowing lawn towards the ivy-covered portico. Her legs feel heavy as she climbs the cracked stone steps; she hopes she has the strength to do what needs to be done. She takes a breath, then opens the rotting door with a firm shove and steps inside.

The echo of her footsteps on the stone floor unnerves her. The hallway is pitch black, the boarded-up windows blocking out any light. Last time Jennie was here, the lights had already been switched on. She gropes around on the wall for where she vaguely remembers the switches are. It takes a while before she finds them and flips them on.

Nothing happens at first. Then she hears a faint humming sound overhead before the fluorescent strip lights flicker into life.

She exhales. It's a relief the electricity is still on. She wouldn't fancy doing what needs to be done in pitch darkness. What she has planned is already risky enough.

Hurrying down the corridor, Jennie steps over a pile of mouldy debris where the ceiling has caved in, and strides through the double fire doors hanging crooked on rusty hinges. She doesn't stop by her old locker this time, instead rushing the rest of the way to the top of the stairs.

She slows her pace and avoids touching the rotten banister as she descends to the basement. The temperature drops as she goes down; the stench of damp gets stronger. Stepping off the bottom stair Jennie coughs, the dust-ridden chewiness of the air creeping into her lungs. A sense of dread is building inside her, just as it did when she came down here the day Hannah's remains were found. This time the dread is for a different reason.

Jennie coughs again, her eyes watering. She clutches her ribs, biting back the pain as the movement aggravates her injuries. She doesn't have time for that right now. This is all about justice for Hannah.

As her heartbeat accelerates, she goes through the open doorway and into the passage beyond. The first door on her left is the room she's looking for.

Jennie pauses. Heart thumping. Then opens the door.

She flicks on the lights and watches the dust motes swirl. The darkroom looks different and familiar all at once. There's no soft red light, and the smell of chemicals is long gone. But the rickety old external door is still there, now reinforced by planks of wood nailed across it. The dark wood-panelled walls have mould growing along them and the old burgundy sofa is years past its best. The long, thin table up against the far wall is empty now: gone is the stack of shallow trays and chemical bottles. The washing line, where they used to peg photographs to dry, hangs flaccid from a hook in the wall, its end spooling on the dusty floor. The damp smells worse in here and the air is even thicker.

As the minutes tick by, Jennie begins to feel increasingly nervous. So much so, that when she hears the voice, she almost jumps out of her skin.

'Jennie? Oh thank God. This place is disgusting.'

She turns to see Lottie. She's impeccably dressed as always – white blouse, camel trousers, nude sandals – with a white Prada handbag slung over her shoulder. Jennie forces a smile. 'Thanks for coming at such short notice.'

'Well, your text intrigued me if I'm honest,' says Lottie, walking across to the mildewed sofa as if to sit down, but then changing her mind when she sees the state of it.

'It's damp in here,' says Jennie. 'I don't remember it being like this when we were at school.'

'Me neither,' says Lottie, frowning as much as her botox will allow. 'Mind you, the chemicals and the weed would've masked it.'

'True.' Jennie arranges her expression into what she hopes looks sympathetic. 'You were pretty upset when I last saw you. How are you doing?'

'I'm holding up, but it's hard, you know?' Lottie's voice cracks a little. She walks closer to Jennie. 'It's been the worst week ever. First Hannah, then dear Rob. I'd only been talking to him an hour or so earlier. He came here especially from London to support my vigil for Hannah and then … that happened, it's just too awful. I can't help but feel responsible.'

Typical Lottie. Making it about her.

'It was a shock,' says Jennie, nodding.

'And you found him. That must have been horrific.' Lottie looks as if she might cry. 'I don't understand why he didn't reach out to one of *us*. Elliott, Simon and I were all there at the vigil, we would have supported him if he'd just told us he was struggling …'

Jennie hardens her heart to the barbed dig. She's learnt from what she's uncovered during the investigation that she was never really a full member of their group. Lottie rubbing it in now isn't going to divert her from the real purpose of this meeting.

'I know Rob had been having a few troubles in his work but surely it would all have been sorted out soon enough,' continues Lottie, gabbling on. 'But I suppose a job like his was very high-pressure and not everyone is equipped to handle the stresses of something like that, are they? I just hate to think of him alone in those final moments, so lost. It's just tragic. And to think he'd been holding onto all that guilt about Hannah for so many years. It must have just eaten away at him. It's just so … I guess you can never *really* know a person, can you?'

Jennie can see how Lottie is trying to frame this, but she doesn't want to go there just yet. Not until it's time. So she nods. Keeps her expression and tone sympathetic. 'It's tragic. Like I said in my message, I do need to clarify some points of evidence with you, if that's okay?'

Lottie nods vigorously. 'Of course, Jennie. As I said before, anything I can do to help dear Hannah.'

There's a noise from the hallway and Lottie jumps. The door creaks open.

'Oh my God, what's that … ?' Wide-eyed and fearful, Lottie moves behind Jennie.

'Hello?' says Elliott, poking his head around the door before pulling it wider to reveal himself and Simon standing in the corridor.

'What the hell are they doing here?' says Lottie, her fear turning to irritation. She looks at Jennie accusingly. 'You didn't say we'd have company.'

'I thought a reunion might be helpful,' says Jennie, giving a small shrug. Forcing a smile, she gestures for Elliott and Simon to come in. 'It's good to see you both again.'

Unlike Lottie, Jennie *is* glad they've arrived promptly. She needs to get this done. In an hour or so, the DCI will release the statement to the press that they've closed the case, naming

Robert Marwood as the killer. If she's going to get to the truth, it has to be now.

'What is this? Why are we all here?' says Simon, suspicious.

'I thought we needed a private conversation so we could speak freely,' says Jennie, injecting as much warmth into her voice as she can muster. 'Just us, here in the darkroom. Like old times.'

Simon, still wary, looks from her to Elliott and Lottie. None of them speak. Lottie bites her lower lip.

Elliott clasps his hands together. In a friendly tone at odds with his rigid posture, he says, 'Sounds good. How can we help?'

This is the moment. Jennie inhales. She makes eye contact with each of her old schoolfriends in turn. 'I have proof you were all here with Hannah on the night she died.'

Lottie's mouth opens in surprise, the rest of her body stays immobile.

'What are you talking about?' says Elliott, wringing his hands together awkwardly.

'This is ridiculous.' Simon flushes red. 'I'm not staying here to be accused of this—'

'If we were here, don't you think you'd have been with us?' says Elliott, with a rueful look. 'Rob and Hannah might have met up here together to do drugs, but the rest of us only ever hung out together, you know that.' Stepping closer to Jennie, he looks at her with those kind blue eyes that had always made her melt, and puts his hand on her arm. 'You were one of us.'

No, I wasn't.

It kills her that Elliott can look so sincere as he lies to her face.

'I have proof.' Removing the photos from her pocket she unfolds them and lays them out one by one on the table where they used to process negatives. Hannah preening for the camera, Rob's shirtless image reflected in her mirrored shades; Thunderbird, vodka, pills and foil packets littered across a small table; Simon in a headband leaning over Lottie pouring vodka into her mouth as she lies on the sofa, while Elliott develops pictures and Hannah dances with a manic look on her face. 'I know now that you all used to party without me.'

'It doesn't mean we had anything to do with Hannah's death,' says Elliott, squeezing her arm.

Simon shrugs. 'That party was a one-off. You were busy or whatever.'

'Rob organised it,' says Lottie, her voice whining, nervous now. 'We honestly didn't realise he hadn't told you.'

Jennie shakes her head. 'You're lying. Just like you lied in your police statements about what *really* happened to Hannah.'

There's a brief silence. Lottie shoots a glance at Elliott.

'This is bullshit,' rants Simon, his cheeks turning puce. 'Those photos were taken before Hannah disappeared. They prove nothing. This is a waste of time...'

'You're right,' says Jennie, resisting the urge to yell back at Simon. 'Those pictures were taken earlier in the week that Hannah went missing.'

'So you don't have proof?' says Elliott, cautiously. Seemingly unaware of the implication of his words.

I do now.

'It must have been a good party, because you did it again three days later. And you were *all* here.'

Lottie's shaking her head.

Simon swears loudly.

'What do you mean?' asks Elliott. 'We weren't—'

Jennie keeps talking, ignoring their protests. 'In his statement, Rob told us he had been watching *Four Weddings and a Funeral* that evening, but there was no sign of the ticket stub he said he'd given to the original misper investigation as proof,' says Jennie, assertively. 'I doubted he'd have seen that film again, because he didn't think much of it when we watched it as a group the week before. So we dug a bit deeper. Turns out the cinema had projector issues that day and was forced to close. So Rob's alibi was fake.'

Lottie nods. 'Well, yes, that's—'

'Simon told us he was at work,' says Jennie, interrupting Lottie. 'But EDT Logistics confirmed he didn't show up that night and had his wages docked. Elliott said he was here in the basement darkroom, but although he claimed to have seen Paul Jennings and that he left him here with Hannah, I don't believe that's true. And you, Lottie, were allegedly at the youth club disco in Farnby Square, but I know you weren't because I *was* there. Like me, none of the people I've spoken to who were there that night saw you.'

'It's true,' says Lottie, her voice smaller, shakier now. 'We did meet up a few times without you.'

Elliott shoots Lottie a warning look.

Simon grimaces. 'So bloody what? It's a free country.'

'We need to tell her the truth,' says Lottie. She meets Jennie's gaze. 'You're right, we were there on the night Hannah died.'

Simon shakes his head. Swears under his breath.

Emotion builds in Jennie's chest. She blinks rapidly. Needs to stay focused. Fighting to contain her fury as she asks, 'What happened?'

'It was just a party, a few drinks and a bit of weed. At first, anyway,' says Lottie, hesitantly. Her eyes start to tear up. 'But Hannah was so *wild*. And Rob always did encourage her, always wanting to push the boundaries. That night they were out of control. Rob kept on saying it was our "big bang" before the exams started. He said it was going to be the best night of our lives.'

Lottie pauses. Elliott is shifting his weight from foot to foot. Simon looks ready to punch someone.

Her voice gentle, Jennie asks, 'Was it?'

Lottie looks away. Her eyes fill with tears and she shakes her head, sadly. She puts her hand against her chest and takes a couple of breaths. Then she looks back at Jennie. 'Hannah had taken a load of stuff – pills, weed – then her and Rob chased the dragon. Hannah had this scarf tight around her neck. Rob was banging on about how you could reach a better high if you limited your oxygen. The rest of us were drunk and high, not really paying attention to what they were doing. But whatever did happen, their game went horribly wrong. One minute they were dancing around like wild things, the next Hannah fell and the scarf got caught... Her neck was snapped instantly.'

Jennie's heart races as she pictures the scene. Her best friend, so vital and alive, having the life snuffed out from her so suddenly.

Elliott looks ashen. 'It was horrific.'

'I *told* her not to be so reckless,' says Simon, his rage barely contained. 'But Rob always encouraged her to be a daredevil. She didn't bloody listen to me and it killed her.'

There's a clanging noise overhead. The four of them flinch, and look up.

'It must be the old pipes,' says Jennie. It has to be that; there's no one else around. Down here in this dank and derelict basement, they are completely isolated. The thought makes her feel suddenly vulnerable. If things turn bad, it's three against one; those aren't good odds. Careful to keep her tone sympathetic, she asks, 'What did you do next?'

'Rob was crying, howling, he couldn't believe what had happened and he felt responsible,' says Elliott, his tone solemn. 'Hannah was dead, there was no bringing her back.'

'We helped Rob bury her,' says Lottie. She shudders. 'It was awful, putting her into that muddy trench...'

'That bastard pretty much forced us to help him,' says Simon, the fury clear in his voice. 'I told him we should call the police, tell them it was an accident, but no, he wouldn't have it.'

Elliott looks upset. He puts his hand on Jennie's. 'Yes we were there, and yes we're guilty of helping cover up what happened. But you have to believe us,' he says, his voice becoming more insistent, 'we only did it to protect Rob. You'd have done the same if you were there, Jen. You'd have wanted to protect him. It was an awful accident but it's what Hannah would have wanted.'

Jennie stares into Elliott's eyes. She thinks of all the good times they shared in that year of upper sixth: how he'd taught her to develop her own photos, how he listened to her talking tearfully about her dad and how much she missed him, how he never judged her or mocked her but always treated her with kindness.

She yearns for that time again. That feeling of friendship and belonging and hope.

Then she thinks of Hannah, her heart sister, her best friend, reduced to the bones dug up from the muddy trench she'd been dumped in all those years before. Her resolve hardens.

Jennie narrows her gaze. Lets go of Elliott's hand. 'What about the acid?'

Chapter 42

Elliott stares at her, frowning. 'What do you mean?'

'The forensic report on Hannah's shirt showed a high saturation of hydrochloric acid,' replies Jennie. 'We used that in the darkroom; it was your favourite intensifier. So I had the delivery logs checked. They showed a bottle of hydrochloric acid was part of the supplies you took delivery of on the day Hannah went missing, but also that you ordered *another bottle* just two days later. Why would you need to replace the bottle so quickly?'

Elliott takes a couple of steps back from her. His pupils dart from side to side. His hands are clasped together. Simon is looking at him, furious. Lottie, wide-eyed and still tearful, seems to be in a state of shock.

'It took months for us to use a bottle of hydrochloric acid,' Jennie insists. She looks pointedly at Elliott's hands. 'Why do you have acid burns on your palms?'

'It happened the day after Hannah went missing. I was distracted, clumsy,' says Elliott, falteringly. 'The new bottle had a faulty seal. I didn't check it and paid the price; it spilt over the floor and as I tried to prevent more damage, it splashed over my hands.'

'Bullshit.' Jennie stares at Elliott. His anguished expression makes her want to stop this, but she can't. She's onto the truth. She knows it. 'You were always so careful. I remember how insistent you were about correct procedure and safety protocols. You *never* handled the darkroom equipment without protective gloves.'

Elliott looks away. Lottie avoids eye contact with him, as if distancing herself. Simon gives a small shake of his head.

Jennie looks from one old schoolfriend to another. Her voice is firm. 'Tell me the truth about what happened that night.'

They all stay silent.

'Did you argue about Hannah spreading rumours about you?' says Jennie, stepping closer to Elliott. A muscle pulses in his jaw. She needs to push him harder. 'Did you throw acid at her in revenge?'

'I didn't do anything,' blurts out Elliott, his expression horrified. 'I'd never have hurt Hannah. It was Lottie.'

Jennie looks at Lottie. 'What did you do?'

'You can't say that, Elliott,' protests Lottie. 'I didn't *do* anything. I loved Hannah.'

Jennie turns to Simon, who's seething with ill-concealed rage. 'If it wasn't Elliott and it wasn't Lottie, was it you, Simon? Did Hannah's affair with Duncan Edwards make you lose it? Or did she finally dump you like she'd been threatening for months? Did you kill her in a jealous rage? Or—'

'I never bloody touched her,' shouts Simon, his face turning a darker shade of puce. 'Don't look at me, Elliott's right, it was all Lottie's fault.'

Lottie gasps. 'No, you promised...' Her voice breaks. Tears stream down her face.

'Tell me the truth. Please,' says Jennie, her voice soft and encouraging.

Lottie shakes her head. 'Simon's lying. It's like we said before, it was a tragic accident.'

'I loved Hannah too,' says Jennie. 'I just need to know.'

'We told you already.' Lottie's gaze flicks to Elliott and Simon as if looking for confirmation. 'If anyone's responsible, it was Rob.'

Jennie keeps her eyes on Lottie. 'I don't believe you.'

Lottie's eyes widen. 'But you have to believe me. We're friends, Jennie. Haven't we always been friends? I'd never lie to you.'

'But you've already lied,' says Jennie, calmly. 'Your alibi was a lie and saying the darkroom crew didn't meet without me was a lie. It's obvious your story about Hannah, the drugs and the scarf is a lie. You need to tell me the truth. After all these years don't you *want* to tell the truth? Keeping it a secret didn't do Rob any good, did it?'

Lottie shakes her head. 'No, no, you're wrong. It's not—'

'For God's sake, Lottie, just admit what you did,' screams Simon, his voice raw with emotion. 'Hasn't this gone on long enough?'

'It *wasn't* my fault,' Lottie yells at Simon, the tears starting to fall again. She turns, pointing at Jennie. 'It was yours.'

What the hell . . . ?

'I didn't kill Hannah,' says Jennie, feeling as if a knife is twisting in her heart. 'That's ridiculous.'

'You might not have done it, but you caused it,' Lottie says between sobs. Her mascara-smudged eyes are teary and bloodshot. 'We'd planned to have a party, but when Hannah arrived, she was carrying a rucksack. She said she wasn't staying and was only there to say goodbye.' Lottie glares at Jennie, her hatred clear in her eyes. 'She said she was leaving White Cross and starting a new life in London with you.'

She was coming. She didn't abandon me.

Tears prick Jennie's eyes but she blinks them away. She has to get the truth. 'Why didn't you let her go?'

Lottie sighs. 'I was afraid. I begged her not to go. Honestly, I literally got on my knees and begged. But she didn't care. She said she was sick of me clinging to her and she wasn't going to let me hold her back – she was going to be a supermodel.' Lottie's voice breaks into a sob. 'She told me to buy some other friends because paying someone was the only way I'd get them to hang out with me.'

'What happened next?' asks Jennie, fighting the urge to shake

Lottie or worse. The woman has lied for thirty years about Hannah's death. They all have.

'It was my worst nightmare,' says Lottie, her voice getting louder and higher-pitched. 'I was already drunk, and her words tipped me over the edge. I said maybe I could be a model too and we could go on jobs together, but she told me I wasn't model material. I felt utterly crushed. I mean, how could she say something so cruel? She only seemed to care about modelling and *you*.' Lottie takes a breath. 'She wouldn't shut up about how her face was her ticket out of White Cross and I ... I just couldn't take it any more. I was desperate for her to stay. I wasn't thinking straight. I just grabbed the nearest thing to me and I threw it right in her face.'

'The hydrochloric acid?' says Jennie, her voice a whisper.

Lottie nods. The tears cascade down her face. 'I was so angry at her. I thought maybe if her face was messed up then it'd ruin her chances of being a model. Then she'd have to stay here, with me. I never meant for it to do *that* to her.'

Horrified, Jennie reluctantly imagines the scene. Hannah screaming blue murder from the agonising burns, the others in shock at what Lottie had just done. Then all of them panicking that someone would hear – afraid to be exposed for their drug-taking, their drinking and now this horrific violence.

That wouldn't have killed her, though, and the acid certainly couldn't have broken her hyoid bone. As she looks from Lottie to Simon and then Elliott, she realises what happened next.

Elliott must have stepped in and strangled Hannah – that's why only he has acid burns on his palms. But Jennie doesn't believe it was an altruistic act. She holds his gaze. 'It was you?'

Elliott doesn't deny it. He stays silent as he wrestles with his conscience, with the knowledge that his life is about to implode.

Then the tension goes out of his shoulders, as if he's finally freed from carrying the burden of what he did thirty years ago. His expression is earnest. His tone sincere. 'She was screeching in pain; I've never heard anyone scream like that before. It was awful; I can still hear it in my nightmares. The logical, most humane thing to do was to stop her pain. No one should ever have to endure that.'

Devastated, Jennie fights to keep her emotions in check. Elliott – her friend, a man she'd always thought of as kind and honest, someone she felt love for – had calmly snapped Hannah's neck because it was the 'logical' thing to do. 'Why didn't you call an ambulance? Why didn't you get her help?'

Elliott closes his eyes a moment as if reliving the horror of the past. 'Hannah wouldn't, couldn't, stop screaming. Her face was a mess, she didn't look like herself any more. She was in agony, and it was sickening to watch. We were all afraid the janitor would hear and come to investigate.' His tone hardens. 'I did what had to be done.'

What had to be done?

Jennie swallows down her rising nausea. Murder is never an act of kindness. Elliott was meant to be Hannah's friend. He should have called an ambulance, they all should. But instead they only thought of themselves, fearing the repercussions of their lawbreaking just as they were about to take flight as young adults. Awfully, selfishly, they snuffed out Hannah's life and buried her. It wasn't 'what had to be done'. It was a heartless, grim act of betrayal.

She bites her tongue, too afraid her anger would be obvious in her voice, in her words, and would stop his confession. Nodding, Jennie waits for Elliott to continue.

'It was Simon who buried her.' Elliott looks over at Simon. 'He got down into the trench the construction workers had laid the pipes in and dug a section of it deeper. He put Hannah's body in the hole he'd made, then covered her up. With the pipe on top, no one was any the wiser.'

'If Rob hadn't insisted we have another big-bang party that

night, things wouldn't have kicked off,' says Simon, bitterly. '*He* was to blame. Rob caused Hannah's death.'

'No,' says Lottie, shaking her head. She glares at Jennie again. 'It was *your* fault. If you hadn't filled Hannah's head with dreams of running off to London, none of it would've happened. We wouldn't have argued, and Hannah would still be alive.'

Jennie stares at her, unable to comprehend how Lottie can be so utterly delusional as to blame her for Hannah's death. She loved Hannah like a sister. They had a future all planned out: how they'd escape White Cross and their shitty family lives. But Lottie's actions destroyed that. Elliott killed that life dead the moment he choked the breath from Hannah.

'Like hell it is.' Fighting back emotion, Jennie tries to keep her voice calm. 'You're all responsible for what happened. You have to take responsibility.'

'But it was an accident,' says Lottie, tearfully. 'I never meant to hurt her. You have to believe me.'

'I had no choice,' says Elliott, wringing his hands. 'She was in agony. I had to act.'

'We were just kids, and we panicked,' says Simon. 'We were high and drunk. Everyone does stupid shit when they're young.'

'Most kids don't commit murder,' says Jennie, disgusted that the last remaining members of the darkroom crew won't own what they did, even now.

'You're right,' says Elliott, raising his hands. 'What we did was wicked, unforgivable. There's not a day that's gone by when I haven't thought about it.' He looks at Lottie and Simon. '…When *we* haven't thought about it. We've kept the awful secret all these years and it's destroyed us all, one way or another. Rob took his own life because the guilt slowly ate him up. Simon turned to drugs and crime to try and escape. It took me years to commit to a relationship, and I've never been able to be honest with my husband about my past. And Lottie's been in therapy and on medication for her nerves since university. Surely we've paid enough of a price?'

'I've got three kids who depend on me,' says Lottie, her tone pleading. 'Elliott's about to have his first. If you take us in, they'll be robbed of a parent.'

'I've finally got my shit together,' says Simon. 'My charity does great things for people who need help to turn their lives around. If I go back to prison, it'll all be screwed and far more lives will be ruined.'

Elliott moves towards her. He looks so sincere. 'You're one of us, Jennie. You *know* us. Our friendship binds us together and we've always had each other's backs. What good will it serve to put us in prison? We're not murderers. I know you know that. Rob left a note, didn't he? He was willing to make that sacrifice.'

Jennie says nothing. She's waited thirty years to learn the truth about what happened to Hannah, yet her so-called friends knew all along. They only told her when they had to, happy to keep her in the dark for all these years.

What do I do?

The blow that they are responsible feels like a roundhouse kick to the heart, and the fact Lottie blames *her* for causing the rift that led to Hannah's death makes her feel physically sick. She used to care for each of them, especially Elliott. But how can Rob taking all the blame ever be *justice*?

She looks from Lottie to Simon and finally at Elliott. They killed Hannah and they left her rotting in a shallow grave. There's nothing that can justify that.

'Charlotte Varney, Simon Ackhurst and Elliott Naylor, I'm arresting you on suspicion of the murder of Hannah Jennings.' Jennie's voice is firm, and her words clear. 'You do not have to say anything. But it may harm your defence if you do not mention when questioned something which you later rely on in court. Anything you do say may be given in evidence.'

There's a creak as the basement door opens and Zuri, Naomi

and Steve enter the darkroom. Elliott, Simon and Lottie don't resist arrest. They look shell-shocked as the team cuff their hands behind their backs.

Jennie watches as it's done and then, when she's certain they're secured, she turns away. She can't let her colleagues see her cry.

Day Seven

43

Jennie stands at the graveside.

She's glad Paul Jennings chose to bury Hannah in the cemetery at Little Cross, a small village a quarter of a mile outside the main town. White Cross is tainted with the violence that ended Hannah's life and the friends who betrayed her. This place has none of that gruesome history.

The stone and flint church sits nestled between the canal on one side and an organic farm on the other. It's silent here now aside from the clucking of the chickens whose paddock borders the graveyard. The service is finished and the other mourners are long gone. Jennie stands alone, watching as the sun sinks slowly in the sky and finally lets herself grieve.

She remembers Hannah free and happy, twirling in the woodland; taking charge as her personal stylist when they went shopping for a new dress; rescuing her from the bullies when she first joined White Cross Academy. Hannah had really made her feel like she belonged. It was Hannah who encouraged her to follow her dream to be a photographer when no one else cared. She was the one who told Jennie that she'd got bags of talent and that it was her wonderful photos that got her the modelling gig in London. She'd always had faith in her.

Jennie knows now there were things about Hannah's life that her friend had kept secret from her: the drug use, the secret parties, her affair with Duncan Edwards, and the physical violence her dad had inflicted. Teenage Jennie might not have forgiven her friend for keeping her in the dark on some elements of her life, but adult Jennie does. Relationships are complex. Secrets are often held.

Reaching out, Jennie puts her hand on the top of the simple wooden cross at the head of the grave, a placeholder until the earth has settled and the headstone can be laid. The wood is rough against her fingers. Her voice cracks as she tells Hannah, 'I miss you.'

Lottie's accusation that Jennie caused the rift that led to the fatal argument between her and Hannah has weighed heavily on her mind. Rationally, she knows she isn't to blame for Hannah's death, but there is a small kernel of truth in what Lottie said. Unwittingly, the plan they'd hatched to run away together *had* set in motion the events that led to Hannah's murder. When Hannah had disappeared, Jennie felt as though part of her had died – the creative part – as well as the confidence to follow her dream. Jennie had got through those dark days, but she never left White Cross and never allowed herself to be the person she might have been. Stuck in limbo. In arrested development for thirty years. She's never let her guard down. Never fully given herself to anyone or trusted a person with her heart for fear that they'll suddenly disappear on her. She's never allowed herself to be happy in case it jinxed things and she lost that happiness.

Now she knows Hannah really *had* been coming to the bus stop that night; she didn't abandon her on purpose. She didn't betray her. Hannah was stolen away by their so-called friends in heinous actions fuelled by jealousy and resentment.

Kneeling down, Jennie places the bouquet of white roses on the heaped dirt alongside the other floral tributes. She smiles as she thinks that Hannah probably would have preferred a new lipstick over all the flowers, but Jennie wants to give her something beautiful to mark her final resting place. She deserves that.

Jennie presses her hands against the earth, her tears flowing freely now, and whispers, 'I'm sorry I doubted you.'

Chapter 44

At White Cross Police Station after hours, Jennie walks through the now empty office to the incident room. It's weird being the only one here. The space, usually a hive of activity, is still and silent, eerie almost. But she knows the calm won't last for long. This is just a momentary pause in the action. Soon another case will land and the hustle will begin again.

But first, there are things she needs to do.

One at a time, she removes the photos taped to the top of the whiteboard. First, the individual pictures of Rob, Simon, Lottie and Elliott, then the one she took of the darkroom crew sitting on the burgundy sofa. She pauses, looking at her old schoolfriends: Simon with his arm around Hannah; Lottie with her head resting on Hannah's shoulder; Rob sitting on the arm of the sofa beside Lottie, his long, grey coat hanging over the side; Elliott, with his safety glasses still on, beside Simon. Each of them grinning. Who would have guessed from this picture that they'd have turned on each other, and killed Hannah, less than two weeks later?

Not me.

Jennie puts the pictures into the cardboard evidence box. Rob's funeral is due to take place tomorrow, but Simon, Lottie and Elliott won't be attending. The voice recorder on her phone had secretly recorded their confession. Zuri and the team had come straight to the school after receiving Jennie's text; they'd heard the most incriminating part of the conversation too.

A confession is never a hundred per cent guarantee of a conviction, but then there's the supporting evidence: the photos of drug use after hours in the darkroom earlier that week, the extra order of hydrochloric acid, the broken alibis and Rob's suicide note. All of them together make a strong case and the CPS are confident they'll secure convictions that mean Elliott, Simon and Lottie will be going to prison for a very long time.

Jennie takes down the last photo, the picture of Hannah, and holds it in her hands. Hannah's image stares back at her; piercing blue eyes, sun-kissed make-up free skin, tousled strawberry-blonde hair. Even in the still photo she seems so effervescent, so utterly alive, but it's just an illusion. Hannah is gone. Jennie's waited thirty years to find out what happened to her friend, and she's finally done it. She's found the truth, and she's made sure Hannah will get justice.

She bites her lip. Her grief still feels raw and deep. It comes in waves, and there's no predicting when it will crash over her: in the supermarket, cycling to work, or when she's watching some reality programme on the telly. It'll take a long time to fully heal, but something has changed within her. She feels lighter somehow, more loved. The knowledge that the friendship she shared with Hannah was real, and that her friend *didn't* betray her as she'd believed all these years, has finally given her closure.

Putting Hannah's photo into the box, Jennie takes down the rest of the artefacts taped to the top of the whiteboard and then wipes it clean. She carries the archive box across to Zuri's desk and labels it with the case number, adds the original misper file and all her notes and information on the case she led, and then closes the lid.

There's nothing more to do. The case is closed.

Walking across to the DCI's office, Jennie steps inside. She removes from her pocket the folded envelope containing her resignation with immediate effect and places it on his keyboard, so he'll see it first thing tomorrow. Beside it, she puts her office keys and her police ID.

No second thoughts.

Turning, Jennie collects her jacket and new cycle helmet from her desk and heads towards the door for the last time with a bounce in her step.

It's time for a change.

Day Eight

Chapter 45

It's early, not yet seven o'clock, but the morning is already un-seasonably warm. Jennie stands at the safety barrier, a couple of hundred metres back from the crumbling, derelict facade of the original White Cross Academy building. Waiting.

She's not alone. Gradually over the past half an hour, a small crowd has gathered along the barrier. She recognises quite a few of the faces: Carl and Daisy Winkleman, both wearing black; a group of women whose names she doesn't know but she remem-bers as being in the fifth year when she was upper sixth; Dr Fetz from White Cross Surgery; and Belinda, a career school dinner-lady who ruled the canteen back in Jennie's day and, from what she's heard, still does.

An older man and woman stand slightly away from the rest of the group; Paul and Shelly Jennings. Their focus is unwaveringly on the school building. Jennie can see the tension in the rigidity of their stance. She can imagine the conflicting emotions they must be feeling right now.

Outside the aged school building, three construction workers in orange high-vis overalls stand conferring over a clipboard. A pair of red kites wheel in the cloudless blue sky overhead. The trees of the Chiltern Forest stand sentry on the hillside stretching up from the old school site. Sunlight reflects off the chalk cross, as if drawing attention to something important that's about to happen: X marks the spot.

In the distance, the clock in the town square strikes seven. Jennie's stomach flips.

It's time.

A hush falls over the crowd. The high-vis construction workers stride quickly towards a Portakabin at the far side of the site. One enters the cabin, the other two stand to the side of it, looking up at the crumbling old mansion.

A loud siren sounds.

The security officers in yellow tabards move along the safety barrier telling people to stay back. Everyone does as they ask. All eyes are on the building. Anticipation from the gathered crowd seems to crackle in the air like electricity.

Jennie hears a low rumbling as the charges inside the school detonate. For a moment the centre of the stone building seems to wobble. Then it collapses to the ground, sending a huge cloud of dust ballooning into the air around it.

In less than thirty seconds, the original White Cross Academy is gone.

As the dust cloud starts to clear, she can just make out the rubble that is now heaped in the spot where the building once stood. Her eyes start to water, but it's from the grit in the air rather than any emotional attachment to the building. With the secret it hid from her all these years, she's happy never to see it again.

The crowd clap for a job well done, but the mood remains sombre. Jennie senses the town needed the building razed to the ground, too. With it gone, the site has been given a clean slate and the possibility of a new beginning.

'Jennie?'

Recognising the voice, she turns to see Paul and Shelly Jennings approaching. Somehow Hannah's dad looks smaller, frailer than he did the last time they met. Shelly has her arm through his, almost holding him up. The fire in Paul's eyes as he shouted at her in the interview room is long gone, replaced by the subdued resignation of a grief-stricken father.

'I wanted to thank you for finding who took my Hannah,' says Mr Jennings. 'I didn't recognise you at first, but when I read the article in the paper saying how you'd been best friends with

Hannah, I remembered. You came to the house once, but didn't come in, I think?'

Jennie nods. 'Yes, just the one time.'

Mr Jennings exhales hard. 'I wasn't a good dad. I loved Hannah, I really did, but I was angry at the world back then, and sometimes I… I took it out on her. I'm glad she had a good friend, not like those… those…' As the emotion threatens to overwhelm him, Paul Jennings reaches into his jacket pocket. He removes something then reaches out, pressing it into Jennie's hand. 'She'd want you to have this.'

Jennie looks down at the heart-shaped gold pendant, now attached to a new chain, nestling in her palm. *Hannah's favourite necklace.* Closing her fingers around the pendant, she feels incredibly moved. She meets Paul Jennings' gaze. 'Thank you.'

As Paul and Shelly Jennings move back into the crowd, Jennie lets out a long breath to steady herself. Her fingers tremble as she fastens the chain around her neck, but as the gold pendant rests against her skin, she feels a sudden sense of calm.

I'm ready now.

Hoisting her rucksack up onto her shoulder, Jennie sets off along the pavement. She takes a left at the end of the street onto the main road and continues on, past the Cross Keys pub, then over the zebra crossing outside Coffee Shack. She reaches the bus stop just as the number forty-eight bus is approaching, and raises her arm to hail it.

As the bus's indicator flashes and it begins to slow, Jennie feels the adrenaline build within her. She's solved the mystery of what happened to Hannah and she's got her friend justice. She's paid a company to clear the rest of the junk from her mum's house and she'll put it on the market as soon as the probate is through. She's done all she can here. There's nothing left to stay for. Nothing will bring Hannah back.

She's spent too much of her life stuck in limbo, always trying to protect herself from hurt, from loss; never fully trusting anyone and never letting anyone get close. It's time she pursued what she needs. It's time she allowed herself to be happy, to be the person she always wanted to be, *where* she always wanted to be.

Pushing her hand under the top flap of her rucksack, Jennie double-checks her Nikon SLR is safe inside. Dad and Hannah both encouraged her to use her talent; now taking pictures is when she feels closest, most connected, to them. So what if she's a bit older than the average student? That's not going to stop her following her passion.

This is my chance.

Art College here I come.

The bus comes to a halt beside her and the door opens.

Jennie steps inside. She smiles at the driver as she touches the pendant around her neck. 'A ticket to London, please. One way only.'

Playlist

'Ordinary World' – Duran Duran.

'Two Princes' – Spin Doctors.

'The Rhythm Of The Night' – Corona.

'Inside' – Stiltskin.

'The Most Beautiful Girl In The World' – Prince.

'Come As You Are' – Nirvana.

'Nothing Else Matters' – Metallica.

'Blinding Lights' – The Weeknd.

'Come Undone' – Duran Duran.

'Black Hole Sun' – Soundgarden.

'Secret' – Madonna.

'Who Wants To Live Forever' – Queen + Adam Lambert.

'The Show Must Go On' – Queen + Adam Lambert.

'Creep' – Radiohead.

Credits

M.J. Arlidge, Steph Broadribb and Orion Fiction would like to thank everyone at Orion who worked on the publication of *The Reunion* in the UK.

Agent
Hellie Ogden
Oli Munson

Editorial
Leodora Darlington
Sanah Ahmed

Copyeditor
John Garth

Proofreader
Linda Joyce

Audio
Paul Stark
Louise Richardson

Design
Tomás Almeida
Morven Davis
Loveday May
Nick Shah

Contracts
Dan Herron
Ellie Bowker

Marketing
Lindsay Terrell
Hennah Sandhu

Editorial Management
Charlie Panayiotou
Jane Hughes
Bartley Shaw
Lucy Bilton

Finance
Jasdip Nandra
Nick Gibson
Sue Baker

Publicity
Leanne Oliver
Ellen Turner

Sales
Jen Wilson
Esther Waters
Victoria Laws
Toluwalope Ayo-Ajala
Rachael Hum
Anna Egelstaff
Sinead White
Georgina Cutler

Production
Ruth Sharvell

Operations
Jo Jacobs
Sharon Willis

Looking for your next gripping, unputdownable read?
Don't miss *Forget Me Not*, from the Helen Grace
series by M.J. Arlidge!

GONE BUT NOT FORGOTTEN

A gang war grips the city, and the police force is
under fire from all sides. But Detective Inspector
Helen Grace defies direct orders as she becomes
drawn to the case of a missing teenager.

LOST BUT NOT ALONE

Naomi's mother is desperate for help – and Helen
is her only hope. Keeping the investigation secret,
she finds a disturbing trail of questions – and
more who have vanished off the streets…

WILL THEY FIND HER IN TIME?

Sometimes, the truth hides in plain sight. But proving it is
another matter entirely. The clock is ticking – and the only
person looking for Naomi is about to meet her match.

ORDER NOW!

If you loved the twists and turns of *The Reunion*, you'll devour *Your Child Next*, the latest pulse-pounding thriller from M.J. Arlidge and Andy Maslen that asks you how far you'd go to protect the ones you love.